THE OPTICIAN'S WIFE

BETSY REAVLEY

BLOODHOUND
— BOOKS —

ALSO BY BETSY REAVLEY

For Freeman, Matilda and Elodie. You are my world.

'I shut my eyes and all the world drops dead;
I lift my eyes and all is born again'
The Bell Jar, Sylvia Plath

'I love you without knowing how, or when, or from where. I love
you simply, without problems or pride: I love you in this way
because I do not know any other way of loving but this, in which
there is no I or you, so intimate that your hand upon my chest is
my hand, so intimate then when I fall asleep your eyes close.'
100 Love Sonnets, Pablo Neruda

'People like to say that the conflict is between
good and evil. The real conflict is between truth
and lies.'
Don Miguel Ruiz

INTRODUCTION

Inspired by true events

PROLOGUE

I always knew I was different. I've known since I was very small, since I could hold a pencil.

I used to think it was a bad thing. That fitting in was the most important thing in the world. Growing up I wanted to be just like the other girls. It wasn't easy being on the outside looking in. I felt utterly alone. My parents didn't understand me. I had no real friends.

I used to look in the mirror and wish that I had a physical abnormality that would explain why I was different from the rest. If only I'd been born with a huge mole on my forehead or two noses, then I could have made sense of it. But I didn't. I looked normal. Painfully normal.

For a long time I lived my life under the radar, not noticed. I was invisible.

Then I met Larry and my life changed. He saw me. He was the first person to ever really see me. He understood I wasn't like everyone else and he embraced it. Nurtured it.

He taught me how to live. How to feel alive. And I taught him.

That is where it all began.

Now people notice me. Now they remember my name.

PART I

1

I was sitting on a bench in the park eating a prawn sandwich and flicking crumbs off my jumper. The late April sunshine was warm on my face and the ducks on the river busied themselves with their young.

It was my lunch break and as usual I was eating alone. My colleagues from Woolworths all went to a trendy sandwich bar together. I preferred being outside watching the birds. Cambridge is lovely at that time of year. I often spent my breaks sitting by the river on Jesus Green.

When he sat down at the other end of the bench, his hands tucked into his brown coat pockets, I moved away from him, right to the edge. I didn't look up and avoided eye contact.

We sat silently for a while. I fed the ducks and swans the crusts left over from my sandwich. A cocky swan lifted itself out of the water and came padding over, wagging its clean white tail feathers in a show of disapproval. The large bird came so close to me it was able to take the bread right out of my hand. The man on the bench next to me chuckled to himself, amused by the swan's bravado.

'Break your arm if you're not careful,' he piped up. I stayed silent, too shy to respond.

When the bird realised I had no more food to offer it turned and plodded back to the river, the ducks scattering to get out of its way as it returned to join its mate.

'Most people like the swans best. But I like ducks.' He spoke again.

'Me too.'

I felt him turn and look at me.

'Swans think they're all that. Kings of the river. Pushy buggers if you ask me.' He took his hands out of his pockets and placed them on his knees. I tried to sneak a look at him in my peripheral vision.

'Yes.'

'I've seen you around. You're always feeding the birds.'

'I like watching them.' Finally I turned my face to look at him.

He had a nice smile. Broad and open with small dimples in his cheeks. His mid-brown hair was thick and wavy around his square face. He reminded me of George Michael from Wham. His dark chocolate eyes were smiling at me. He was very handsome and I felt myself blush.

'I'm Larry,' he said still smiling and extending his hand, 'It's nice to meet you.' I rubbed my hands together quickly to make sure I didn't have mayonnaise on them before shaking his.

'Deborah.' My cheeks felt hot.

'Do you work nearby?' His eyes were searching mine and I didn't know where to look.

'Not far. In Woolworths on Sidney Street.' I fumbled with the brown paper bag my sandwich came in and folded it into the smallest possible square, pushing out the creases with my thumbs.

'I'm doing my training at the opticians in the centre. Rook's, do you know it?'

'I think so.' I said, lying.

'You have very pretty eyes,' he said as he got up from the bench and plunged his hands back into his pockets.

I didn't know what to say so I said nothing and focused my attention on the rowers who were passing by.

'Sorry. Didn't mean to embarrass you.'

'You didn't.' I tried to sound relaxed.

'Well, I need to get back to work now. My boss is a bit of a slave driver. Maybe I'll see you around, Deborah.'

'Sure. I need to get going, too.' I checked my wristwatch and got up brushing the final evidence of crumbs from my indigo tights.

'I hope so,' he said with a smile before turning around and walking away down the path.

I stood watching as his frame grew smaller and smaller and the distance between us widened.

No one had ever given me a compliment like that before. I hoped our paths would cross again soon.

2

The next day I went into the bakers to buy my lunch. I bought my usual prawn sandwich on brown bread and treated myself to a bag of crisps.

I returned to the same spot by the river in the hope that I might see Larry. I picked at my food, tossing crumbs to the greedy flock of pigeons that descended round me. The swans were nowhere to be seen and neither was Larry. I felt bitter disappointment when I realised I needed to return to the shop. Ever since our meeting yesterday I had been thinking about the friendly stranger.

As I walked over the footbridge that connected Jesus Green to Sidney Street I dragged my feet. I was in no rush to return to work. My job was boring and I hadn't made any friends. It paid the bills though and that was something.

I didn't do well at school. 'You're not academic,' my dad would say. It was his way of calling me thick. But it never really bothered me what he thought. Ever since my mum died six years earlier my relationship with my dad had taken the strain.

'Go on, go out. Meet up with some friends. Get out from under my feet,' he would say so that he could sit at home and get drunk without me knowing. But of course I knew. I would stay in my bedroom and listen to him cry over his beer. He used to talk to a photograph of Mum when he was drunk.

'I miss you, Sue,' he would sob. 'I can't deal with that girl all alone. Why did you have to leave me?'

I knew he meant me whenever he said 'that girl'. My younger sister, Dawn, was the apple of his eye. She could do no wrong. She was perfect.

As I passed by a shop window I caught a glimpse of myself in the reflection. Not usually one to indulge in vanity, I stopped for a moment to look at the girl everyone else saw. My pudgy face stared back at me, my little blue eyes empty of hope. I wondered why that nice stranger even gave me the time of day. I was plain. My light brown hair was so dull it appeared almost grey. Other people had luscious waves. I had frizz. Uncontrollable frizz that makes each individual strand stick out and appear brittle. Still looking at my disappointing reflection I tried to smooth my hair with the palm of my hand. It didn't work. Nothing would tame it.

Everyone else I knew of my age wore make-up. Bright candy pink lipstick and electric blue eyeliner were all the rage then. But those bright garish colours never suited my pallid complexion. And besides, make-up was for girls who wanted to be noticed. Girls who followed fashion and thought that their appearance was the most important thing in the world, spending most of their income on clothes from Topshop.

I went to charity shops for my clothes and wore some old things that belonged to my Mum. My sister, Dawn, didn't want them. They're old fashioned, she would say, and they wouldn't fit her anyway. She was tall and skinny like Dad. I got Mum's figure. Curvy, she used to say with a giggle. I missed her.

Walking away from my reflection I bowed my head, keeping my eyes on the pavement as I made my way back to work. I was avoiding stepping on any cracks. I was always careful and a bit superstitious. Dad said it was stupid to think like that. Maybe he was right.

When I got to the glass doors into the shop I was met by a gaggle of co-workers, chatting and smoking cigarettes. They would say that they were just stepping outside for a breath of fresh air. I never got the joke.

Silvia, a girl a few years older than me with long silky blonde hair, blew her smoke at me as I passed. The girls standing with her sniggered. I felt angry. I wanted to turn around and slap her but that would take courage and I didn't have any back then. Instead, I pretended not to notice and hurried inside holding my breath.

Once indoors I headed straight to the bathroom to clean my face and wash away the foul smell of cigarette smoke. I bumped into Trisha. She was about the only person in the shop who ever bothered to speak to me. She was washing her hands and smiled when she saw me.

'Good lunch?' She checked her perm in the mirror from various angles.

'Fine, thanks.' I could still smell the smoke.

'Stuart is really pushing us at the moment, don't you think? It seems a bit extreme.'

Stuart was our supervisor, a short, balding man with elevated self-worth. He used to bark at people to stop chatting and get back to serving but he never told me off. I was never caught talking to anyone other than a customer.

'He's OK.'

'I think he's a total drag, Debs.' Trisha rolled her eyes. She was the only person who ever called me Debs, other than my sister. I didn't like it but said nothing. 'Oh and you'll never guess what. Sarah has only gone and got herself pregnant. Pregnant! She broke up with Luke a week ago and only just found out she's got a bun in the oven! Awkward or what.'

Trisha had a large mouth that appeared to never stop moving. Her brown eyes were large and framed by too much mascara. Her large bust would heave whenever she laughed and her cleavage was often on show. Sometimes I didn't know where to look.

I didn't have a clue who Sarah was and certainly had never come across Luke. But I was thankful that Trisha talked to me the way she would with everyone else. It didn't matter to her that I wasn't part of the popular crowd. She was happy as long as she could share gossip with anyone who would listen.

'But you didn't hear it from me, OK?' She gave a wink and left me standing alone in the toilets, the door swinging backwards and forwards on its hinges.

I was dreading going back to my till. Silvia sat a few seats away, surrounded by her gaggle of friends. Sometimes they would throw little balls of paper at me when Stuart had his back turned. Too ashamed to do anything about it, I'd tidy away the evidence scattered around my chair. People were much more immature in those days. Not like the young of today.

I straightened my blue polyester tabard and made the long walk back to my till, which was on the far side of the large shop floor.

The best thing about my job was that the shop had windows that went from ceiling to floor. When I wasn't having my ear chewed off by a customer, I could look out across the road at the people walking by. I liked watching people when they didn't know they were being watched. Men and woman going about their business, shopping, collecting their kids from school. Normal life. But it fascinated me and I used to fantasise about what those people were like behind closed doors. I'd give them all roles to play and pretend I was directing them. Once Stuart caught me staring out of the window instead of working. He shouted at me in front of everyone. I was so embarrassed. The others laughed and then he shouted at them.

It was a typical day for me. I'd wake up, have a wash, get dressed, eat some toast and then walk to work. I'd have my lunch, always a prawn sandwich, by the river unless it was raining very hard, in which case I'd sit at one of the bus stops or stay in the back room of the shop. I'd spend the afternoon serving customers until half-past five when the workday ended. Then I'd leave the shop and walk home in time to make tea for Dawn and Dad.

That day was no different.

I scurried out of the shop, keeping a low profile, and made my way along Chesterton Road and away from the town centre. At the time we lived in a small two bed on the northeast side of the city. Dawn and I had to share a bedroom, which we resented.

We moved to Cambridge in 1978, the year after my mother died from cancer. My aunt Mary, Dad's sister, lived in the area and he said he wanted her to help look after us.

Before living in Cambridge we lived in Harlow. I missed it for a long time. We'd had a bigger house and I'd had my own bedroom then. But Dad reminded us that now Mum was gone things had to change. We all have to make sacrifices, he used to say. He would cry a lot then and I didn't want to upset him more, so I stayed quiet and didn't complain.

My mother, Sue Campkin, died in 1977 aged thirty-seven, after a short battle with breast cancer. She had been a loving mother and wife, and worked at a doctor's surgery in Harlow as a receptionist.

I was just twelve years old when she passed away. Dawn was nine. Since my father found solace at the bottom of a bottle it was left to me to keep things running. My father was permanently drunk from September 22nd 1977, the day after she died, right up until he took his last breath. In the end his liver had had enough.

After mum died I became the housekeeper. I cooked and tidied and made sure that Dawn and Dad had clean clothes. My childhood was cut short but I was always older than my years. I wanted to look after them, just like my Mum would have wanted me to. It was my duty, and besides, somebody had to step up to the responsibility. Dad had no intention of doing so.

I have never been sure if Dad was sad after she died because he missed being looked after or if it was her additional income he missed. The rent got too much for him and, so, unable to afford to stay in that house he decided to move us all to Cambridge. Looking back, I suppose he was probably too ashamed to stay locally. He was a proud man. He wouldn't have wanted his friends to see us downsizing. So he decided we needed a fresh start. But Cambridge had other attractions too. Namely his sister, Aunt Mary, who he hoped would be a substitute mother to Dawn and me.

Mary did her best to help out, but she had a family of her own and three young children, including twin boys. To begin with she would come over and bring meals, usually casseroles or pies. She was a good cook. But then as her family grew, and she had her fourth child, she spent less and less time with us.

Dad's drinking didn't help. She hated it when he was drunk. I used to hear her shout at him about it. It never made any difference. It just made things worse. When she left he'd go to the shop and come back with a bag full of beer. Those were the days when I used to take Dawn out to the park until it was dark, until I could be sure he had passed out in his armchair.

When we got back to the house I would get Dawn to take her shoes off and tiptoe past him up the stairs to bed. I remember how creaky the stairs were in that house. We would walk with our backs to wall to avoid waking him up. After we cleaned our teeth and got into our pyjamas, I would read her a bedtime story and tuck her in with her favourite toy, a bunny called Wilson. It had been a birthday present from Mum.

The room was so cold. There was a gap between the window and the sill where cold air would pour through. I took the bed nearer the window and used an extra blanket in the winter to avoid freezing.

Our bedroom was really only a single but Dad had somehow managed to squeeze in two beds so we could share the room. He took the large double room for himself until we grew into teenagers and then he had no choice but to swap. But he was bitter about it and refused to give us any money to buy paint so that I could brighten the room up. Waste of bloody money, he used to say.

The most extraordinary thing was that, somehow, Dad managed to hold a job down. He was a builder and finding work in and around Cambridge was easy for him. It paid the bills and left enough over to cover the cost of his beer intake, a minimum of six cans a day.

Looking back, I suppose I almost understood why he chose to get drunk all the time. It must have been lonely for him and difficult bringing up two girls without a wife. But it was hard for us too. Dawn was so young and I was barely a teenager. Still, I never understood why he picked on me so much. Dawn could do no wrong. He never got cross with her or shouted. His eyes would fill with tears every time he gave her a hug. 'You remind me so much of your Mum,' he would say. It was strange because I always thought I looked more like Mum. 'Dawn got her pretty face,' he said. I suppose that meant I had her chunky figure.

Growing up it would have been easy to resent Dawn, but I didn't. It wasn't her fault he loved her more. It wasn't her fault Mum died. And it wasn't her fault I was plain and unpopular. But as she grew into a woman she seemed to forget the kindness and care I'd bestowed upon her. She started to resent me. The irony wasn't lost on me. 'Why don't you do something with your hair,' she would say. I was not the cool older sister she longed for. Even her friends used to laugh behind my back. As we grew older we grew further apart. She had been the one good thing in my life up until that point. When she stopped making an effort with me I sunk deeper into myself.

It was around that time when I discovered my love of books. I read like my life depended on it. I lost myself in the stories of faraway worlds and would dream of travelling the earth. I read travel journals and history books, romance and adventure. All the things my life was lacking I found between the pages of all those books. They were my friends. They were safe.

I never liked reading books about crime or anything like that. Ghoulish if you ask me. I didn't want to think about all the horrible things in the world and all the nasty people. I wanted my books to take me to far off lands where Princes would battle for fair maidens.

Without even realising it I had arrived at our front door. I didn't remember the walk or how I got to our street. I suppose I must have been daydreaming. Probably thinking about one of the stories I'd recently read.

Our terraced house was situated on Haviland Way, a cul-de-sac in the King's Hedges area of town. The upper level of the house was a painted in a dirty cream colour and the lower level was exposed modern red brickwork. We had off-street parking in front of the house: a concrete space where Dad could leave his van. It was a dull street and home to dull people.

Our front door needed some attention. The faded racing green paint was flaking. Dad had been saying he would do it for as long as I could remember. I put my key in the lock and turned, pushing the door open. I hoped Dad wasn't at home.

The front door led straight into the living room where he

was normally found in his old armchair, holding a beer in one hand and the remote control for the telly in the other. But that day he must have been working late or at the pub. The house was cold and quiet. I knew Dawn was out because the drone of music wasn't coming from our bedroom. She used to play a Madonna single on repeat. It drove me mad but I never said anything. I didn't want to spoil her fun or risk an argument.

I liked it when no one was home. My shoulders dropped and I relaxed a bit. I pretended it was my house and I lived alone. No Dawn and definitely no Dad. Passing through the pokey living room and small, dark dining room I made my way into the kitchen. The cupboard doors were laminate chipboard. The cheapest kind that hung on loose hinges. Landlords got away with murder then. They probably still do.

It occurred to me how unfair the world was. But I wasn't the type to mope. I made my cup of tea then did the washing up that was left festering in the sink. As I put the dishes on the draining board I wondered if Dawn or Dad ever realised I always did the washing up. It probably didn't even register with them. They just assumed that there would be clean plates and saucepans. And there were. There were always clean dishes and an empty sink after I came home. I did it without thinking or questioning. It was my duty.

As I dried the last cup I looked out of the grubby window above the sink. The garden was seriously neglected. We had a small concrete paved patio. The rest of the square garden was laid with overgrown grass. No one ever used the garden. If mum had been alive, it would have been nice. She would have taken care of it. The pots that she once tended were now overgrown with weeds. I remember realising that Dad or someone, probably Aunt Mary, had taken the trouble to bring them from our old house.

The garden was always mum's department. She took pride in

it when she was alive. I felt so removed from myself looking out at this neglected patch. Mum had never set eyes on this house. She'd be upset if she had. She was a good housekeeper, proud of her little corner of the world.

Roses were her favourite. She liked the pink ones the best. Pretty in pink, she used to say when they were in bloom. When I grew up, I would have a garden with pink roses in it. I didn't have the green fingers that she did but I figured I'd be able to nurture a rose bush or two.

'They are tough plants,' she used to say. 'They might not look like it by they are. Be like a rose, Debbie.' She was the only one who called me that. 'Look nice but remember you have thorns,' she would say. That was her advice to me. I never really understood what she meant. How could I be like a flower? Did she want me to stay still and remain silent? I did for a long time. I stayed invisible.

I dried the crockery before putting it back in the cupboard where it belonged. Then I went into the garden. I never did that. None of us did. It would only remind us of Mum and what we were missing. But on that day I was compelled to go.

It was about half past six. The sun was setting and the sky was littered with dirty lilac-coloured clouds. I stood on the weed-ridden patio. Unwelcome plants had seeded themselves in between the paving stones, fighting for dominance. The place was a characterless mess.

I'd taken on many of Mum's roles but it had never occurred to me to look after the garden. She took pride in how things looked. Mum was no great beauty but she always wore a smile. People liked her. She was loved.

When we lived in Harlow, our front garden was the envy of the street. The bins were always lined up neatly and there was never a blade of grass out of place. I used to wonder where she found the time. Later in life, I realised she probably threw herself into her gardening so she could escape Dad. For a long time, I told myself that he broke after she died but the truth was that he had been like that for as long as I could remember.

Standing in that miserable garden I made a promise to myself. I didn't want to be there any more. I was tired of looking after everyone. I was tired of being me. Aged seventeen I was old enough to fend for myself. I'd save my money and move out. No one would miss me, until I left. Then they would realise. Then they would see how much I did for them. The dishes wouldn't get washed; their laundry would pile up. Dad would discover his lunch box was empty in the morning. Dawn would wonder why her bed wasn't made.

I'd had enough.

3
_____

The next day I went to work as usual. It was raining as I walked along the busy main road to work.

That morning I broke with tradition. I always used to wait until lunchtime before going into the bakers and buying my sandwich, but on that day I decided to go in before I started work. As I was taking the coins out of my purse, I felt a hand on my shoulder. I fumbled my money and my coins fell to the floor as I turned around. There stood the handsome stranger I'd met by the river.

'Hello.' He smiled as I began to scrabble about on the floor, collecting my loose change.

'Hi.' The floor was cold and hard on my knees. From the corner of my eye I realised a queue had formed behind me. An impatient-looking man was scowling at me.

'Sorry.' I stood up, deciding to sacrifice the remaining coins.

'I'll get that for you.' Larry reached into his inside pocket and removed his wallet. He handed the woman behind the till a note and waited for his change.

I was dumbstruck. No one had ever done anything like that for me before. The woman in the apron put my sandwich into a brown paper bag and handed it over, never breaking eye contact with Larry. I remained unnoticed.

'Thank you.' I felt myself blushing as I moved to one side and let the next customer pay for his loaf of bread.

'Fancy bumping into you,' Larry cocked his head to one side. He really did look like George Michael, without the earring, back then. 'You on your way to work?'

'Yes.' I checked my wristwatch, feeling self-conscious.

'I'll walk with you.'

'How do you know we are going the same way?' It was out of character for me to be so direct in those days.

'I don't, but I'm prepared to take a risk.' He grinned, flashing a row of white teeth. He held the door for me.

Once out on the street, I wrapped my sandwich tightly and put it into my navy canvas rucksack, the straps of which I slipped over my shoulders.

'I'm going this way,' I said signalling left.

'Then so am I.' His confidence unnerved me but I was pleased to see him again.

We walked in silence for a while. He splashed through the puddles in his laced-up shoes while I avoided them.

'Horrid weather.'

'I don't mind the rain,' I said.

'Like a duck?'

'Yes. Like a duck.'

As we got closer to the shop my heart began to sink. I didn't want our time together to end.

'Is this you?' he asked, as I came to a stop.

'Yep.' I found it hard to look him in the eye.

'Well,' he shifted on his heels, 'I suppose this is goodbye.'

'Yes, I guess it is.' There was a lump in my throat.

'OK.' He looked down the road in the direction he wanted to go. 'See you soon.'

'Bye.' I turned and headed for the door. I wanted to watch him walk away but didn't have the guts.

Then, just as I pulled the door open, I heard him call. 'Do you have plans for lunch?'

I swung around in time to see Silvia approaching.

'Not really,' I mumbled, avoiding looking at Silvia who was paying careful attention to the conversation.

'How about I meet you here and we have lunch together? What time do you break?'

Silvia stopped walking and stared at Larry. He didn't appear to notice her.

'Twelve-thirty.' I hated having her there.

'OK. Twelve-thirty it is. I'll meet you right here. OK?'

'OK,' I echoed.

'See you then,' he called, turning away.

'Who was that?' Silvia demanded, still standing a few feet away.

'Just a friend.' I couldn't meet her eye.

'A friend?!' she spat. 'You don't have any.' Silvia flicked her blonde hair over her shoulder and pushed past me. But nothing she said could kill the joy I felt inside.

The morning seemed to drag on. I watched the slow minutes circle the clock before it got to twelve twenty-five. Springing out of my chair, I went into the ladies to inspect myself in the mirror.

My reflection was as unimpressive as always. *What are you doing?* I asked the bland face staring back at me. *Who are you kidding?*

Things like this didn't happen to me. Handsome men didn't want to spend time in my company. They didn't notice me. They noticed girls like Silvia and Dawn. I wondered if it was all a joke set up by one of my colleagues. It wouldn't have surprised me.

Poor little Deborah standing outside waiting for someone who isn't coming. I imagined them all standing by the window watching and laughing at me and suddenly I felt scared but I decided it was worth the gamble. I would go outside and wait. Only for three minutes. If he was late, so be it.

When I stepped out into the cold, he was there, waiting for me. I couldn't believe it.

'Twelve-thirty exactly.' He smiled and took a step towards me.

'I don't believe in being late. My Mum always said that being punctual was good mannered.'

'Very sensible woman,' he said cheerily. 'So where shall we go?' He looked up at the grey sky.

'The river?' The cold never really bothered me.

'The river it is.' He sunk his hands into his pockets and I realised he didn't have a bag with him. Where was his lunch?

'Back to the bench where we met?' His question sounded intimate and I liked it.

'Sure.' I let him lead the way.

'So Deborah, how long have you worked at that place?'

He remembered my name.

'Six months.'

'Do you like it?'

'I can't complain. It's OK.'

'Well I love my job. I get to spend my time looking into people's eyes. Literally.' He laughed.

I imagined beautiful women queuing up to get their eyesight checked by him and it made me feel invisible again.

'You can tell a lot about a person from their eyes.'

'Windows to the soul?'

'Exactly.' He nodded. 'Happiness. Fear. It's all in the eyes.'

We crossed over the footbridge and followed the path along the river until we reached our bench. He signed for me to sit down first and so I did.

'Pick a side.'

'A side?'

'Everyone has a side they prefer.' He was serious.

'OK.' I said sitting down on the left side of the bench.

'Well, what do you know?' he chuckled to himself, 'I always choose the right. That's neat, isn't it?'

The bench was damp and I felt the wetness soaking through my uniform. He didn't seem to notice.

'No grumpy swans in sight.' He looked down the river past the houseboats.

'No ducks either.'

'They'll come.' He was confident.

I opened my rucksack and removed my sandwich, which was slightly squashed.

'Don't you have any lunch?' I asked, biting down into the crusty bread. Mayonnaise spilled out of the sides and on to my fingers.

'No. I forgot to bring any.' He was still looking at the river.

'We could share mine.' I suggested brushing crumbs off my coat before tearing the sandwich in two.

'Thanks.' I handed him his half and he took a large bite. 'Nice,' he said, his mouth full.

We sat and ate in silence for a while, enjoying the food and each other's company until we felt the first raindrops. I looked up at the clouds and cursed the weather for ruining our moment.

'April showers.' Larry pulled his brown coat collar up around his square jaw. 'Shall we go to a café?'

'I'm not sure I have time. I can't be late back for work. My boss will be angry.' I wished I could have been braver.

'All right then.' He didn't even try to convince me to stay and the disappointment I felt was bitter.

I got up from the bench. The rain was coming down more heavily then. 'I'll see you around.'

'Why don't we meet for lunch tomorrow?' He stood up, raindrops running down his nose. 'I owe you half a sandwich. My treat.'

'OK.' I found it hard to contain my happiness.

'Great. I'll meet you outside Woolworths tomorrow. Twelve-thirty again?'

'Sure.' He was looking at me with such intensity I felt uncomfortable. He had a searching gaze and when he looked at me everything else seemed to melt away.

'Great. It's a date then. See you tomorrow.' Without any warning he leant over and planted a small kiss on my cheek. I felt my face flush with colour as I turned around and quickly walked away. I had never been kissed before, let alone been on a date.

4

Things with Larry carried on like that for some time. Every weekday we would meet for lunch and, if it wasn't raining, return to our bench. As the spring retreated and made way for summer I felt myself growing in confidence. Larry seemed genuinely interested in learning all about me. He wanted to know everything there was to know. For the first time in my life I felt special.

I told him all about my family and my mum's death. He listened intently and never interrupted. He was curious to know about my childhood and what Harlow was like. He grew to know my likes and dislikes and paid attention to it all. Larry had a wonderful memory. He never forgot even the small details.

In turn I learnt all about his life. He was born in 1960 in Peterborough. His father, Jim, and his mother, Linda, moved the family to Cambridge in 1981 when Jim wanted to move job. He was a science teacher. He hated his previous school. The kids there had no respect, Larry said. No doubt he was echoing his dad.

Linda was a homemaker.

Larry had a younger brother, Eric, who, he told me, he got on well with. It seemed Eric had a weakness for gambling and the horses. Larry told me he spent a lot of time in Newmarket at the racecourse. My mother would have described him as a rogue. 'Stay away from men like that, Debbie,' she would have said. But it wasn't Eric I was interested in.

Larry's family lived in a Victorian house they owned in the Romsey area of Cambridge, just off Mill Road. It had three bedrooms and two bathrooms. He came from a better family than I did.

Larry talked all about how he was going to be an optician. He loved eyes, he said. For as long as he could remember he'd been fascinated by sight. He wanted to help people keep seeing, he would say. To have no vision would be scary, he thought, and I agreed. I'd never known anyone have such enthusiasm for anything.

The fact that he loved his job came as real surprise to me. Working in Woolworths was OK, but I couldn't say I loved it. Larry said I needed to find my calling. He said he'd help me. I told him I liked books and he said I must love eyes, too, because without eyes you couldn't read. I'd never seen it like that before I said, and he laughed.

'There's lots of different ways of looking at the world. You just have to find your own way of seeing it,' Larry said once. I didn't really understand what he meant by that back then.

By June we had grown close but those were the early days and our relationship moved at a snail's pace. He was very respectful. I wasn't ready for kissing and heavy petting then. I had to get to know him first, to be able to trust him. I was still a virgin and the thought of being anything different terrified me.

I hadn't met his family and he hadn't met mine. I liked it just the way it was: the two of us in our private world uncompli-cated by adults. Although he was twenty-three and I was seventeen, we still felt like kids inside. But Larry was more grown up than I was. He was older and he had his head screwed on. He knew what direction he wanted to go in. He had plans. I was still working out who I was. Sometimes I used to think that I would never know. But having him in my life helped me to focus. I was caught up in his positive outlook. It started to rub off on me.

On that day as we sat by the river enjoying the warm sunshine, Larry turned to me and said, 'I think you should hand in your notice at Woolworths. It's no good for you, Dee.' That was his nickname for me.

'I can't. What else would I do? I need the money.'

'I know what you should do. You should get a job working in a bookshop. Then you could read all the time.'

'I don't know–'

'Sure you do. It would be perfect. If you worked in the bookshop in the centre you'd be closer to the opticians and I could pop in all the time. It would be great.'

'They probably don't have any vacancies–'.

'They do.' Again I was cut off. 'I went in yesterday and asked the woman behind the desk. I told her all about you. How much you love reading, how you don't really like your current job and she said you should go in and give her your CV. I'll help you write it, if you like. I'm really good at that sort of thing. I know just what people want to hear.'

I looked down at my chubby pale knees that were sticking out just below the hem of my blue tabard and noticed my legs needed shaving. I'd never shaved my legs before or even thought about doing it. I felt self-conscious and tugged at the skirt hoping Larry wouldn't notice.

'What do you think?' He leant in with his eyebrows raised.

'Well, I'd need to check with Dad.' I knew he wouldn't approve.

'Rubbish. Look, as long as you have a job I don't think he will mind where you're working. I'm sure he'd want you to be happy.'

The idea was laughable. I pictured him scoffing at the prospect. 'What do you want to work in a bookshop for?' he'd say, 'You need to get your head out of the clouds and step into the real world, my girl.' I could imagine the whole conversation.

'I'll do it.' I felt a burst of pride and strength. 'I'll go and speak to the people in the bookshop after work today.'

'That's the spirit!' Larry put his arm around my shoulder and pulled me into him. I could smell his musky aftershave and inhaled. 'You should think about yourself more. Stop worrying what your dad will think. I'm proud of you.'

It was the first time I'd heard anyone say that since my mum had died and I felt my bottom lip quiver.

'What's wrong?' He lifted my chin in his hands.

'I'm just happy.' A large tear rolled down my cheek and he wiped it away.

'Not as happy as me.' He kissed my lips, lingering a moment longer than usual. 'You are so special, Dee. You can do anything you set your mind to. You just have to believe.'

I told Stuart that I had a headache so I could leave work half an hour early. The bookshop closed at five-thirty and I wanted to make it there in time to talk to the manager.

As agreed, Larry met me on the corner and we walked through the town past Sydney Sussex College and on to Trinity Street where the bookshop was located. Freeman's Bookshop had been there for years. It was the place I always went to browse for my next read. It was the most popular bookshop in the town, always full of students looking for textbooks and bookworms in search of fuel.

As we approached, I started to feel my nerves getting the better of me. The cream stone building was old and I found its history suddenly daunting. Larry picked up on it and linked his fingers with mine.

'It's just an informal talk. Relax.' His tone was soothing.

'I've only ever had one interview before and that was at Woolworths.'

'This isn't an interview, Dee. You just have to introduce your-self and tell her you want to apply for the job. Simple.'

The street was busy with shoppers and kids who were killing time together after school.

A cyclist passed too close to me, almost knocking me over.

'Idiot!' Larry called out. The cyclist kept up his speed and didn't look back.

'It's OK.' I'd never seen him look cross before. It unnerved me.

I was used to close calls with bikes. Everyone who lived in Cambridge needed to have eyes in the back of their head. Cyclists were everywhere but not all of them were very consid-erate of pedestrians. I can't count the number of times I'd been knocked over or had to jump out the way of an oncoming cyclist.

'Still,' Larry said calming down, 'he should look where he's going.'

I was still too worried about going into the bookshop to be bothered by the selfish student.

'Ready?'

'Yes.' I hoped I sounded convincing.

'Good luck. I'll be waiting for you out here.'

I nodded and pushed the door open.

It was nearly closing time and the last few customers were queuing at the till waiting to pay. It suddenly dawned on me that I'd not chosen the best time to come in. I stood there for a moment wondering what to do. I looked around to see if I could see someone else who worked in the shop, other than the middle-aged woman who was behind the till. There was no who else who obviously worked there. I wanted to turn and leave and never look back but I was more worried about appearing foolish in front of Larry than being dismissed, so I straightened my skirt, made sure my peach T-shirt was tucked in and went to join the line.

As I walked across the shop I noticed how shiny the dark wooden floor was and wondered how many people had passed through over the years.

When I reached the line there were two people in front on me. A man in a green tweed jacket, who looked like he might be a doctor, was being served. He had grey hair and a kind face. I imagined myself serving him and I liked the idea of it. Between us stood a young woman who was absorbed in the book she was holding. She wore a smart grey skirt suit and her brown hair in a neat bun on the top of her head. She had an air of intelligence about her that I admired even though it intimidated me.

It was then that I realised that both the people in front of me shared one thing in common. They looked presentable. I looked down at my peach T-shirt tucked into my knee length beige corduroy skirt and wondered if I was making a huge mistake. The lady who was serving them was also well turned out in her white blouse. She had a small brooch just above her left breast. It was a little diamanté fox with red jewels for eyes. I thought it was really stylish.

On the far wall, above the entrance, a large old round clock hung. It was five-twenty and the shop would be closing in ten minutes. Panic set in when I realised how little time I had left. I wasn't even wearing the right clothes. If only Larry hadn't been outside I could have left.

I was so busy worrying that I didn't notice that both the people in front of me had paid and left the shop. The woman behind the till stood there looking at me with her head to one side.

'Can I help you, dear?' Her impatience was tangible.

'Oh, sorry,' I mumbled, 'I came to– my friend said– I mean, I wanted to talk to you.'

She folded her arms across her chest and raised her salt and pepper eyebrows. On a second glance she was older than I first thought.

'I haven't got all day.' It was not going well.

'Ms Faulks,' Larry's voice echoed through the room. 'This is Deborah,' he said, sauntering over wearing his charming smile, 'my friend who we talked about earlier. She's here to inquire about the job.' I watched in amazement as the expression on the woman's face instantly softened.

'Why didn't you say?' Ms Faulks turned to me. Her breath smelt of instant coffee and her small grey eyes peered through her gold-framed glasses, which sat at the end of her pointy nose.

'I was about to.' I dug my nails into the palms of my hands.

'This is Dee. She'd be perfect for you.' Larry was leaning on his elbows on the desk looking relaxed and I realised that they knew each other.

'Have you worked in a bookshop before?' she asked, her gaze unflinching.

'No, no I haven't.' I could tell immediately that she didn't like me.

'But she's got lots of experience dealing with customers, haven't you, Dee?' I was grateful for Larry's presence.

'Yes. I currently work in Woolworths. I have to talk to customers all the time.'

'But never about anything other than loo brushes,' Ms Faulks cut in.

'No, that's true. But I love reading. I read all the time. I'm never late and I'm respectful of others.' I wasn't ready to give up just yet.

'I see.' Ms Faulks turned her attention to a pile of books to the left of the till while she considered my response.

'Some people think it's easy working in a bookshop. It's not. You need to keep on top of things.'

'Very organised aren't you, Ms F?' Larry winked at me. 'She's only asking for an interview,' he continued, still fighting my corner.

'Very well.' The spinster turned to me. 'You can come back on Saturday morning at nine a.m. before the shop opens and we can have a proper discussion then. Make sure you bring your CV.'

'I won't be late, I promise, thank you–'

'And, dear, a piece of advice. Try not to look so, so...' she was searching for the word, 'dowdy next time. Never wear a T-shirt to work. That might be fine in Woolworths,' she couldn't disguise her disgust at the mention of it, 'but here we have standards.'

'Ah, thanks Ms F. You won't regret it. Dee's a really hard worker.'

Once outside I was able to finally relax my shoulders. The intensity of the woman's stare had been too much for me. I was dreading the formal interview.

'There you go,' Larry removed a large red apple from his bag and bit into it, 'easy as pie.'

'Why didn't you tell me you knew her?'

'Didn't think to. She comes into Rook's to get her glasses prescription. Got a bit of a soft spot for me, I think.'

'I don't think she liked me very much.' I didn't hold out much hope for getting the job.

'Ah, take no notice. She's a pussycat when you get to know her. You'll see.'

I doubted he was right.

5

JULY 16TH 1983

On Saturday morning I woke at seven. The sun was making its climb, warm rays flooding through the green leaves on the branch that overhung our garden in front of my bedroom window.

Dawn was still fast asleep, her satin eye mask blocking out the light. She was sleeping in her favourite Frankie Says Relax T-shirt. She must have got home late last night. I didn't hear her come in and I stopped reading at about ten o'clock. Dad never told her off for coming home late. He was always too drunk to notice. I suspected Dawn had a boyfriend, not that she'd ever confide in me.

Pulling the covers back I got out of bed. I was wearing the mint green V-neck short-sleeved polyester nightdress I always wore. Looking down at my feet I could see that my toenails needed cutting. Tiptoeing out of the room, so as not wake Dawn, I pulled the door closed quietly behind me. From Dad's bedroom I could hear snoring as I went into the bathroom.

Our bathroom was as dated as the rest of the house. All the taps on the moss green suite were loose and drippy. The floor was grey speckled lino that looked dirty no matter how often I mopped it. I opened the mirrored cabinet above the sink and hunted for the toenail clippers. The shelves were filled with Dawn's products. I didn't know what most of them did but one thing was for sure, she always looked and smelt nice. Behind a large bottle of bubble bath I eventually found what I was searching for.

Sitting on the edge of the bath I lifted one knee up to my chin and started to trim my nails. The hard crescent clippings fell to the floor and collected in a pile. I couldn't remember the last time I paid attention to my feet and wondered why I was bothering on that day. Ms Faulks would not be seeing my toes.

After having a quick shower, I brushed my teeth. I watched in the mirror as my hair dried in front of my eyes until it stood up in the usual halo of frizz around my head. Even though I was clean, I looked like a mess. Determined to make a good impression at the interview, I opened the cabinet again and pulled out the box containing Dawn's vast collection of hair accessories. Fingering through the content I wondered what some of the knick-knacks did. How they fixed into your hair was a mystery to me. But then I found a black Alice band that would do the job. I did my best to flatten my hair then placed it carefully on my head before inspecting myself in the mirror. I looked so different with my hair pushed back from my face. My skin was so pale and my cheeks lacked colour. I toyed with the idea of applying a little bit of make-up but didn't want to risk putting it on wrong so decided against it.

With a towel wrapped around my body, I crept back past Dad's room and into my bedroom. Dawn was still in the Land of Nod as I carefully opened the wardrobe door and removed an old white shirt I used to wear to school. Since I didn't have a suitably smart skirt to go with it I reached for a pair of black cotton-mix trousers and got dressed as quietly as I could. I didn't want Dawn to see me leaving the house looking like that. She would ask questions.

It wasn't impossible that I would have time to go the interview and make it back to the house in time to change before either of them rose from their pits, but I didn't want to take the chance. I stuffed a long brown cotton skirt and blue T-shirt into my rucksack before putting on my old black lace-up school shoes. I would change in the public toilets on the green before I came home. Just to be on the safe side.

Once downstairs in the kitchen I prepared my breakfast, which consisted of a bowl of Ready Brek, a glass of water and an orange. On the hob I warmed the milk and water before plunging the oats in to cook. There was something quite soothing about watching the grains expand in the liquid. Gradually they turned into a grey mush and I added half a teaspoon of sugar before removing them from the heat.

Mum always used to make me porridge when I was little, especially when it was cold. It made me feel close to her repeating the habit and so it became my tradition every morning, whatever the weather.

Dawn only ever ate fruit. Better for my skin, she used to say. I'm sure she was right but I pitied her. She didn't remember mum the way I did.

I put my empty bowl into a sink full of water to soak while I turned my attention to the orange. Taking a knife out of the cutlery drawer I sawed carefully through the waxy skin of the fruit. When the metal met the juicy flesh I took my time. Watching the juices spill out and drip down the blade was hypnotic.

When all that was left was the dimpled skin of the fruit on a plate, I tidied away the evidence of my breakfast and got ready to leave. It was eight-twenty. I had forty minutes before I was due at the bookshop. On a warm sunny day, like it was, it would only take me twenty-five minutes to walk there. That meant I wouldn't be late. That was a good thing. The interview was going to be challenging enough without my timing being brought into question.

As I left the house I was convinced that I heard someone stirring. It would be just my luck if on that day one of them decided to get up early. The world was against me, and I wondered why I had always ignored this fact until now.

Pulling my rucksack over my arms, I tugged the door closed behind me and stepped out on to our bland street. Even in the sunshine, when it should have looked its best, it was uninspiring. No wonder most of the people who lived locally had issues with alcohol.

Determined not to let my new-found resolution take a hit, I marched along the concrete pavement towards my future. It was as exciting as it was sobering. I did my best to forget my first encounter with Ms Faulks. She clearly had a soft spot for Larry and I hoped that might extend to me, too.

It wasn't worth dwelling on the types of questions she might ask. Honestly, I had no real experience and couldn't possibly second-guess what it was she was looking for. But she was a difficult character and I found it hard to imagine that many people would be willing to work for her. That was something I had on my side. That and Larry.

Despite the fact it was before nine a.m. on a Saturday morning there was a reasonable amount of traffic. Of course, nowadays the roads are permanently gridlocked. Even in those days we noticed that there were more and more vehicles on the road. Cars where everywhere and more than that, they were a status symbol. German cars were the most sought-after for some reason. Although I remember reading somewhere that a lot of the big German car companies started off making vehicles for the Nazis. Not that it really bothered me. I didn't drive nor could I imagine any time when I might have my own little car. I never pictured myself driving anything flash. A second-hand Ford Escort or something like that would have been nice.

As I turned on to the bridge that linked Chesterton Road to Jesus Green I started to feel butterflies. I wondered what I was doing, being so brave and taking such a risk. I was content in my job. It was safe. Trying for the position in the bookshop was so unlike me. So unsafe.

My head bowed, looking at my feet, I didn't notice Larry approaching me from the opposite end of the path. I was so busy tussling with the idea of turning around and going home that I jumped when he laid his hand on my shoulder and spoke.

'Hello you.' He was wearing a white T-shirt and denim shorts. The first thing I saw were his legs, which looked tanned and were covered in fine, dark hairs. 'Sorry,' he apologised exaggeratedly stepping back, 'I didn't mean to scare you. I don't bite very often.' His grin was broad and white and I was reminded yet again of George Michael. I never went in for pop stars but if I had, George Michael would have got my vote. Dawn loved him too. She hid posters of him under her mattress. Dad would not have approved.

'Nervous?' Larry slipped his arm through mine and we carried on walking together.

'Yes, a bit.' I chewed my bottom lip and kept my eyes on the ground.

'You'll be fine. Honestly. The job is yours. Larry says so.' He winked and pulled my arm gently. 'You look really smart.' He popped a piece of gum into his mouth before offering me a piece. I declined.

'No thanks, I don't think Ms Faulks would like me chewing gum.'

'Probably right. You don't miss a trick, do you.' I liked him flirting with me. It was a welcome distraction from my nerves. 'Your hair looks nice. You've done something different to it?'

'Yes.' I was so pleased he had noticed.

'I like being able to see your face properly. And those pretty eyes.'

Self-consciously I adjusted the Alice band as we approached the front of the bookshop. He let go of my arm and took a step back.

'So, here we are.' He had tucked his hands into his pockets and looked sheepish suddenly. 'I'll wait in the coffee shop round the corner on King Street. Meet me there when you're done.'

'OK.' I clung on to the straps of my rucksack to stop my hands from shaking.

'Break a leg.' He blew me a kiss before turning and walking away.

The centre was strangely quiet. Very few shops were open and the normal bustle of people on their way to work was missing. I checked my watch. It was five to nine. Standing on the pavement I looked up at the shop front and wondered whether I should knock on the door or just try to open it.

Since Ms Faulks was expecting me I peered in through the glass to see if I could see her. The bookshop was as empty as the street. I tried the door to see if it would open. It did.

Walking in the soles of my shoes echoed across the wooden floor. Suddenly it seemed like a spooky place, full of ghosts. I slipped my rucksack off my back and held it in front of me before finding the courage to call out.

'Ms Faulks?' No reply. 'Hello, Ms Faulks, it's Deborah. Deborah Campkin. I'm here for my interview.' Silence.

I stood still for a few moments wondering what I should do. The door was open so surely she must be there. I decided to go to the back of the shop to investigate. I knew if I was more than a few seconds late it would give her the ammunition she needed to grill me.

Passing by rows and rows of neat bookshelves I came to a door that led into a back room. The sign on it read 'Staff Only' so rather than go through I thought it best to knock.

'Yes.' Her shrill voice called out from the other side of the door. 'Come in.'

Holding my breath I pushed the heavy wooden door open to find Ms Faulks sitting stiffly in a chair at a desk.

'I thought you were going to be late, but I see that you are punctual. Take a seat.' Her navy patent leather heeled shoes stuck out from her green tartan trousers. She was wearing a pale blue blouse and the same diamanté fox brooch I had noticed a few days earlier.

I sat down unaware that I was still chewing my lip.

'So,' she looked down at a piece of paper through her small spectacles, determined not to grace me with eye contact, 'why do you want this job?'

There were no niceties. She cut right to the chase.

'Well, I really like reading books.'

'Sit up straight, please. I can't bear it when girls slouch.'

'Sorry.' I felt myself going red.

'What else?'

'What do you mean?' Her attempt to make me feel foolish was working.

'I like food, but I have no desire to work in a supermarket. Just because you read it doesn't mean you are suited to working in a bookshop. Tell me why I should employ you.'

'I am young and eager to learn.' I was determined not to let her cold stare put me off. 'I have experience working with customers. I'm used to using a till and I'm a fast learner.'

She sat back in her chair and took a long look at me.

'If that's the best you can come up with then I really don't think this is right for you. I need someone intelligent, who can communicate with the people who come into the shop. Someone who can advise the customers which books to buy and who can help the students find what they are looking for. I'm just not sure you are made of the right stuff.'

'But if you give me a chance, I can show you that I could do this job justice.' My bravery came out of nowhere and I stunned even myself.

'I will not be persuaded by insolence,' she growled talking the wind out of my sails. 'It's brains this job requires not balls. If I had wanted to hire a man I would have done so.'

'Well,' I got up and put my rucksack over one shoulder, 'thank you anyway.'

'Where on earth do you think you're going?' Ms Faulks bellowed.

'But I thought this interview was over–' by then I really was confused.

'Sit down,' she barked.

I stood glued to the spot unable to move or speak. It had taken her all of two minutes to tear me down and now she wanted me to stay. It didn't make sense. I was shy and lacking in confidence but I was no masochist.

'Why? Why should I sit down?' I stood over her and started to feel more certain of myself. 'You've called me stupid and insolent all in the space of a few minutes. I came here for a job interview not a character assassination.'

Ms Faulks sat in her chair looking up at me with disbelief.

'I wanted this job and I know I could have done it well but you aren't prepared to give me a chance so no, I won't sit down. If I want abuse, I can get that at home.'

Ms Faulks stood up; the space between our bodies was less than two feet. 'I've decided you don't have what it takes to work here. Kindly leave. Now.'

I shrugged my shoulders and turned away. Just as I reached the door I heard her say, 'No one that unattractive should be foist upon the general public. Can't imagine what a nice boy like Larry sees in you.'

I stopped with my back to her and my hand on the door-knob. For the first time in my life I was overcome with anger. My hands were shaking but no longer from nerves. For a moment I imagined what it would be like to spin around and slap her hard across the face. Gritting my teeth, I pushed the door open and marched out of the shop.

Once outside again the full force of the adrenaline hit me. I shook all over and had to go and lean against a wall to steady myself. In the few minutes I had spent in the shop Cambridge had come to life. People were beginning to fill the street and vans loaded with goods for the market traders crawled along the narrow cobbled road.

I tipped my face up towards the sky and let the sunshine soothe me. Facing Larry was going to be difficult. The thought of disappointing him filled me with dread.

The coffee shop he had mentioned was less than a hundred yards away but the journey there felt like the final steps of a prisoner on death row. I no longer felt anger. Only shame. I knew my bubble would burst. The last few weeks spent in Larry's company had been like a dream. Girls like me didn't get the leading man. We were extras wheeled in to make the female star of the show look even better.

As I turned down the alley I could see that Larry was sitting in the window of the coffee shop. He spotted me and jumped out of his seat, pushed past the breakfast crowd and bounded out of the door. It was so unlike him. Normally he was the pinnacle of cool.

'So, when do you start?' he called out, taking broad strides towards me.

I stopped dead in my tracks and waited for him to join me. As he got closer he must have noticed the expression on my face and his smile melted away.

'I don't.' My voice was meek and I couldn't look him in the eye. He stopped about a metre away and examined me.

'What happened, Dee?' He was no longer the boisterous young man he had been the moment before.

'She hated me.' I was trying not to cry so that he wouldn't see my misery.

'Come on,' he moved closer to me and put his arm around my shoulder, 'let me buy you a hot chocolate. Then you can tell me what went wrong.'

6

I'd followed her home the day before but kept my distance. She lived in a maisonette in one of the Victorian houses off Chesterton Road. From the other end of the street, I watched her let herself in and go indoors. I didn't even know why I'd followed her. I was curious, I suppose. I wanted to see where she lived.

On the Sunday I waited around, hoping to catch sight of her. Fate played her card. The old woman came out of her house holding a bag as if she was about to go shopping. It was a clammy day. It felt like thunder was in the air and a storm was approaching. Making sure she didn't see me, I stayed behind her, following as she took a bus to a supermarket. She was smartly dressed; just like she had been the first time I'd laid eyes on her. She never had a hair out of place.

She went about her business unaware that my attention was focused solely on her. She didn't seem aware of my presence. That's when it dawned on me. That's when I knew what I wanted to do. I left her to her shopping, returned to her street and waited.

An hour later she returned carrying an armful of bags and went into her house. Still managing to conceal myself at the other end of the street I noticed the noise coming from the river. A gentle lapping of water. Hoping the old woman would stay put for a while, I decided to go and investigate. I needed to plan my next move.

I passed one of the university rowing houses as I made my way down towards the water. The angry grey sky above was reflected in the surface. Transfixed by the beauty of the movement I bend down and dipped my fingers into the river. It was cold but not as cold as I had been expecting. Taking my hand up to my nose I tried to get a scent from it. A couple in a rowing boat looked at me strangely and I retreated from the river's edge, not wanting to draw attention to myself.

At the end of her street, Kimberley Road, was a narrow walkway that led down to the river. I decided I would wait there until it was dark. The clouds were rolling fast across the sky, tumbling towards their final destination.

The hours dripped by slowly until eventually dusk fell over the city. I watched as birds returned home and the people of the river started to disappear until there was no one. Only me.

At half-past ten at night I decided to make my move. I was cold by then and I was getting impatient.

I took a deep breath, relishing the buzz of adrenaline, as I approached her front door. I knocked once, loud enough that she would hear.

Seconds later her grey face appeared in the open doorway.

'Hello?' Her voice was clipped but tinged with uncertainty.

Before she had a second to react I put my hands around her throat and shoved her inside, pushing the front door closed behind me using my foot. I was surprised by my own strength. Her little beady eyes filled with horror as I continued to tighten my grip. Her cheeks started to turn red as her hands scrabbled at my arms in vain. I was not going to let go. Not until it was over.

Beneath my palm I could feel the pressure of one of her veins and the blood trying to pump around her body. Every ounce of strength she had was fighting to stay alive. But my desire was stronger and I squeezed harder still.

After a minute her body started to relax and go floppy. Still I held on to her neck until I was sure I had seen the life leave her body. As she died with my hands around her throat her body grew heavy. Refusing to let go and wanting to keep the moment alive for as long as possible, I collapsed on top of her still gripping her throat.

We must have lain together like that for some time in her hallway. Eventually I pulled myself off her and sat back to look at her body. My breathing was heavy, almost a pant.

She was so still. Her eyes were bloodshot and staring. I sat with her there for a while stroking her hair. Then I got up off the floor and went to explore her home. I turned the television off in the sitting room before walking into the kitchen. There, lying on a draining board was a clean plate, a saucepan and a small kitchen knife. I picked it up, mesmerised by the shine of the metal, and ran my finger along the sharp blade. It had been calling to me and at last I knew what I had to do.

Returning to the body I knelt down beside it and stroked her hair for one last time before carefully inserting the point of the knife into the skin below her left eye. I moved the blade around the socket until eventually I was able to lever the eyeball out.

The jelly mass lay on her cheek still attached to the nerves. I was amazed by the intricate anatomy. My fingers were covered in blood and bits of skin so I wiped them on her blouse before hacking through muscles and veins that were attached to the eyeball itself.

When I had finished removing both eyes I stood up to admire my work. She would never look at me like that again. Two hollow bloody caves stared back at me and I felt a grin spread across my face. I returned to the kitchen, washed my hands and the knife before putting it back where I'd found it. Then I searched for something to put the eyeballs in. I would keep them. They would be a reminder.

For lack of anything better, I used a plastic bag to wrap them in *before putting them into my pocket. Checking the time on my wrist-watch I saw that it was nearly one o'clock in the morning.*

Stepping over her corpse I went over to the front door and opened it a fraction. Outside the night was dark and quiet. I ran my eye up and down to the street to check nobody was about, before taking hold of her ankles and dragging her heavy weight down to the river. It was only twenty yards but my heart was thumping hard in my chest from a mixture of the effort and the next wave of adrenaline.

I rolled her on to her back to look at her one last time and noticed the little brooch on her blouse glinting in the moonlight. A keepsake.

Using all my strength I rolled her little body into the water and watched for a second as it started to drift away.

Then I slipped back into the night taking with me my treasures.

7

JULY 19TH 1983

By the time Tuesday arrived I had started to forget about my interview from hell. Larry had done a brilliant job of consoling me. Silly old bat, he'd said. It made me feel much better. But still I couldn't quite shake the memory of her forbidding stare and cutting words.

It wasn't the first time in my life that I'd suffered rejection, and it wouldn't be the last, but it had never come from someone I expected to respect before. I couldn't make sense of it. My mere existence seemed to be at the root of her hostility.

Before I met Larry I'd been invisible. I might not have liked that but I was comfortable with it. It was all I'd ever known. Then he burst into my life and things started to change – both for the better and for the worse. It seemed that my association with him was having a ripple effect on my life. It was as exciting as it was scary.

As usual I had agreed to meet Larry for lunch. It was a dull day. The air was close and the sky threatened rain. On my way to buy my sandwich I passed a newsagent's. Propped outside beside the entrance was a billboard with a headline in large black capitals.

BODY OF WOMAN FOUND IN RIVER

I never normally paid attention to the local news but it was such a sensational story that I felt compelled to go into the shop and buy a paper. I paid for a copy of the *Cambridge Evening News* and left the shop. The sky was darker than before and ominous clouds were collecting above the rooftops. Shoving the paper into my rucksack I made my way towards the café I often met Larry in. I would read about it later.

When I reached the café Larry was standing outside leaning against a wall talking to a beautiful brunette, who curled a long lock of hair in her fingers and giggled. I stopped just out of sight, uncertain whether I should interrupt. The young woman was wearing a pale pink vest and denim shorts that showed off her long thighs. She dropped the cigarette she had been smoking and stubbed it out with one of her clean white sneakers before sauntering away. When I was sure she was gone I scurried out from my hiding place and approached Larry.

'Hi Dee.' He hugged me.

'Sorry I'm late.'

'Only a minute or two. Doesn't matter. I just bumped into Lorna.'

'Who is she?' I tried my best to disguise my jealousy.

'One of Eric's girlfriends.' Larry rolled his eyes.

'How many does he have?'

'Too many. Lorna was trying to find out what he'd been up to and why he hadn't contacted her.'

'Oh.' Relief washed over me.

'I really don't understand where he finds the time to juggle all those ditsy girls. One girlfriend is enough for me.' It was the first time he had referred to me, as that and I loved how it sounded.

I was someone's girlfriend.

'I've been thinking,' he continued, 'it's about time you met my family.' I was horrified and thrilled all at the same time. 'Why don't you come over for Sunday lunch? My ma does a good roast.'

'If you think it's OK.'

'OK? I've told them all about you. They're dying to meet my mystery woman.'

'OK then. That sounds nice.'

'Great. I'll tell Ma to set another place at the table. She's going to be so excited.'

This was a big step. It was huge. I was going to meet his family. My stomach filled with butterflies.

'Now,' he put his arm around my shoulder and started to guide me away from the café, 'I want to buy my girl something to wear for the special occasion. We want you looking your best.' Was he really suggesting we went clothes shopping? I hated the idea but remained silent as he led me by the hand towards the shopping centre. 'Come on, look, Topshop has a summer sale.'

I had never been clothes shopping with anyone other than my mum and certainly never somewhere like Topshop before.

'I don't know.' I freed my hand from his and stopped outside. 'I don't think it's really me.'

'Sure it is. Just come in and have a look. If you don't see anything you like we won't buy anything.' His boyish enthusiasm was hard to refuse.

'OK. Just looking.'

When we entered the shop we were subjected to loud music blasted out of speakers on the wall. David Bowie's 'China Girl' filled the air. The room was filled with racks of clothes all hanging neatly. It was so colourful. So unlike what I was used to. Gaggles of girls stood fingering through the clothes. They all looked like adverts for the store. I stood out like a sore thumb in my Woolworths uniform. One or two of them looked at me with disdain.

'Over here,' Larry called out. He was standing holding a pink dress with puffy arms and frilly skirt. I'd never seen anything like it. 'What about this?'

'No, I couldn't.' The idea of it was horrible.

'Too much?' he examined the dress.

'Just a bit.' I didn't want to be rude but there was no way I was going to wear something like that.

'OK. So we keep looking,' he hung the dress back on the rack. 'Seen anything you like?'

'Not so far.'

'Let's keep looking.'

I followed him around the shop as he picked up clothes that I continued to reject until finally I spotted something bearable.

'This is nice.' I held up a plain white cropped T-shirt.

'OK.' He didn't sound convinced. 'I suppose that's a start.'

I clung on to the top for dear life hoping that the shopping trip would now end. But it didn't.

Larry went over to a row of shelves on the wall and removed a pair of denim shorts with frayed hems. They looked very similar to the ones Lorna had been wearing.

'These would be perfect with the tee.' He held them up against me.

'They look a bit small.' Shame hit me like a fist to the face.

'So, find them in your size.' He wasn't going to take no for an answer so I went through the pile until I found a pair of size 14. It was the largest size they had.

'Are you going to try them on?'

'No!' the idea of going into the changing room was terrifying. 'I'm sure they will fit. I can always bring them back if they don't.'

'OK.' He was looking at the price tags. He had offered to pay but I wondered if he really meant it. Too embarrassed to ask I opened my rucksack and searched for my brown purse.

'Don't be silly. Put it away,' he said, dismissing it with a gesture. 'It's my treat.'

Grateful but unaware of how to show it, I put my purse back into my bag.

'Now, to the shoes.' Larry marched over to the display at the back of the shop.

I had never seen so many shoes before. There were heels in all shapes and sizes. I'd never worn stilettoes before and didn't plan on starting any time soon. Luckily he made his way over to the sneakers. He picked up a pair of bright white ones with pink laces.

'These are perfect.' Larry held them out for me to inspect.

'Not really me.' I refused to take them.

'Nonsense. They will be perfect with the outfit. What size do you wear?'

'Six.' I didn't have the energy or the inclination to disagree.

Larry approached a girl wearing a nametag who was picking at her nail varnish.

'I'll take these in a size six.'

I watched as the girl disappeared into the back of the shop to fetch the shoes and it occurred to me that the shoes were a lot like the ones Lorna had been wearing. Just like the shorts.

Larry paid, handed me the bag and we left the shop. My stomach was rumbling since we hadn't had lunch. My sandwich was sitting in my rucksack getting warm.

'Right. Next.' He checked his Casio wristwatch.

'Next?'

'Come with me. I've got a surprise for you.'

I followed him through the shopping centre and back out on to Sidney Street. We passed Woolworths and continued on to

Bridge Street. The sky was even darker and the rain was imminent.

Larry stopped outside a hairdresser's and held his arms out. 'Surprise!'

I didn't understand.

'I've booked you an appointment to have your hair done.' He must have seen the look of horror on my face. 'You looked so lovely the other day, with your hair back, I thought maybe it was time for a change. You are so pretty, Dee. You don't know how pretty you are. I think a haircut is just what you need to help you make the most of yourself.' He brushed my frizzy hair back off my forehead. 'A new style will make you feel like a new woman.'

He held the door open and I stepped in. The smell of flowery shampoo filled my nostrils. Larry approached the desk.

'Dee has an appointment for twelve-fifty.'

'Yes, that's right.' The receptionist said checking her diary. 'With Lucy. Please take a seat.'

I went over to a row of chairs and sat at the end. Larry came and sat beside me.

'I really don't think I can afford it Larry.' The panic was beginning to set in. 'I don't get paid until the end of the month.'

'My treat, I said.' He rubbed his trousers with the palms of his hand then picked up a magazine that was lying on the small coffee table. He flicked through before stopping on a page and showing me the picture. 'What do you think?'

There was a photograph of a pop star I vaguely recognised.

'Very nice.' I didn't really understand what he meant.

'Good. We'll tell Lucy that's what you want: a Sheena East-on.' He put the magazine down, open, on the chair next to him, folded his arms and sat back.

'You mean the hair?'

'Yes, of course.'

'Oh, I'm not sure,' I felt like I was losing control.

'You'll look great. We'll ask her to dye it to. Would you rather go darker or blonde?'

'Um,' I'd never thought of dying my hair and wasn't sure I was ready to do so then. 'It's just a bit shorter than I normally like.' I referred back to the photograph of the pop singer's cropped hairstyle.

'Change is good. Otherwise you're always just standing still.' He always used to say that.

Before I could object Lucy appeared and guided me over to a chair. Larry followed casually holding the magazine. I sat obediently down in front of the mirror. Lucy, standing behind, smiled at me in the reflection.

'So what can I do for you today?' She was chewing gum.

'That.' Larry held the picture out to show her. 'Just like that.'

'Oh lovely.' Lucy was lifting first one section of my hair and then another. She nodded. 'I love it when a client comes in who wants a new look.'

'I'm not sure it's really me.'

'I think it will really suit the shape of her face.' Lucy continued paying no attention to my objection. 'Are you wanting to dye it?'

'Yes.' Larry was standing next to her and smiling at me in the mirror. I didn't want to disappoint him.

'Yes.' I echoed.

'What colour would you suggest?' he asked the hairdresser.

'Nothing too dark. Maybe a few highlights here and there.' Lucy had her head tipped to one side.

'What about blonde?' Larry looked eager.

'Yes, that could work.'

I sat in silence while the two of them discussed what should be done to my hair. It made me feel foolish, not being included in the talk. Larry had never made me feel like that before. As if sensing my disappointment Larry interrupted Lucy, who was suggesting maybe auburn would suit me.

'What do you think Dee?' he smiled at me and squatted down so that his face was level with mine. 'What do you want?'

'I think blonde would be good,' I suggested hoping that would please him.

'Blonde it is.' Larry stood up. 'Right, I'll leave you girls to it. I'll see you back here in...' he checked his watch.

'Give us until two-fifteen.' Lucy said fighting with a tangle in my hair.

'But work! I'm meant to be back at one-thirty.' There was no disguising the panic in my voice.

'I'll go in and tell them you went home because you didn't feel well. Relax, it will be fine.' Larry turned and sauntered out before I had a chance to disagree. Before I knew it Lucy had my head in a sink and was energetically washing my hair. After she had lathered my head in shampoo and conditioner she wrapped a small blue towel tightly around my dripping wet scalp and led me back to my chair.

While she disappeared off to fetch one product or other I removed the newspaper from my rucksack and started to read the main story.

BODY OF WOMAN FOUND IN RIVER

In the river by Stourbridge Common, a dog walker made the grim discovery of a body in the early hours of the morning, the *Cambridge Evening News* can reveal.

A massive police investigation was launched after the body of the woman was found at the site to the east of the city.

The dead woman's identity has not been released, but our sources say she worked in a shop in the city centre.

Detectives set up a major crime scene and scoured woods in the area.

It is believed they were looking for a weapon after finding several wounds on the body.

The site was cordoned off during the investigation, with walkers and cyclists arriving at the site to use the paths being turned away.

Police spent hours at the site and it remains un-opened after officers declared the death was suspicious.

The Cambridgeshire force has contacted the victim's next of kin.

A police spokesman said: 'The body of a woman was found by a man who was walking his dogs at the time. The death is being treated as suspicious and we are advising the public to remain vigilant.' The force spokesman added that detectives would conduct a thorough investigation and were asking for anyone with information to come forward.

I folded the newspaper and sat back stunned, thinking of the people I'd seen working in Freeman's.

By the time Lucy had finished with me I didn't recognise myself. For the first time ever I looked my age. I stared at the girl with the peroxide hair staring back at me.

'Do you like it?' Lucy asked holding a mirror up to show me the back of my head.

'Yes.' I really wasn't sure.

'We've got some really nice products that will help to keep it lovely and soft. Helps with the frizz. We sell make-up too, if you're interested.' I got the hint.

She removed the cape from my shoulders and blew the last remaining hairs from my neck.

'Just go over to reception to pay.' It was the most she had said to me since Larry left. I'd sat static in the chair pretending to read a gossip magazine so I could avoid eye contact and didn't have to watch the chunks of my hair falling to the floor.

'Thank you.' I picked up my rucksack and went over to reception, avoiding looking in any of the numerous mirrors.

Larry was already there, leaning on the desk talking to the receptionist.

'WOW!' He stopped and let his mouth hang open. 'You look incredible.'

'You like it?' I touched my hair self-consciously and shuffled on the spot.

'Love it.' He held his arms out and beckoned me. I did as I was told but felt uncomfortable with the public display of affection. 'Right, what's the damage?' he asked turning back towards the till and removing his battered leather wallet from his back pocket.

Embarrassed that Larry was paying for me again, I moved towards the door to wait for him. I didn't want to know how much it cost.

'Come on you,' he slipped his arm around my waist, 'let's go before it starts to bucket down.'

Once outside we headed for shelter. The rain had just started to fall and the black clouds looked angrier than ever.

'Bloody miserable. Thought it was meant to be the summer.' He chuckled pulling me down so that I was half sitting on his lap in the bus stop.

'Thank you for today.'

'You're very welcome. I can't wait to see you in your new outfit.' I felt something hard digging into the back of my leg and froze. Larry felt me stiffen and adjusted his erection.

'What time shall I come to lunch on Sunday?' The words fell out of my mouth fast as I tried desperately to lighten the awkwardness I felt.

'About one will do. But I'll check with Ma.'

'Will your dad be there?' I thought it strange he rarely spoke about his father.

'Should be.'

We stayed in the bus shelter for a while until the worst of the rain subsided. I kept looking around nervously, terrified that someone from work might see me and tell Stuart that I was bunking off. I'd forgotten how different I looked. No one would have recognised me.

Above us the clouds crashed together and thunder echoed across the sky.

'Let's get out of here.' Larry stood up. He was at least half a foot taller than me.

'Where do you want to go?'

'I've got a great idea. Come on.' He led me through the rain and into the park. Water dripped down my neck and made me feel naked suddenly. 'Over there,' he indicated to the public toilets near the river, 'you can try on your new clothes for me.'

By then I was tired and hungry. I hadn't had any lunch and felt exhausted.

'I'd rather try them on at home. You'll see me in them on Sunday.'

'Don't be shy.' He pulled me along the path eagerly towards the small public building.

'I'm not sure.'

When we reached the toilets Larry pushed me up against the wall and started to kiss me. He put his tongue into my mouth and pressed his hand against my crotch. The feeling that ran through my body was something I had not experienced before. It felt good.

'Now Dee, go in there and show me what a pretty girl you are.'

Breathlessly I nodded and did what I was told.

When I went into the first cubicle I didn't notice he was right behind me. He shoved me in and pushed the lock across the door.

The toilet was tiny and there was hardly room for the both of us.

'Take off your dress.' He ordered.

I was shivering all over and stood there unable to move. Then he got on to his knees and lifted my dress. He pulled my white cotton pants down and started to kiss my special place. The pleasure was so intense I thought I might faint.

When he had finished doing that he turned me round and bent me over the loo. I didn't know what was happening but was powerless to resist.

'Dee,' he grunted. He ran his hand through my short hair as he thrust into me. I yelped but it only encouraged him.

Minutes later it was all over. He pulled his trousers up and left the cubicle. I sat down on the toilet in pain and in shock. Removing some tissue from its holder I wiped away the fluid that dripped down the inside of my thigh before pulling up my pants and straightening my clothes.

When I stepped out of the toilet I caught a glimpse of myself in the mirror. The girl looking back at me wasn't Deborah. Deborah was gone. Dee had taken her place.

8

JULY 24TH 1983

Sunday came around quickly. I'd met Larry every day in between and we returned to the public toilets to practise. That's what he called it.

After having sex we chatted like we always did. I recounted the reaction Dawn and my Dad had to my radical new haircut. Dad nearly dropped his beer. It was almost funny.

'What on earth you done to your barnet?' He wiped the froth from his moustache with the back of his sleeve and I was reminded of my favourite book as a child; *The Twits*.

'Do you like it?' I knew I would regret asking the question.

'Like it? You look like a toilet brush.'

Dawn's reaction wasn't much better. 'Why did you do it? It's not very you,' she said applying her lipstick in our bedroom mirror.

But I didn't care what they thought. Larry liked it and that was all that mattered.

As I got dressed in my new clothes and did my best to make my hair look the way it had done when I left the hairdressers, Dawn was in our room also getting ready to go out. She was meeting up with some of her girlfriends and they were going to the cinema to watch *Staying Alive*. John Travolta was the main role. I hadn't seen many of his films but I did enjoy *Grease*.

In order to avoid having to talk to me Dawn turned her old Roberts radio on.

After a song I didn't know ended the voice of a newsreader filled the air.

'After the shocking discovery of the body of Daphne Faulks, aged 58 from Cambridge, on Stourbridge Common, police are searching for the killer. A dog walker found Ms Faulks, who lived alone and worked at Freeman's bookshop in the city centre, in the early hours of Monday morning. The inspector in charge of the investigation said that the brutal nature of the crime meant they were using all their resources to find the person responsible. As of yet no arrests have been made. In other news...'

I sat down on my bed and looked down at my brand new sneakers. I couldn't believe they had found her body. It seemed so unfair.

Dawn turned and looked at me.

'What's wrong with you?' She fluffed her hair with the palm of her hand.

'It's horrible about that woman.'

'I guess.' Dawn looked so uninterested.

'Someone killed her.'

'I know. But better her than me.' Dawn shrugged and left the room.

I sat there for a moment thinking about my experience with Ms Faulks. She was not a nice person. Maybe Dawn had a point.

Larry met me at midday at the Drummer Street bus station and walked me to his house. The sun was shining and the streets were busy with weekend shoppers and people out enjoying the warmth.

'Did you hear about Ms Faulks?'

'Sure did. Pretty grim. Did you hear that the killer stabbed her eyes out?' He seemed strangely aroused.

'Really? That's disgusting. I wonder why anyone would want to kill an old woman?'

'She wasn't that old,' Larry laughed.

'No, I suppose not.'

'Probably had it coming after the way she treated you.'

As we walked along the road past Parker's Piece he spotted a bench and suggested we sat and basked in the warmth for a moment.

The slats on the bench were warm against my pale bare legs. The shorts I'd got from Topshop were a little tight around my waist. I noticed my stomach bulge over the top of the denim and tugged on the white T-shirt to disguise it.

Larry put his arm around my shoulder and slid closer to me.

'I've been thinking Dee,' he was looking out over the green, watching a group of young men kick a football, 'I think we should get married.'

A first I thought he was joking and laughed but when he turned to look at me I could see he was deadly serious.

'I could tell you were a virgin when we met. I liked that about you. Not like the other girls, all putting it about and opening their legs for anyone.'

'Was I bad?'

'No. We need to keep practising, but that's not what I meant. You haven't been spoilt, tainted by anyone else. I don't like the idea of you ever being with another man. You and me, we are good together. I think it makes sense to get married. What do you say?'

I'd read about romantic proposals in books and always wondered what it would be like. Larry had not exactly swept me off my feet by suggesting it off the cuff, sitting on a bench. He didn't even have a ring.

'Well, either you want to be my wife or you don't.' He grinned at me and I melted.

'OK.' I couldn't believe anyone wanted to marry me. Let alone someone as handsome and clever as Larry. I was in shock.

'Is that a yes?'

'Yes. It's a yes.' I wanted to cry.

'Perfect. We'll tell my mum and dad at lunch.' Larry put his hand on my knee and gave it a squeeze.

His family home was halfway down Mackenzie Road, off the top of Mill Road. Hollydene was a terraced brick Victorian house with a bay window and neat, tiled front garden. A large pot with a small pruned bay tree sat next to the mid-blue front door. There were no chips in the paint.

'There's a path down there on the right that leads into the cemetery. I'll take you there after lunch if you like,' Larry signalled with his head while he slipped his key into the lock. 'Ma, I'm back,' he called out, ushering me in to the hallway.

The first thing I noticed was the smell of home cooking. The waft of a chicken roasting in the oven filled the house.

'Come in, come in.' Larry's mother appeared, wiping her hands on a tea-towel.

She was a tall slim woman and I could see the family resemblance. Her hair was short and dark. She wore a patterned blue and green dress that swished whenever she moved.

'Ma, this is Dee.'

'Hello, Dee. I'm Mrs Miller, but please call me Linda. Well, it's really lovely to meet you. Larry hasn't stopped talking about you.'

'Nice to meet you, Mrs Miller.' My throat felt unnaturally dry.

'Linda, I insist.' She gave a wide smile, showing all her large teeth. 'Come on through and have a seat in the dining room.'

As I followed Mrs Miller through the hallway, past the lounge and into the dining room it occurred to me that I was meeting my future mother-in-law. The idea scared me senseless. What if she didn't approve?

'Is Eric joining us?'

'No. He's not.' Linda turned to her son and they shared a relieved look.

Lunch was long. Mr and Mrs Miller sat at either end of the table with Larry and I sandwiched between them. She was warm, the perfect hostess. Mr Miller didn't say much. He just chewed his food.

The chicken was the size of a turkey. I'd never seen such a big one. Mrs Miller placed it proudly on the table and asked Larry to carve. She and Mr Miller could barely look at one another. You could have cut the tension with a knife. Thankfully, Mrs Miller wasn't short of things to say and her idle chatter helped the time pass.

I kept expecting Larry to announce our engagement but he didn't. I put it down to the atmosphere between his parents.

Linda Miller was very friendly but a bit overbearing. She talked with her mouth full, never pausing for breath. I watched the potatoes and broccoli journey around her mouth and tried to concentrate on what she was saying.

It was nice sitting round with a proper family having a civilised meal even if the grown-ups weren't talking to each other. I couldn't remember doing anything like that with Dad and Dawn. Not since Mum died.

When we'd all finished our food and Larry had stopped mopping up his gravy with a piece of sliced bread, I helped Mrs Miller tidy the plates away. She seemed grateful for my offer to help. Larry got up and left his father sitting there alone. He seemed unwilling to allow me to be alone with his mother.

Once in the small kitchen, at the back of the house, I piled the crockery next to the sink while Mrs Miller ran the hot tap and put on an apron.

'You dry.' She smiled, handing me a tea-towel.

Larry leant against one of the cupboards watching us both, nursing his beer. I didn't know he drank. He looked so grown up holding a pint.

When all the dishes were clean Larry kissed his mum on the cheek and told her we were going for a walk. I was disappointed I didn't get to see his bedroom. I thought he'd be eager to show me. But he seemed distracted and we left the house, never saying goodbye to Mr Miller.

'Sorry about that.' Larry rubbed the back of his neck with his hand. 'Let's go to the cemetery.'

I'd never really visited that part of the town before. There had never been any need. We followed the pavement until we came to a small path on the other side of the street.

'Come on,' Larry grabbed my hand and pulled me along.

I was expecting a small churchyard but what I saw was something very different. It was a large open green space with long grass and a few wild flowers, interspersed with headstones. We walked for a while hand in hand silently looking at the names of people long gone.

'I think we shouldn't have a big wedding.' Larry stopped by one of the graves and bent down on his heels so he could read the stone. 'Look at this, Dee, a husband and wife buried together. That's nice.'

I stood awkwardly, my shorts feeling even tighter since consuming a large helping of roast dinner.

'We won't do it in a church. I'm not religious and you're not either, are you?'

'My mum was Catholic, but lapsed. So no, I'm not.'

'We'll go to the registry office and do it there. I'll go in the week and see when they can fit us in.'

'I think we need to tell our parents first before we make any plans.' The reality of telling my dad was dawning on me and I was wondering what had stopped Larry mentioning it at lunch, like he'd said he would.

'I'll tell Mum tomorrow before I go to work. I think she's had an argument with dad and I don't want to get in the middle of it.' He stood up and kissed me on the nose. 'You can tell your dad when you get home.'

'You're not going to be there with me when I tell him?' I was horrified.

'I don't think it would be a good idea if the first time I meet him is when we announce our engagement,' he laughed. 'Much better if you tell him first and then introduce us.'

'OK,' I agreed meekly.

'Oh, and next week speak to your manager and see if you can get more shifts. We need to start saving.'

'I suppose we do. Weddings are probably expensive.'

'Not for the wedding.' Larry was laughing at me and I felt foolish. 'We need to save for somewhere to live. We can't stay living with our parents.'

'No, I suppose not.' I hadn't made that leap yet. It hadn't occurred to me. Everything was happening so quickly.

9

S he was pretty, that was for sure. I'd seen her about. Flirting with all the men, like she didn't have a care in the world. It made me sick. She would be my second. I knew that the minute I laid eyes on her. This time I knew exactly what I wanted to do. I had a plan. She was going to be punished. I would see to that.

The afternoon I'd spotted her I'd followed her home. She worked in the centre but lived off Barton Road to the southwest of the city, in a little place on Hardwick Street. She wasn't very old, probably in her early twenties, and lived in what appeared to be a shared house.

On that day I finished work and walked straight through the town. It was dark so early and that gave me an advantage. I knew the way she went home on her bike. She cycled through the town and cut across Lammas Land, that large grassy area where homosexuals meet in the bushes at night to do their filthy acts.

That evening I found myself lingering behind a large shrub waiting for my opportunity. I didn't have to wait long before I saw her tootling along the path on her bike. I stepped out from the bushes and waited for her to get closer. I began to walk so that we were both heading in the same direction. In my right hand I gripped a thick stick I'd found beneath a bush. The path was nice and narrow and so the

66

moment I heard her approaching me from behind I readied myself. From my peripheral vision I caught a glimpse of her passing and just at the right moment I swung the stick with all my might sending it crashing into her skull. She went flying off her bike and ended up in a heap on the ground a few feet away.

It was dark but it was still early evening so I had to act quickly. She groaned on the grass, trying to sit up. I sat on top of her and punched her repeatedly until she wasn't moving. Despite the fact it was freezing cold she'd chosen to wear a short denim skirt. Slut. Quickly I pulled if off of her and wrapped it tightly around her neck and twisted the fabric. Eventually I heard a pop in her spine and she was gone.

From my trouser pocket I removed the penknife I'd brought with me and set to work on her eyes. I had to work fast. There was no time to prolong things with her. After her eyes were removed, I dragged her half-naked body to the edge of the river and pushed her in.

Then I calmly returned to her buckled bike and wheeled it into the bushes. It was like she was never there. I straightened my clothes and casually made my way home.

10

W e were married in August 1983. It was a low-key affair. From my side Dad, Dawn, Aunt Mary, her husband and kids came. When I told Trisha, at work, she was so excited I ended up inviting her. Her brown eyes shone with excitement and her bosom jiggled up and down as she hopped on the spot with delight. She appointed herself my maid of honour and insisted on coming dress shopping with me.

Dad's reaction took me by surprise. He was normally so damning but in that instance he said it was time I grew up and moved out. I realised he was pleased that I was no longer his responsibility. It freed up more money for beer.

Dawn had been shocked. The look on her face was priceless. When it sank in she, too, was pleased. It meant she would have our bedroom all to herself.

Larry's parents and brother were at the ceremony along with his boss from work and an old school friend who I'd never met before.

I wore a beige crêpe crochet lace maxi dress Trisha picked out at the charity shop. To begin with she was horrified I wasn't going to buy a new dress. But I explained we needed to save money to afford a home. I told her I didn't want to wear white. Larry said it was wrong since I wasn't a virgin. I didn't tell her that.

Trisha insisted we went into a florist to order a bouquet. I told her that it seemed like a waste of money but she said I'd already cut too many corners.

'You only get married once,' she said. She helped me to choose some pink roses. I was carried away by her enthusiasm.

Larry looked so handsome that day. He wore a dark blue pinstripe suit he bought from Debenhams, with a white shirt and black tie.

We were married in the morning at the Shire Hall register office and went to a pub down the road from the council offices for lunch. Dad got drunk and offended Larry's mum and Dawn flirted outrageously with Larry's brother. He lapped it up and that annoyed me.

We didn't really have a honeymoon. Larry's mum was very kind: she insisted we should spend our first night as a married couple together and booked us into a smart hotel in the city centre. Clearly she was desperate for a grandchild.

A week after the wedding we moved into a two-bed, on Gunhild Way in the south of the city. I couldn't believe it when Dad offered to help us with the rental deposit. I was grateful even though he couldn't disguise his pleasure at getting rid of me.

The house was sparsely furnished with old cheap furniture but I didn't care. It was home. Over the months I did my best to make it look nice and welcoming. I bought knick-knacks and furniture from junk shops and Larry would restore them. I discovered he was good with tools and a paintbrush.

Larry was still a trainee optometrist and would take his final exam in the autumn. I was so impressed and proud of him. He was happy working at Rook's. Mr Rook was a great mentor, Larry said.

Another body was found in the river. I heard about it from Trisha at work.

'You know they dragged another body from the river yesterday?' She was loving the drama.

'No I didn't know. What happened?'

'A young woman apparently. Found in Grantchester Meadows by some kids bunking off school. One of them was my friend's friend's little sister and apparently the body was really beaten up.' She moved closer and whispered. 'The eyes were missing.'

'How horrible.'

'It's like something out of a film, isn't it,' she mused. 'I'm going there after work.'

'Where?'

'To the site of course. Apparently there's loads of police and it's all taped off, but I'd like to see the action. It's quite exciting really.'

I didn't share her enjoyment.

'Do they know who she is?'

'Apparently but they haven't come out and said yet. I suppose they need to tell the family and stuff first.' She picked at her chipped purple nail varnish. 'Do you want to come with me?'

'No thanks. I've got to get home to make Larry's dinner. He loves it when I cook for him. Says my food is almost as good as his mum's.'

'Proper little wife, aren't you?'

11

JANUARY 10TH 1984

The next day it was all over the news. Journalists were speculating that there was a serial killer on the prowl. The police refused to comment on the possibility. All over the city people were talking about it. There was fear in the air and people were being cautious with strangers.

The victim was a woman called Jane Shanks, aged twenty-two. She had worked in a record shop. Her parents had reported her missing two days earlier when she didn't come home. The officer on the case said women should remain vigilant and not walk alone after dark.

That evening Larry told me he knew Jane. 'Yeah, I knew her. She worked in the record place on Bridge Street. I go in there to browse albums sometimes. She was really nice. Friendly girl, always happy to stop and talk.'

'When did you last see her?'

'A few weeks ago, I think. Popped in one day after work.'

'I didn't know you liked music that much.'

'As much as the next person.' He chewed his dinner. 'How come you are so interested all of a sudden?' Larry pushed the peas around his plate with his fork.

'Just sad what happened to her.' I didn't have much of an appetite and slid my plate away.

'Something wrong?' He stopped eating and put his fork down. 'You don't seem yourself.'

'Was just thinking about her. That's all.'

'It's not nice but there's nothing to worry about.'

'I know that. It's the idea of her being in that freezing cold water.'

'She was naked apparently.'

'Naked? Had he hurt her?' I hadn't heard that before. 'How do you know?'

'Overheard a conversation between Mr Rook and a customer. He works with the police. Had some inside information.' He picked up his fork and shovelled some pie into his mouth. 'She had been strangled with her own skirt. It was still around her neck when they pulled her from the river. They think it's linked to Ms Faulks. Similar wounds or something like that he said.'

'A serial killer?'

'That's pretty much what he said.' A piece of mushroom was stuck in his white teeth.

'Did he say anything else?' My stomach felt like a washing machine and I suddenly felt very sick.

'Like what?'

'Oh I don't know. Did he talk about suspects or evidence or anything like that?'

'Nah, he didn't. It's not like you to ask so many questions. Why are you so interested?'

'Well, I mean, you know... if there's someone going round killing women...'

'Hey. No one's going to hurt my girl.' Larry winked. 'You're safe with me.'

12

I discovered I was pregnant in April of 1984. Larry was over the moon but I was shocked. We hadn't been using protection but we hadn't been trying either. It wasn't something we'd discussed. But Larry had a way of making even bad news seem good. 'Change is good,' he would say. My purpose in life was to make him happy. He was my world.

For the first few months the morning sickness was debilitating. I had to take time off work and Stuart, my supervisor, was less than understanding.

Larry's mother was thrilled. Linda was longing to be a grandmother. I was pleased to be able to give her a grandchild but not that happy when she started to turn up at the house more and more often, with gifts and suggestions.

She had always been very respectful and never interfered before. The news that I was expecting seemed to send her into overdrive. With hindsight, I believe she saw it as a good excuse to spend less and less time at home with her husband. They were having problems. Big problems.

Jim Miller had been suspended from his teaching position after an allegation of inappropriate behaviour with a student.

The thirteen-year old girl had complained to her parents that Mr Miller had come on to her. Jim denied it but the school had no option but to suspend him while they investigated her claims. After this all came out Larry confided in me that his father had left the last school under a similar cloud. Jim Miller would never get a job in education again.

Poor Linda, who was a good honest woman, had moved out of their marital bedroom and into the room Larry left vacant. It turned out that our wedding was a blessing for a number of reasons.

I asked Larry if he thought his parents would divorce. He didn't know but it was clear then that he disliked his dad. Finally, I understood where all the tension in the family stemmed from.

By September I was really beginning to show. I'd always been overweight but now my stomach was bigger than ever before. I loved the feeling of my baby moving around inside of me. I would talk to my bump for hours, stroking my belly.

Until then my sex life with Larry had been extremely active but the moment he discovered I was pregnant he refused to touch me. It was as if I was made of glass. I couldn't help but feel neglected and unattractive. As the months passed he came home later and later. I knew he couldn't be at work. Mr Rook kept very strict hours and the moment half-past five arrived the shutters came down. I used to wonder where Larry went. Every night I made his dinner and sat at our dining table waiting for him in vain. I didn't understand what had changed. I loved him and he was the most important thing in my life.

At the weekends he was spending hours in the shed. His man-den, he called it. I never went in. There was no reason to even open the door. He kept his tools in there and tinkered away at this and that. He started to make a bit of extra income doing up bikes and selling them for a profit to students.

On that Saturday he appeared home with a cot.

'I picked it up from the dump.' He said proudly taking it off the roof of his burgundy car. 'Bit of work and it will be good as new.'

I looked at the dilapidated base and pushed away my feeling of bitter disappointment. I wanted something better for our baby.

'Look,' he sensed my apprehension, 'it'll be good as new. I promise. We need to tighten our belts, Dee, especially if you are going to give up work.'

'Give up work?' It was the first time he'd mentioned it.

'Yes. You need to look after the baby. You can't manage a job as well.'

'I suppose.' I hadn't really thought about it. 'But how will we afford to live?'

'I've spoken to Mr Rook. He's going to give me a rise as soon as I become a fully qualified optician.'

I stood in the sunshine on the small concrete driveway that led up to the front of the house and stroked my belly.

'I'll take care of you both.' Larry carted the cot towards the gate that led straight into the back garden. I knew he meant it. He was a natural protector. It was one of the things I adored most.

'Put the kettle on, Dee.' He fiddled in his pocket for his keys. 'I'm parched.'

Doing as I was told, I turned and went back into the house while Larry wrestled with the rusty lock.

As I watched the teabag leak into the water I thought about leaving Woolworths and the idea made me feel sad. I'd never really liked it, but not working there meant I'd hardly ever see Trisha. She had become a good friend.

Larry appeared in the doorway and wiped sweat from his brow with the palm of his hand.

'Hot out there today.' He took a glass from the cupboard and poured himself some water.

'I've been thinking,' I dropped the teabag into the bin, 'I thought we could paint the baby's room yellow. What do you think? I know your mum thinks pale green would be nice but I prefer yellow.'

'Pay no attention to mum. She's just excited, that's all.'

'Do you think she'll ever work things out with your dad?' I prayed they would.

'Maybe.' Larry shrugged as I handed him his tea.

'She has been spending a lot of time here.' I did my best to hide my frustration.

'I know.' He frowned. 'I'll have a word.'

'Thanks.' I leant heavily against the worktop. 'I thought maybe we could go shopping for a pram.'

'Not today, Dee. I want to make a start on the cot. Besides we've got a while yet and we don't want it sitting in the hall, getting in the way for the next few months do we?'

'No. I suppose you're right.' Larry was always right. I never doubted that.

'Anyway, Eric says he has a friend he might be able to get one off. Probably be stolen but that won't matter to the baby.' Larry laughed spilling a little bit of tea. 'Right, thanks for the tea. I'll be in the shed for a while.' I knew that meant stay away.

'But I thought I'd make some sandwiches and we could have lunch together.'

'Maybe later.' He came over and ruffled my hair with his hand before leaving me alone again.

13

I watched her with her clients. *Disgusting whore. In a dark alley, dropping her knickers and letting them fuck her against the rough brick wall. The whole time I kept my eyes on her face. She didn't smile, didn't moan, didn't even react. As if she was standing in a line waiting to pay for her shopping or something. She looked bored. That made me angry. I couldn't wait to get my hands on her. She was going to feel pain and I was going to enjoy it.*

14

W hen I got to work on Monday morning Trisha came bounding over, her face all lit up.

'They've found another.' She couldn't contain her excitement.

'Another what?' I really wasn't in the mood for any of her idle gossip.

'Another body! What if it's someone we know? What if we know the killer?'

'Hmm.' I hung my rucksack up on my peg and sat down in a chair to take the weight off my feet for a moment.

'Is that all you can say? The police have admitted it's a serial killer. Here in Cambridge.'

I'd heard of course. Everywhere you turned it was there in the papers, on the radio and in the news broadcasts. Murder fever had gripped the whole of the city. Sales of penknives doubled, with young women desperate to protect themselves. As if a penknife was the answer when facing a madman.

Even the pubs and bars had seen a dip in sales. Women in particular were less eager to stay out late and face the danger of walking home alone. In every shop you went into you would hear a conversation about it. 'Who was next? Why weren't the police doing their job?' It was the usual nonsense that civilians always grumble about. Why blame the perpetrator when you can hold the police to account? Everyone had a theory. Some of them were laughable. I tried not to pay too much attention but it was hard to escape the topic people whispered about.

'I'm sorry, Trisha, I'm just a bit tired.' I rubbed my temples with my fingers.

'Are you all right?' She sat down next to me and cocked her head to one side. She'd recently got a new perm and the curls flopped across her face.

'There's something I need to tell you.' I felt miserable.

'Go on.' She had quickly gone from being a giggly schoolgirl to an understanding woman.

'I'm going to hand in my notice. Larry wants me to stay at home and look after the baby. He's right of course. How could I keep working?'

'Oh I see.' She studied my face for a moment. 'But you don't want to?'

'It's not that.' I wasn't really sure what was bothering me. 'I'll miss you.'

'I'll come and see you all the time. Try and keep me away. I love babies and besides, who else will listen to me babble on the way you do? You're my best friend.' Hearing those words made me want to cry.

'Don't get all emotional on me.' She cackled and made a cross with her fingers. 'Just because you've got baby brain, I can't deal with anyone crying.' She gave my shoulder a gentle shove and stood up. 'Come on, before we have Stuart breathing down our necks.'

By lunchtime I felt better. Knowing that I would still see Trisha made all the difference. Her friendship had become so important to me, especially since Larry was spending less time in my company. I told myself that when the baby came things between us would go back to normal.

On that day the city was busy with tourists, stopping to take photographs of the university buildings and Market Square with their cameras. On the corner near Rook's Opticians, a young man stood holding a billboard offering tours of The Backs on punts. I'd only been punting once and that was with Larry last autumn. He was good at poling the boat along the Cam. We'd stopped for a picnic on the riverbank and watched the world go by. It had been a good day.

Larry came out of Rook's with his face buried in a newspaper.

'Hi.' He folded it quickly and kissed my cheek. 'How are my two favourite people?' he said resting his hand on my bump.

'Fine thanks.' I was so unused to his touch that I flinched. He took a step back, his dark brown eyes searching my face.

'What's wrong?'

'Nothing. I'm just tired.' And I was. 'I told Stuart I would be leaving at the end of October. He said he'd fill the position easily and didn't seem very concerned.'

'That's good news.' Larry ignored my disappointment.

We made our way to our usual spot by the river and I unwrapped my cheese sandwich. Ever since the pregnancy I couldn't stand the smell of prawns or anything fishy.

Larry sank his teeth into his BLT and opened a can of coke.

'Want some?' He held the drink out.

'No thanks.' I didn't want to put on any more weight than I already had. I suspected that was the reason he was no longer sleeping with me. I looked down at the folded newspaper that lay on the bench between us.

'I was just reading about the latest murder. They're pretty

sure it's a serial killer now. This is number three.' He wiped some tomato seeds from his top lip with a napkin.

'Yes I know. Trisha was talking about it at work.' I watched as a pair of swans floated past. 'You don't think it can happen where you live.'

'I know what you mean.'

I reached for the newspaper eager to learn more about the reported killer stalking the streets of Cambridge.

CAMBRIDGE KILLER STRIKES AGAIN

Rowers discovered the body of a woman, named by police as Rose Delaney, in the city centre in the early hours of Sunday morning. A section of the river, from Jesus Green to Magdalene Bridge, has been cordoned off. Emergency services and an inflatable dinghy were on the scene.

Police said the woman, aged twenty-two, was a known prostitute. The *Cambridge Evening News* can reveal that the victim was sexually assaulted and had her eyes removed before being strangled in what is described as a frenzied attack.

The detective, DCI Frank Wilkinson who is in charge of the investigation, admitted that police were exploring a link between the case and the discovery of two female bodies in the river in previous months.

A police spokesman made a plea for information: 'Anyone who was in the area and might have seen something is encouraged to come forward. No matter how small the detail may seem it might hold the key to catching the person responsible. We advise that the public remain cautious and call the police if they see anything suspicious.'

'Makes for pretty depressing reading.' I handed the paper back to Larry who'd finished his sandwich.

'Doesn't seem they have a clue who they are looking for,' he pondered.

'Bit of a change though, isn't it, going from normal women to a prostitute.'

'Maybe it was just easier.'

'Probably. I didn't even know there were prostitutes around Cambridge.'

'Oh Dee, you're so naïve. There are prostitutes everywhere.'

'Well I've never seen one.'

'They don't all walk around holding signs you know. They just hang out in places where punters know they'll be.'

'You seem to know a lot about it.' I immediately regretted the throw-away comment.

'I don't like your tone.' Larry turned to me, rage burning in his eyes.

'I didn't mean anything,' but it was too late. The damage had been done.

'I'm going back to work.' He stood up and dusted himself off.

'But I haven't finished my lunch.'

'So?' His eyes were cold. He turned and walked away. I felt the anger coming from him despite the distance between us.

After work I went food shopping for dinner. Even in the supermarket I couldn't escape the chatter about the killer. The woman serving behind the till was happy to impart her so-called knowledge to a customer who stood there transfixed by the details about the latest death. The conversation was holding me up and it bored me. These people clearly didn't know what they were talking about. They wasted their breath throwing clichés backwards and forwards as if that was going to change anything. I clung on to my basket of groceries and bit my tongue waiting for the idle gossip to come to an end.

I wanted to cook Larry his favourite. I had some making up

to do. I'd never seen him so cross and I'd felt bad about it all afternoon.

When I got home, I went straight into the kitchen. The house was quiet. Larry hadn't returned from work, even though he finished the same time as I did. I hoped he wouldn't be late back as I set to work preparing a fish pie. Although the smell made me gag I was determined to push on. I pulled the skin off the smoked haddock fillets and felt the flesh for any bones. On the hob next to me a pan of potatoes boiled furiously.

I cut the cod and haddock into chunks, put them in the pie dish and sprinkled a few frozen prawns over them before adding a white sauce I'd made. By the time I'd made mash and spread it on top it was seven o'clock. The sun was descending in the sky and I looked out of our kitchen window at the peach, pink and lilac streaks in the sky. Birds flew by in silhouette, making their way home to roost.

As the smell of fish pie filled our small kitchen, I checked the clock on the wall. It was nearly half past. Larry should have been home by then. Wanting to escape the nauseating smell I stepped out into our garden to soak up the last minutes of warmth before the large sun sank below the horizon.

Sitting down on a rusty iron bench Larry and I had found in a junk shop, I wondered what had inspired me to speak to him like that. I deserved to be sat there alone. He was probably in the pub or wandering through the park, avoiding coming home to me. I was being punished.

15

NOVEMBER 23RD 1984

I had stopped working at Woolworths three weeks before. My tummy was huge and I felt like a whale. I was suffering from swollen ankles and fatigue and was grateful to have the time to rest. The baby was due in a few short weeks and I was enjoying the calm before the storm.

It gave me the opportunity to put the finishing touches to the nursery. I did a lot of reading to pass the time. The anticipation was tinged with fear. Larry suggested we didn't go to the ante-natal classes. Full of know-it-alls, he said. No doubt he was right but it would have been comforting to know what to expect from the labour. If my mum had been alive I would have asked her.

Women have been doing it for thousands of years, how hard could it be? At least that is what I told myself.

It was just after nine in the morning and I was mopping the kitchen floor when I felt the first twinge. I put the mop back into the bucket of dirty soapy water and rubbed the bottom of my back. Maybe mopping wasn't such a good idea.

I emptied the bucket down the drain outside the back door and returned to the living room to pick up my book, Barbara Cartland's novel, *Love on the Wind*, a historical romance set in

Victorian India. A girl tormented by her cruel uncle meets a mysterious man on a voyage to Calcutta. It was very romantic and encouraged me to daydream about far off lands. Places like India. Places I would never get to visit.

I read fifty more pages before realising the throb in my stomach wasn't going away. It was getting stronger. Putting my book back down on the coffee table I paced backwards and forwards to ease my discomfort. Waddling a bit like a penguin, I made my way up the stairs to the nursery to look at my hospital bag and double-check I had everything I needed.

The baby wasn't due for a few weeks but I knew I was in the early stages of labour. Standing in the yellow box room I stared down at the refurbished cot. Larry had done a wonderful job. He was so talented and clever. It looked new. That was the first time that it really dawned on me how much my life was going to change. The next time I stood in that room there would be a new life in the world. A life for which I was responsible.

Larry was twenty-four years old. I had only turned eighteen in October. Suddenly I felt very sick. I put it down to the labour and tried to ignore the claustrophobic fear that had its hands around my throat.

Unable to face being in the same room as the cot I took myself downstairs and drank a large glass of cold water from the kitchen tap. Outside in the garden a blackbird hopped around on the cold ground looking for food. The frost had thawed leaving a thin wet layer over everything.

Listening to the silence in the house unnerved me. I didn't want to be alone. I went back into the lounge and wondered if it was too soon to call Larry. It was only eleven o'clock and my labour hadn't really taken off yet. Still, I wanted him there, but the fear of upsetting him stopped me from picking up the phone. Larry had given me the telephone number for Rook's so I could call in an emergency. Did this class as an emergency? No. Not yet. I would suffer alone until it became too much.

A book from the library about labour and birth had taught me that I needed to wait until the contractions were five minutes apart or my waters had broken before showing up at the labour ward. Neither of these things had happened yet so I sat back down and picked up my book. I couldn't really concentrate but I had to do something. Clock-watching would have driven me mad.

I sat alone in the house for hours, dealing with the increasing pain until three twenty-five when I felt a rush of wetness down the inside of my legs. My waters had broken. Although my contractions were not yet that close together, I thought it best to call Larry.

I picked up the phone and dialled the number he had scribbled on a piece of paper.

'Hello Rook's Opticians.' Mr Rook's voice travelled down the line.

'Oh, hello, Mr Rook. It's Deborah, Deborah Miller. Can I speak to Larry please?'

'He's just taking a payment from a customer. Can I pass on a message?'

'Would you mind if I held on?' I wasn't doing a very good job of disguising the panic in my voice.

'Is everything all right, dear?' The old man asked.

'Yes. I just need to talk to Larry.'

'He might be a few minutes. Why don't I get him to call you back when he's done?'

'OK. That's fine. Thank you, Mr Rook.'

'I'll pass the message on the moment he's finished with Mrs Rice.'

'Thank you.' I put the receiver down and hoped the old man didn't forget to tell Larry to call.

Minutes later the phone rang.

'Larry?' I picked up the receiver hoping to hear his voice.

'Everything OK, Dee?'

'Everything's fine. It's just I think my waters have broken.'

There was a long silence.

'Are you sure? You're not due for a few weeks.'

'I know. I'm fairly certain.'

'OK. Go and get your hospital bag and jump on a bus. I'll meet you at the entrance.'

'You aren't going to collect me?'

'No point. It will take longer for me to get home and for us to go in the car. And the car park will be expensive. Just get a bus.' He was always the sensible one.

'OK.' I was embarrassed that my clothes were wet. 'I'll change and then walk to the bus stop.'

'Good girl. I'll be there soon.' The line went dead.

When I arrived at the hospital Larry was waiting outside, in the cold, just like he'd said he would. Putting his arm around my shoulder he led me inside. Reception directed us to the labour ward where a friendly-faced midwife greeted us. She showed us to a room that had two unoccupied beds in it.

I was handed a gown and told to get changed. Larry sat down on the chair near the bed, folded his hands behind his head and put his feet up on the clean sheets. I was too uncomfortable to lie down so I stood bent over the bed huffing and puffing.

A little while later the midwife returned and told me she needed to check how dilated I was. I felt like a prize cow, lying on my back with a strange woman's hand feeling about in a place meant only for Larry. She said I was five centimetres and I still had a while to go. I dreaded how bad the pain was going to get, as I sucked hard on the gas and air from a tube attached to a large metal canister.

Seven hours later, at ten fifty-five pm, our first child was born with the help of forceps. They had to cut me to get her out. It would not be the last time she caused me trouble.

Sue-Ann weighed six pounds and two ounces. She had a thick head of dark hair, just like her father. Larry cried when he held her in his arms. I lay there exhausted and in pain watching father and daughter meet for the first time. I just felt numb inside.

16

MAY 17TH 1986

By May 1986 our life had changed even more. In March, a few months earlier, I gave birth to our son, Robert 'Robbie' Miller. He was a difficult child and cried continuously. What with Sue-Ann walking and getting into everything and Robbie refusing to sleep through the night, I was a shell of the girl I'd once been.

Larry had been working hard and passed his exams. He was a fully-fledged optician. Mr Rook made him a junior partner and increased his salary. I was so incredibly proud. We had more money coming in but I never saw the benefits of any of it, until Larry announced that he'd put down a deposit on a house.

His parents divorced in 1985 after a miserable final few years together. The separation had been messy. Linda acquired a lawyer who persuaded her to go for everything in the settlement. Jim, who was by then an unemployed teacher with a career in tatters, didn't put up a fight. After the divorce was finalised he moved back to Peterborough alone. Linda sold the house and moved to Bournemouth. I was so pleased not to have her breathing down my neck. She wanted a new start, away from

Jim and the shame of it all, and before she left she gave a chunk of money each to Larry and Eric. Linda wanted to know she was leaving her children with some financial security.

Eric quickly pissed his away his on cheap women and gambling. Larry hardly ever saw him although he said they used to meet up in a pub from time to time. Eric was as hopeless an uncle as he was a brother and a son. He couldn't hold down a job and got by doing dodgy deals. At the time I suspected he might have been involved in drugs.

Occasionally, for some unknown reason, Eric would show up at the house and come in for a cuppa. This usually always happened when Larry was at work. I think Eric missed his mother and liked having a woman he could talk to. I didn't mention our coffee mornings to Larry. It would only have upset him.

Spending time with Eric I got to know him properly. He wasn't the rogue I'd always thought he was. Sure, he didn't lead a conventional life and he would rather make a living doing something illegal than hold down a proper job but I came to realise he was the product of his parents. Larry had always been the golden boy. Linda and Jim, on the other hand, had written off Eric at a young age. He wasn't academic or ambitious and that frustrated them. I could relate to how he was made to feel growing up and I saw a softer side of him. He was the perfect example of self-fulfilling prophecy.

On that Saturday morning Larry woke up in an unusually good mood. He made us breakfast, bacon sandwiches, and even changed Sue-Ann's nappy. I was so tired from the night feeds that I felt like a zombie wondering around in someone else's life.

'I've arranged with Mr Rook that I can have the day off. I'm due some holiday time.' The smell of frying bacon filled our small chaotic kitchen. I had tried to keep up with the housework but I was so worn down by the children that I'd lost control of the place. The sink was full, the surfaces dirty and the floor hadn't been mopped for far too long.

In the early days of our marriage Larry used to worry about the appearance of the house and I worked hard keeping it neat to please him. Looking around at the mess I wondered when everything changed.

As Larry stood cooking breakfast Sue-Ann sat at his feet munching on a piece of bread he had given her. She wore a faded pink vest that was covered in stains. Her chubby little fingers forced the food into her mouth.

'I've got a surprise.' Larry turned to me with a boyish smile and I was reminded of the man I fell in love with.

'Oh?' I tried my best to sound enthusiastic but I was too exhausted to muster the effort.

'We're going on a little trip.' Larry placed the bacon butties down on the table and handed Sue-Ann a sliver of back bacon out of his own sandwich. Sticky ketchup covered her chin. 'Eat up, put a dress on and get the kids ready. We're leaving at nine-thirty.' He chewed with his mouth open and I watched the meat being ground up between his teeth.

'OK.' Robbie was hanging off my exposed breast. Using my free hand, I picked up the food took one bite and then pushed the plate away. Any desire I'd once had to please Larry no longer existed. It had evaporated, along with the confidence I'd found when we met.

Carrying Robbie in one arm and Sue-Ann with the other I went upstairs, leaving behind my food and half-drunk cup of tea. I didn't much feel like getting dressed and would have happily spent the day in my dressing gown but Larry seemed so excited and, even though I envied his energy, I didn't want to burst his bubble.

Pushing the nursery door open using my foot I was greeted

by yet more mess. Dirty babygros and used nappies lay on the floor by the changing mat. I put Robbie down in Sue-Ann's cot. He immediately started to cry but I ignored it as I searched through the chest of drawers for something clean for her to wear. At the back of the drawer there was a brand new outfit Trisha had given her that had somehow been forgotten. It was a sweet little yellow dress with a duck on the front. The label said it was for twelve to eighteen months and I held it up. It looked a bit small for her but it would have to do.

She wriggled on her changing mat, refusing to lie on her back. With one elbow I leant on her chest to hold her still while I managed to twist her arm into one of the holes. Sue-Ann gave out a little cry but I was too tired to feel any guilt. Once the dress was over her head I left her blubbing on the floor while I dealt with Robbie who was screaming in the cot. His little face had turned beetroot red. Flinging him over my shoulder and patting his back in a half-hearted attempt to soothe him I carried him into the other bedroom, leaving Sue-Ann alone on the floor to entertain herself.

Our bedroom was at the very top of the stairs I could hear Larry downstairs in the bathroom, brushing his teeth and gargling. Closing the door behind me I placed Robbie down on the bed and went in search of clothes. Larry wanted me to wear a dress, so I would wear a dress.

As I opened the cupboard the door almost came off its hinges. The landlord, had neglected Gunhild Way over the months, and it was beginning to show.

Flicking through the hangers I eventually found a denim dress and pulled it roughly down. I'd bought it from a charity shop a few weeks earlier. To my disappointment I discovered I was a size sixteen. In those days that was really big. It was no wonder Larry hardly ever looked at me. It was a miracle Robbie was conceived. It must have been the only time he had touched me in months.

I dropped my dressing gown to the floor and stood looking at myself in the mirror. I had on a flesh coloured nursing bra and grey pants, that were once white. The dimples in my fat tummy revolted me and I noticed, for the first time, how many stretch marks I had.

My hair had grown and was shapeless and my roots needed some serious attention.

Robbie lay on the bed behind me gargling to himself. He and Sue-Ann had done this to me. Trying not to drown in my own resentment I turned away from the mirror and continued getting dressed. I didn't bother to change my underwear, even though I had been wearing the same set for days. None of it mattered any more.

I went back into the nursery to retrieve Sue-Ann, who had moved over to a chair and was trying to climb on to it, before taking both kids downstairs.

Larry was waiting impatiently in the kitchen, his arms folded across his chest. He was wearing his jeans and old Timberland-style boots.

'Ready?'

'Yup.' I handed him Sue-Ann and grabbed muslin to throw over my shoulder, in case Robbie was sick.

Stepping out in the spring air I took a long deep breath. I couldn't remember the last time I'd left the house.

Larry put Sue-Ann in the back of the car and strapped her seatbelt on. In those days we didn't have all the rules and regulations that exist now. I sat in the front passenger seat and held on to Robbie who was starting to drift off. Larry got into the driver's seat and started the engine of his burgundy Ford Cortina. Before pulling out of our concrete driveway he leant over, planted a kiss on my cheek and squeezed my knee. I was dumbstruck. What had come over him?

We drove into the city in silence. Staring out of the window I watched people go about their daily business. I felt so removed from the world.

Larry double-parked on St Andrew's Street.

'I need to stop here for a minute and pick something up. Won't be long,' He slammed the car door loudly and disappeared up the high street. The noise woke Robbie who screamed with protest.

Undoing the buttons on my denim dress I unclipped one side of my nursing bra and shoved a nipple into his mouth. It shut him up instantly. Peace again.

Moments later Larry returned. He didn't appear to have anything with him.

'Got it,' he said cheerily. He started the car and pulled a U-turn. A bus was forced to stop and wait. The driver glared angrily at us and beeped his horn. Larry gave him the finger as we drove away in the opposite direction.

'That's my boy.' Larry glanced at Robbie and smiled. 'Always eating.'

We followed the traffic out of the city until making a right turn on to Long Road and heading west.

'Nearly there.'

Nearly where, I wondered.

A few minutes later we were on the outskirts in an area known as Trumpington. The car pulled on to a small street called Alpha Terrace and stopped.

'Come on.' Larry removed the keys from the ignition and got out. I followed, almost banging Robbie's head on the roof of the car as I manoeuvred myself out.

Alpha Terrace was a narrow Victorian street with slate-roofed grey stone houses.

'Come on.' Larry held hands with Sue-Ann and led the way. Stopping fifty yards down he turned to me. 'Here!' he proclaimed pointing at a green-painted front door before reaching into his jeans pocket and removing a set of keys.

'Welcome home,' he said unlocking the door and stepping inside.

I remained on the street looking into the house.

'I bought it. It's our new home.' He smiled proudly. 'I wanted it to be a surprise.'

Not really believing what was happening I followed him inside. The house was empty of any furniture and my battered old sneakers creaked on the wooden floorboards in the hallway.

'What do you think?' Larry raised an eyebrow.

'This is ours?'

'Yep. All ours. We can move in immediately.'

I was speechless.

'Go on,' he urged, 'go and explore.'

I handed him Robbie, who I had to physically remove from my breast.

On my left was the entrance to the lounge. The room had a wooden floor and a small Victorian fireplace. I went over to the window and pulled back the net curtain to see the street again. It was so quiet.

Then I returned to the hallway, went past the staircase and then through to the next room on my left, where there was an eat-in kitchen. The floor was covered in old terracotta tiles and I knew that with a bit of care they would look lovely once cleaned up. I let the excitement start to take over as I went through to the bathroom at the back of the house. It had seen better days but there was something to work with.

Returning to the kitchen I heard Larry call, 'It's got three bedrooms,' I poked my head around the door to find him standing by a door under the stairs, 'and a large cellar.' He produced a heavy old key, handed Robbie back to me and unlocked the door. Flicking on the light, a single naked bulb that hung from the ceiling, I peered down the old staircase into the darkness. I wondered what on earth we would need a cellar for. Still, the extra space was luxurious. I'd never lived anywhere that had a cellar before. It felt exciting.

'Come on,' Larry pulled the door closed and locked it again, 'let's take a look upstairs.'

Sue-Ann, who'd been left to her own devices, was already beginning the steep climb. Larry scooped her up in his arms and led the way.

There was beige carpet on the landing, which led to three rooms.

'I'll show you our room.' Larry guided me to the front of the house and opened the bedroom door.

It was a large, light room with two windows that looked down on to the street and on either side of the grubby old fireplace were built-in cupboards, modern and out of place.

'Lots of storage.' Larry plonked Sue-Ann on the floor and swung the cupboard doors open.

'Is this really ours?' It still hadn't sunk in.

'Yes, Dee. All ours.' He came over and wrapped his strong arms around me. 'It's going to be a new start for us, Dee.'

'How did you afford it?' My head was a mass of questions.

'Ma's money and the help of a mortgage. The repayments are a bit more than the rent we've been paying but we'll manage.'

I didn't care if we had to starve in order to be able to afford it. It was exactly what I'd always wanted. A house to call my own.

'I can't believe it.'

'Believe it.' He bent his face down and kissed me properly for the first time in ages. With my free arm I held on to his buttock and pulled him closer to me.

'I want to fuck you,' he whispered.

Taking a step away from him I pulled Sue-Ann out of the room with my spare hand and took both children into one of the other bedrooms. Leaving them both on the floor I pulled the door shut. They would be safe in there for a few minutes.

Returning to our bedroom I unzipped Larry's jeans and got down on my knees.

17

When I saw her floating by I knew I had to have her. She was so wholesome, so pure. She smelt like vanilla. I got close enough to touch her but didn't. I would wait. My time would come.

And then it did. I followed her for a few days. She was more complicated than the others. She didn't really have a routine. That made it hard. I kept close and had to bide my time. It would have to be a spur of the moment thing. I prefer plans but needs must.

She was young. But she had a look about her. Like she knew she was fuckable. She carried it with her everywhere she went, temping men to look, but not to touch. She brought it on herself. I was going to enjoy this one. I would take my time with her.

18

W e had moved into number 11 Alpha Terrace a week earlier. Larry negotiated with the landlord so that we could end our tenancy early. He was so clever like that. I could always count on him to sort out any problem.

I felt like a new woman. I'd been to the hairdressers and started to take more pride in my appearance again. As a result, our sex life returned to what it once was. We couldn't get enough of each other.

The move was fairly easy. Larry hired a van and we did most of it ourselves. We didn't have that many belongings since most of the furniture belonged to the landlord of Gunhild Way. Eric showed up and helped for a very short while, bringing with him a second-hand double mattress for Larry and me and a sofa, which looked like it had fallen off the back of a lorry. It was a start and better than nothing.

That Thursday morning, as I went to retrieve the milk delivered by the milkman, I opened the door and saw the postman on the other side of the street carrying his bag of letters. He smiled and crossed the road to talk to me. I was still in my dressing gown, my hair hadn't been brushed yet and I felt self-conscious.

'Morning Mrs Miller.' I was taken aback by his knowing my name.

He handed me some junk mail and smiled. He had a round friendly face and nice blue eyes. He was considerably older than me, probably in his forties. Although at times I felt like an old woman, I was still only twenty years old. I'm sure that anyone who laid eyes me would have been very surprised to discover that.

'Heard the latest?' He shuffled a pile of mail in his large hands.

'Latest?'

'Yep. 'Nother body found in the river. Awful, just awful.'

I hadn't thought about the murderer, nicknamed The Eye-Sight Killer by the national press, for a while. I didn't follow the news and didn't go out much so it had passed me by. I'd grown sick and tired of listening to people speculate.

'Poor girl. Only seventeen. Hope they find the animal and string 'im up. Vote to bring back the death penalty if I could.'

'How many now?'

'How many what?'

'Victims. How many victims?'

'Fourth. He slowed down for a bit and some people thought he'd stopped. I knew there'd be more. Evil don't stay buried for long. Has a habit of rearin' it's head when you least expect it.' I could see how much he was enjoying imparting his words of wisdom but I wasn't impressed. I couldn't understand why average people were so fascinated by killers.

'Well, have a nice day.' I bent down to pick up the two bottles of milk on the doorstep and smiled before closing the front door on him. He would have been better off talking to Trisha about it. She shared his morbid interest.

I missed her company and decided I would call her that evening. It would be good to see her and have a catch-up, even if that only meant listening to her gossip about the other people at work or friends of hers who I'd never met. I'd not seen her for over six months but we'd spoken on the phone a few times.

Back in the kitchen I returned to feeding Sue-Ann her breakfast. While I'd been out of the room she had smeared a boiled egg all over the tray of her highchair. Yolk dripped on to the floor as she banged her beaker loudly on the surface, hammering a piece of toast into the wood and sending drops of milk flying through the air.

Robbie had been awake a lot of the night but was thankfully asleep upstairs in his cot. Dealing with one of them was bad enough. Ignoring the shrieks of laughter, I left the kitchen and went to fetch the mop and bucket that lived on the stairs leading down to the basement.

Feeling about in the darkness I searched for the light switch with my fingers. The exposed brick wall was rough. After finding the switch the stairway flooded with light. Old dusty cobwebs hung from the underside of the stairs up to the first floor. Reaching for the mop I looked down into the cellar. I didn't like the dark and hated spiders, so never ventured down there.

That night, after I'd cooked dinner, I went and sat in the lounge and dialled Trisha's number.

She lived in a shared house off Newmarket Road, to the east of the city. Her housemates were a motley crew of strangers who'd all ended up living together by chance. She was a local girl, born and bred. Trisha moved out of her parent's house in Waterbeach, a large village outside of Cambridge, when she was eighteen and had never looked back. I'd always envied her confidence. Although she was scatty she knew what she wanted and how to get it. She was nobody's fool.

''Ello.' A male voice answered.

'Hi. Is Trisha there?'

'Dunno. Hang on a sec.' Moments later I heard faint footsteps echo down the line.

'Hello?'

'Trisha! Hi. It's Debs.'

'Debs, hi. How are you?'

'I'm fine. Well actually. You?'

'Can't complain. Stuart is still the bastard dictator of Woolworths but I know how to handle him.'

I didn't doubt it.

'Any news?'

'We moved house. In fact, we bought a house.'

'Oh my god, I can't believe I didn't know this!' She was so over the top. 'Why didn't you tell me? When did this happen? Where are you living? Have you left Cambridge?'

'No. We haven't left Cambridge. I wouldn't leave without saying goodbye. We're living in a house in Trumpington. It's got three bedrooms and a decent garden. We only moved in a week ago. It all happened really quickly.'

'You're such a grown up,' she mocked. 'I'm still stuck here sharing with Alan the junkie and Donna the tart.' I had to give it to her; Trisha had a way with words. I could picture her large mouth flapping as she spoke.

'It would be really nice if you came over. I'd like to show you the place.'

Since neither Dad or Dawn had bothered to visit I wanted to be able to show off my house to someone, even if it wasn't properly furnished yet.

'Sure. I'm around on Sunday afternoon. Does that work?'

'Sunday isn't ideal.' I didn't want to admit to her that I'd rather see her when Larry wasn't going to be around. 'Saturday afternoon would be better.' There was every chance Larry would be fishing somewhere. It was a hobby he'd recently taken up although I had no idea where he fished, or who with. Come to think of it I'd never seen his fishing pole.

'Sure. Saturday works for me.' Trisha chirped down the phone. 'Give me an opportunity to see those lovely kiddies. How are the little angels?' I presumed she was talking about Robbie and Sue-Ann.

'They are fine.'

'How old are they now?'

'Sue-Ann is eighteen months and Robbie is five months.'

'Wow. How time passes.'

'Right, well,' I didn't fancy a long discussion about the kids. I'd called her because I was craving adult company. Larry was due back late. He'd spent the day with Mr Rook at an optometry conference in London. As usual I was alone. Even though we were closer again I still felt isolated and dreamed of going back to work. 'I'll see you on Saturday.' Then I told Trisha the address and we said our goodbyes.

Putting the cream handset back down I sat back in the tatty armchair and listened to the silence. For once both the children were quiet. The chair smelt of mothballs. Larry had spotted it discarded on a street somewhere nearby. It belonged in the dump but we were short for cash and beggars can't be choosers.

Enjoying the peace, I leant back and closed my eyes. The stink coming from the chair interrupted what should have been a tranquil moment, so I got up and moved over on to the stolen sofa.

Talking to Trisha had got me thinking. Why couldn't I go back to work? At least part time. We needed the money and I needed something other than dirty nappies in my life. I decided I would talk to Trisha about it when I saw her at the weekend.

Stuart had never been my number one fan but there were other people he hated more and, besides, I knew Trisha would put in a good word for me. She could be very persuasive. It occurred to me that I'd started to feel down after I'd left work. Being stuck at home with two small demanding children was hard work, especially since Larry worked such long hours and I didn't have any family around me for support. Things would have been very different if my mum had been alive. She would have made a lovely nana.

I got up and went into the kitchen to make myself a cup of tea. Our old kettle was filled with lime scale and little flakes of it always ended up floating in the mugs. I cursed being broke. I'd been so happy when I knew we had the house but quickly the happiness disappeared when the reality of our finances became apparent.

Standing sipping a cup of gritty tea I decided it was about time I took control of my own life again and going back to work at Woolworths was a good place to start. Larry couldn't keep up with the mortgage alone. We needed to share the burden. I tried not to think about what we could do with the kids if I was out. Surely we'd find a way around it. Larry was full of bright ideas and always had an answer for everything.

19

On Sunday morning, despite yet another disrupted night with Robbie and Sue-Ann, who seemed to take it in turns waking me up, I sat in the kitchen smiling to myself. I'd had a lovely afternoon with Trisha. She could talk the hind legs off a donkey but she had a way of picking you up and carrying you along with her. Her bubbly personality was infectious and I would have defied anyone not to succumb to her charms. In that way she was a bit like Larry. People liked her, even if they didn't want to.

We'd sat for hours in the garden enjoying the warm summer weather while she wittered on about her latest fella.

By the end of the afternoon I could have told you his inside leg measurement. I learnt more than I ever wanted to know about Andrew, an estate agent she'd met in a bar one night. She told me he drove a flash car, a Mercedes no less, and that had sealed the deal for her. I was shocked when she said she slept with him only hours after their first meeting. But she explained she got carried away when he offered her a lift home in his soft-top. They did it in the back seat. Any girl would have done the same, she said.

I was taken aback by how prudish I felt talking about sex with her. Larry and I had done some wild stuff in private and he'd taught me everything I knew. My eyes were well and truly open, but that was something private. Something we kept behind closed doors. It shouldn't be discussed over tea alongside celeb gossip.

Larry was upstairs in our room still snoring in bed. He must have come home after I'd gone to bed. I didn't remember saying hello or goodnight to him. Whenever I woke up I couldn't get out of our bedroom quick enough. It was so sparse. Against the wall facing the windows that looked out over the street below we laid the mattress on the floor. Our clothes and other random belongings were stuffed into the built in cupboards. Cardboard boxes, still not unpacked, were piled high against the wall on the left. I had no idea what was in them and didn't care. Everything we needed, we had. It was basic but the set up worked and I wondered if it was worth filling the house with expensive furniture just because that was the status quo.

Even so, I wanted to go back to work. I missed the company. Woolworths had not been the most exciting environment to spend time in, but it beat staying at home and waiting for one of the children to demand something.

Years later it was clear I had been suffering from post-natal depression but back then it wasn't talked about so openly. Nothing was.

Larry suddenly appeared in the doorway, wearing his boxer shorts and nothing else. In one of his tanned muscular arms he held Sue-Ann who was wiping the sleep out of her eyes. He looked like a pin-up and I had to catch my breath. How did I get that lucky? He yawned and stretched with his free arm, the muscles in his hair-scattered chest flexing. His arms were a deep brown colour and stood out next to the pale white of his torso.

'Morning.' He wandered over to the fridge and opened the

door. I got up, went over and kissed his bare back while he hunted for something to eat. 'Here, take this will you?' Larry passed me the baby.

'How about some eggs?' I ran my fingers through my hair and tried to look less dishevelled.

'Why not.' He pushed the fridge door closed and sat down in the only other chair we had around our melamine table. Nothing matched, and for a moment that seemed to poignantly reflect our relationship. 'Did you have any luck yesterday?' I was referring to the fishing expedition.

'Some you win.' He scratched at the five o'clock shadow around his chin. For as long as I had known him, Larry had always been clean-shaven. I stood by the stove for a moment looking at the man I'd married, the father of my children and wondered when he'd changed. I still loved him but things felt different.

'The eggs?' The frustration in his tone interrupted my train of thought and I went back to whisking.

'Did you hear that there was another body found in the river?' We'd been silent for too long and I was desperate to break the tension.

'Really.' He chewed his toast and feigned interest.

'A few days ago, some poor girl was found. The postman told me.'

'The postman?' Suddenly Larry's interest was aroused.

'Oh yes, you know,' I tripped over my words, 'I bumped into him on the doorstep.'

'I see.' Larry sat glaring at me. 'When was this?'

'I told you, a few days ago,' I watched Sue-Ann scrabble about on the floor near his feet. My heart was in my mouth but I didn't know why.

She stood up using the table leg as a prop and made a grab

for her father's thigh. I watched in slow motion as her filthy hand gripped his fine leg hair and pulled.

Without thinking Larry turned and slapped her hard across her cheek with the back of his hand. For a moment she was too shocked to cry. Then the tears came. Accompanied by a scream.

'Get her out of here.' He growled, watching the tears stream down her face, unmoved.

Adrenaline rushed through my veins and without thinking I did what I was told. I picked Sue-Ann up roughly and carried her upstairs. Not thinking, I put her down in the same cot Robbie was sleeping in and returned downstairs.

Larry was still sitting at the kitchen table. The fruit bowl was now in a pile on the floor. I bent down avoiding his eyes and started to collect the shattered pieces of crockery.

'Sit the fuck down.'

I'd cut my finger on a serrated edge of china but did what I was told. The warm red blood dripped on to the floor, creating a trail. It made me think of Hansel and Gretel.

'I love you Dee,' his voice was deep and serious, 'but if you ever speak to another man again without my permission I will put my hands around your throat and squeeze until the last breath has left your worthless body.'

My hands were shaking uncontrollably.

'Do you understand me?' It seemed as if the windowpane shook. His anger was tangible.

'Yes, my lord.' I looked up, meeting his dark stare and couldn't keep the smile from my face.

Larry stood up, the chair he had been sitting on slid backwards screeching against the tiles, and his large frame dominated the room. Stepping forward he grabbed me violently by the wrist and pulled me out of my chair.

'Upstairs. Now.' He whispered in my ear before biting down on my neck.

Twenty minutes later we were lying upstairs on the mattress, spent. His chest rose and fell with each exaggerated breath. His penis lay flaccid and moist.

'I'm going to go back to Woolworths.' I turned on to my stomach, cushioned by the rolls of fat and let the air dance around my bare bottom. 'I want to help bring some money in. You have too much on your shoulders. It's not right.'

'No.' Larry turned on to his side and propped his head up with his elbow. 'You are my wife and I say no.'

'Why not?' It's fair to say it was not the response I was expecting.

'I am the man.' He scratched his testicles with his thumbnail.

'Yes but...' my protest fell on deaf ears and I stopped before finishing the sentence.

'No but. Your place is here with the children. Not working beside that hussy Trisha.'

I wanted to disagree but couldn't find my voice.

'You know what it's like growing up without a mother around. Do you really want that for our children?' He was making sense. 'Think how different your life would have been if she'd been around. No. I won't have it.' He had put his foot down and that was that. He knew best and I wasn't going to argue. I trusted his judgement.

I nodded and rested my head on his chest. I could smell the faint whiff from his armpit. Sweat mingled with sex. I slid my hand down his stomach towards his tired penis.

'Not now.' He swatted my hand away. 'I'm cross.'

I rolled over and looked up at the ceiling searching for answers. All I saw were swirls of plaster. Disappointment took over again.

'Clean yourself up and go and check on the kids.' He didn't

look at me. 'And I suggest you call Trisha. Tell her you won't be going back to Woolworths.'

I sat up, the springs from the mattress sticking into my bottom, and looked at him. Larry pulled the poly-cotton sheet up to cover his man parts. His eyes were firmly closed.

'But why?' Trisha pleaded down the line. 'You seemed so keen earlier.'

'I know, but I've talked to Larry,'

'Oh here we go,' she interrupted. I was taken back.

'What do you mean?'

'Every time he says jump, you say how high. It's always the same Debs. I don't get it.' She did nothing to hide her frustration.

'That's not true.'

'Yes it is.' She paused while she ordered her thoughts. 'If Andrew ever told me what to do I'd end it. Honest, I would. No one gets to tell me what to do.' I wondered if this was more about her than it was about me. 'Look, I like Larry, he's a great guy but you should not let him dictate. That's all I'm saying.'

'I'm not sure you are in a position to judge.' I knew it was inflammatory but couldn't help myself.

'What is that supposed to mean?' Her defences had shot up.

'It's all very well for you with your easy life. Passing judgement. We're not all like you, you know. You sit there handing out advice. What do you know about my life? What do you know about anything?' I couldn't remember a time when I'd been so confrontational. I liked it. It felt good.

'If you want to be a Stepford wife, be my guest. But don't expect me to like it or keep my mouth shut. I thought you were better than that. You are better than that.' Her compliment was lost in the moment.

'Go and suck a dick.' I had no idea where the words came from. It didn't sound like me.

'What did you just say?' Her shock echoed down the phone.

'You heard me. Go. And. Suck. A. Dick. Find some scumbag with a nice car to blow and keep your opinions to yourself.'

Before she had a chance to respond I had slammed the phone down. For the second time that day I was shaking. And for the second time that day I felt more alive than I had done for ages.

20

Christmas was just around the corner. The weather was cold and it was getting dark earlier and earlier. I hated that time of year. Christmas meant presents and presents meant money; Money that we didn't have.

Over the past few months we managed to make the house a bit more comfortable. Larry brought back bits of random furniture that he found or Eric offered him. He could be so thrifty. Nothing matched but I stopped caring about appearances. We rarely had anyone over to the house anyway.

Robbie was crawling and Sue-Ann had begun to be able to put words together. She was a slow developer – much like I had been, according to Dad. 'Daft as a brush,' he always used to say to me. He said it so many times I believed it was true. Only after I met Larry and got away from him did I realise my own potential. I wasn't as hopeless as I'd been taught I was. Larry helped me to see that.

I left the children playing on the floor in the kitchen and went into the lounge.

A few weeks earlier Larry came home with a surprise. It was a television he'd bought on credit from a shop in town. He was so generous and I admired that about him. It was a really modern one that looked expensive. The large set sat pride of place in the lounge. Until then I'd read books to pass the time while I waited for him to get back from work. Having a television to watch felt like luxury. Every spare penny we had was used to make the mortgage payments and I worried we wouldn't be able to afford the television as well, but Larry assured me it wasn't a problem. 'I'll take care of everything,' he used to say and I believed him.

My favourite programmes were *Blockbusters* and *Blankety Blank*. I still read a lot but I liked the noise of the television. It made me feel less alone and helped to block out the sounds the children made.

I sat staring at the set, not really taking in what was on, and replayed a conversation I'd had about Christmas with Larry. I'd suggested we had Dad and Dawn over for lunch on Christmas Day. We never saw each other and rarely spoke on the phone. I had this cosy idea of the family all sitting round together, even if we didn't always all get on.

We had a proper house at last, the kind of house that people did gather in to celebrate. I liked the idea of being able to host them. To show them both that I wasn't a failure and that I'd made something of myself.

'It's a nice idea, Dee,' Larry scratched the back of his neck with his dirty fingernails, 'but the food will be expensive. And you don't want to have the hassle of all that cleaning up afterwards.'

He was right, of course, but I was still a bit disappointed.

'Do you think we'll be able to get a tree?'

'Sure.' He cupped my chubby face in his hands. 'Eric has got some he's selling to make a few extra quid. I'll get him to give us one at a discount.'

That made me happy. We didn't have decorations but it

didn't matter. I could make some. It would be something to do. I was good at recycling stuff.

I started to collect jar lids to turn into ornaments I could hang from the branches. We didn't drink alcohol very often but when we did I would save the corks from wine bottles and bottle caps. I dipped them in glue and glitter. They would look pretty on the tree. I used clothes that the children had grown out of to sew little stockings with and put them around the small fireplace. I wanted that Christmas to be special for us.

Although I loved our home I couldn't help but feel we were living beyond our means and the onset of Christmas only solidified my fears.

When Larry came home after work he was fuming. I'd never seen him so angry.

'That bastard,' he shoved a chair across the kitchen floor before kicking a cupboard.

'What's wrong?' I wiped yoghurt from Robbie's face. His little blue eyes were wide and watching the tirade cautiously.

'Bloody John Boyle. Who does he think he is? Marching into Rook's and demanding money from me. If old Mr Rook hadn't been there I would have punched his lights out.'

'Calm down,' I soothed. 'Who is John Boyle and why does he want money?'

'The fucking television.' Larry spat. 'I missed last week's payment. I told him I only needed a couple of days when we spoke on the phone yesterday. Then this afternoon he comes into the shop and picks up a pair of glasses, one of the expensive pairs, and he snaps it in half, right there, and drops the bits on the floor. Luckily Mr Rook was out the back and I managed to hide it before he saw. But then John started shouting that he was going to make me regret it if he didn't see the money owed him by tomorrow.'

Robbie had stopped eating and sat silently in his high chair watching his father rant. He looked scared.

'Can't we just give him the television back? He could sell it to someone else.'

'It's not that easy.'

'Why not?'

'Because John Boyle is a loan shark.'

I would never have thought that a television could cause so much trouble. Larry and I sat up late into the night coming up with a plan to keep Boyle at bay. Larry went out and got some beer to drink. He wanted to drown his sorrows but it seemed to me that spending money on beer was not the answer. Still, I bit my tongue and let him get on with it. He had never let me down before and I had no reason to doubt he would then.

I told him I'd sell my wedding ring, a simple gold band. Larry wouldn't let me. He was a proud man.

'This is my problem and I'll find a way to fix it.'

'We are in this together.' I reached across the grubby kitchen table and held his hand. He pulled it away and opened his fourth can of beer. The suds bubbled up over the lip and spilt on to the table. The liquid pooled on the table. Neither of us made a move to clean it up.

'Maybe we could just kill him.' Larry laughed but his expression was serious.

'There has to be something we have that he wants.' I ignored his last comment.

'The only thing John Boyle likes is money and pussy.'

21

DECEMBER 6TH 1986

The next day I woke up feeling sick. Everything was so uncertain. I didn't know if our plan would work. I lay in bed wondering how long Larry had been up. He usually slept in on Saturday mornings. I looked at our little plastic alarm clock and saw that it was only seven. It was still dark outside. I rolled over and pulled the duvet up over my head. It smelt of sex and stale sweat and I couldn't remember the last time I washed it. Robbie was crying in his cot in the other room and moments later Sue-Ann joined in the cacophony. I put my fingers in my ears and lay there in the darkness for a while thinking about what I'd agreed with Larry. The plan was simple.

Eventually I dragged myself out of bed and went to check on the children. Sue-Ann had quietened down but Robbie was still screaming at the top of his lungs. When I picked him up he stopped crying and I noticed the babygro was sodden. His nappy had leaked. The smell then hit me and I put him back down. He immediately started to cry again. Sue-Ann was standing in her cot shaking it and calling me. Ignoring her I went over to the disorganised chest of drawers and searched the top drawer for a dummy. Eventually, right at the back I spotted one and shoved it into her mouth. Her dark brown eyes looked sad as she sat back down in her cot and cradled a threadbare teddy.

Robbie continued to cry. I left them both upstairs in their room while I went downstairs to make myself some coffee. I couldn't deal with stinking nappies until after I'd had my caffeine fix.

Larry was sitting at the kitchen table his hands wrapped round a steaming mug of tea. I padded over to the kettle and flicked it on. The sound of screaming water quickly filled the silence. As I turned to pour coffee granules into my chipped mug I felt Larry's hands around my large waist.

'Morning, Mrs Miller.' He grabbed one of my breasts through my nightdress and caressed my nipple. His erection was sticking into my lower back. 'Remember what we talked about last night?' his face was in my hair and I could feel his warm breath on my neck.

'I do.'

'Good girl. Just remember what you have to do.'

'I know.' I stirred the water in and watched the instant coffee dissolve.

'Is that Robbie?' Larry pulled his head away from mine and listened.

'Yes. His nappy leaked all over him again. I'll do it in a bit.'

'OK. I'll call Boyle and arrange the meeting then I'll get dressed and nip out. There are some things we are going to need for tonight.'

At eight o'clock sharp there was a knock on the door. I sat stiffly on the sofa in living room while Larry answered it. Boyle was prompt if nothing else.

Through the top half of the window, that didn't have dingy netting across it, I could see a few scattered stars in the sky. The night looked black and oppressive. It seemed appropriate.

On the coffee table in front of me sat a bottle of red wine and three glasses. The lighting in the room was low with only the table lamp next to the television turned on. Through the closed door I could hear muffled voices and I felt myself tense. This was my moment and I didn't want to let Larry down. I heard the front door close and two sets of heavy footsteps approaching the lounge.

As the door opened I felt myself holding my breath. Larry entered first his eyes burning into me. A small ginger haired man with a beard and red cheeks followed him in. John Boyle was older than I was expecting, probably approaching fifty. His small eyes looked shocked to see me sitting there.

'This is my wife.' Larry introduced us and I got up from the sofa to shake his rough hand.

'Nice to meet ya.' His voice was gruff and he looked distinctly out of his comfort zone. I felt empowered by his weakness.

'Have a seat.' I sat back down on the sofa and patted the spot next to me. 'Wine?' I offered, pouring Larry and myself a glass.

Boyle stood for a moment looking at me before turning to Larry. He didn't accept my offer to sit down.

'I'm here for my money, Miller.'

'John, John, relax please. Let's be civil. Have a drink. Take a seat.' I admired how cool Larry was being. He was so at ease. So manly.

'Fine.' Boyle sat on the sofa as far away from me as possible and took a glass from the table. I reached over and poured the wine for him, flashing him my most attractive smile. He stared blankly back at me before taking a large gulp. 'This is all very nice, but where's my money?' he slammed the glass down on the table, spilling some wine.

'That's the thing,' Larry sat forward in the armchair and rested his elbows on his knees, 'I haven't got it.'

Boyle leant back, crossed his legs and folded his arms.

'Now there's a surprise.' He chuckled, clearly feeling as if he'd regained some control over the situation.

'I can get your money, but it won't be until next Friday at the earliest.' The men eyeballed one another, neither willing to back down. The tension in the room was tangible and it felt as if it might erupt at any moment.

'That's simply not good enough, old chum.' Boyle drank the rest of his wine in one go and stood up. 'I hate to do this, you seem like a lovely couple,' his sarcasm cut through me, 'but it looks like I'm going to have to ask the boys to pay you a little visit.'

'No.' The word left Larry's mouth with force. 'No,' he put his hands up in defeat. 'You don't need to do that, John.'

'You owe me money. You can't pay me what you owe. It all seems pretty simple to me.' I noticed how black his teeth were as he spoke.

'How about we come to some other arrangement?' Larry looked more relaxed again and in control.

'What can you possibly offer me?' Boyle looked bored.

'Dee.' Larry signalled to me.

'I stood up and moved closer to Boyle. He was wary at first, until he understood what was happening.

I dropped my dressing gown on the floor and revealed a polyester silky slip. It was tight around my bust and my waist. Boyle smiled and licked his chapped lips.

'Oh,' he rubbed his beard with his hand, 'Now I see.'

'Dee here is going to take you upstairs, John.'

'Is she now?' Boyle stood there smiling and undressing me with his eyes. I smiled back, doing my best to hide my disgust.

'Do whatever you want.' Larry appeared turned on by the prospect of his wife sleeping with another man. 'Then we're even.'

'You think one session with this whale is enough to cancel out a debt worth two hundred pounds?'

I turned to Larry unable to hide my shock. He ignored my stare.

'Have as many goes as you want.' His eyes were cold and gave nothing away. 'Come back whenever you like.'

Boyle stood there looking at me and contemplating the offer.

'Don't you have kids?' He was still looking at me. I didn't answer. 'I suppose that's your affair. Fine,' he turned to Larry, 'you got yourself a deal. She better be clean.' He took hold of my hand roughly and led me out of the room.

22

It had taken us a while but at last we were financially secure. Larry still worked at Rook's. He was a pillar of the community. I made money by selling sex. Our spare bedroom became my office.

Since my first time with John Boyle, it became a regular thing. Boyle knew plenty of men who were willing to pay for it. It was easy money. I didn't even have to leave the house and I was paid well for what was usually only ten minutes' work at a time. Some of them were rougher than others but Larry was always in the background ready to intervene if I needed him to. Occasionally he sat on a chair in the room and watched. The punters didn't seem to mind. Some of them quite liked it.

Back then I only worked evenings and weekends. It was difficult during the day. Even though Sue-Ann was at nursery some of the time I still had Robbie under my feet.

I was making good money and Larry, with a bit of help from his brother Eric, had started to deal drugs, heroin mainly. Often my clients became his and vice versa. Neither Larry or I ever touched the stuff though. We weren't that stupid. We saw what it did to people, how it wrecked their lives.

There was money stuffed under mattresses and floorboards. We didn't have to pay the taxman and we bought whatever we wanted and went out more. I got nice clothes and jewellery, things I'd never dreamt of owning. We bought a caravan and used to go away to Norfolk for weekends. The extra income also meant that we could afford a babysitter whenever we wanted.

Alice, a spotty, awkward teenager who reminded me of myself at her age, used to come and look after the kids. She'd just finished school and was grateful for the money. She lived a few doors down from us. It was the perfect set-up.

The negatives were that I'd gotten pregnant a few times and had to have four abortions. Some of my clients didn't like using protection. It was a hazard of the job and although I didn't really mind having to go to the clinic, it was inconvenient.

That Saturday morning we were getting ready to go to a wedding. Dawn had met Ian McCarthy a year ago. He was a truck driver. She got pregnant 'accidently' and now they were having a shotgun wedding. It made me happy to see her putting on weight. She'd always been so skinny and smug about it.

Ian was a Catholic, so the ceremony was being held in Saint Laurence's Church off Milton Road in the north of the city. Dad finally had rid of both of us.

Dawn had never paid much attention to my kids but wanted Sue-Ann to be her bridesmaid. I didn't mind, as long as she didn't expect me to pay for the dress.

At ten o'clock Larry, Sue-Ann, Robbie and I pulled into the church car park in the Ford. It was a grey day and rain was starting to drizzle. Getting out of the car in my jade coloured suit and matching hat that I'd bought from C&A I looked up at the church. It was an unimpressive modern building that looked more like a cross between a barn and an office block than a place of worship. Outside a few people congregated by the door, some of them smoking cigarettes. I didn't recognise any of them. I'd only met Ian twice.

Larry and I approached the group and smiled at the various strangers in their wedding attire. Sue-Ann, wearing a maroon faux silk dress, went over to a puddle in her new patent black shoes and started to splash. Larry went over and gave her a little clip round the ear before pulling her away.

I held firmly on to Robbie's hand. He wanted to join his sister in the puddle until he saw her being scolded. Then he stopped wriggling and stayed by my side. He looked quite sweet in his little white shirt and bowtie. People on the day said so.

We seemed to hang around in the car park for quite a while. Eventually Dad showed up and shuffled over to us. His eyes were bloodshot and he looked old suddenly. He didn't even bother to wear a tie. If mum had seen him like that it would have broken her heart. It was a solemn realisation and the first time in my life that I was grateful she was dead. For her sake.

At about ten-twenty Ian showed up in his suit and we were ushered into the church. It was nicer inside than it was out but I felt a bit weird being there. I never went to church. All that history and fire and brimstone gave me the creeps.

Robbie sat sandwiched between Larry and I, his finger shoved firmly up his nose. Sue-Ann had been taken away by Dawn's maid of honour, a pretty blonde girl in the ugliest dress I'd ever seen. Larry paid special attention to her. He might as well have had his tongue hanging out.

Sitting in the uncomfortable wooden chair I looked at Ian, stood at the front of the church fiddling with his buttonhole, and wondered what he was like. We'd spent so little time together I really didn't know him. He had a closed face and it was hard to tell what he was thinking most of the time. I hoped that he and Dawn would be happy. Even if my sister and I had grown apart I still remembered her as the little girl I looked out for after mum died. It made me wonder whether she ever felt the same affection towards me. Her behaviour towards me suggested not.

As the piano sounded the room went quiet and we all stood. The doors at the back of the church opened and Sue-Ann appeared holding a basket full of flower petals that she sprinkled along the aisle. As she made her way towards the front the onlookers cooed.

Next came the maid of honour. Her long blonde hair was piled high on her head in tight curls. She smiled lovingly as she floated past the people on either side, her pale blue taffeta dress swishing as she went. Larry couldn't take his eyes off her and I found it hard to contain the rage I felt seething away inside. Did he have to be so bloody obvious?

Once the pretty blonde, whose name I still wasn't sure of, took her seat, Dawn appeared with Dad. I noticed he was wearing a tie. Someone had plucked one from somewhere. Dawn looked like a great big meringue. The dress did something very unflattering to her figure. It emphasised her ungainly bump and made her body look out of proportion. A large stiff veil covered most of her face. Despite the absurd dress she was glowing and she looked happy. It made me think of my own wedding day, which had been an altogether different affair and I felt a tinge of jealousy. Why did she get the big white dress and the fairy-tale ending? Dad didn't even bother to walk me up the aisle.

After the ceremony, which seemed to go on forever – I suppose that's Catholicism for you – we all made our way to the reception in a nearby hall.

Upon entering the room, which reminded me of a school sports hall, our eyes were met by three long tables already laid out. There were more balloons than I'd ever seen; Bunches of pink and white helium hearts tied to many of the chairs. It looked more like a little girl's birthday party than an adult affair.

Larry followed me into the room. Robbie was sitting on his shoulders eating a chocolate bar someone had given him. His hands and new white shirt were both filthy. Sue-Ann was nowhere to be seen. The maid of honour, whose name I'd learnt was Becky, had taken her under her wing, which I was very grateful for. That meant I could relax and have a few drinks. Larry and I had insisted on paying for some cava to welcome the guests with. It was our wedding present to Dawn and Ian and my way of showing them I'd come up in the world. A few gawky teenagers stood looking awkward holding trays of the bubbly and in the corner of the room was a DJ with his decks.

After a few glasses I started to relax. I didn't care that I didn't really know many people. I was proud to be out showing off my husband who always attracted the attention of other women.

At one o'clock we were all seated. There was no seating plan thankfully so we just sat where we wanted. Larry was on my left and for a few minutes the seat on my right remained unoccupied. I chatted happily to a woman sitting opposite me. It turned out she was the groom's aunt. She was a brash woman wearing an equally loud floral pattern dress that only exacerbated her size. She was clearly rather drunk and it amused me. She chewed my ear off, telling me what a lovely little boy Ian had been, slurring her words and continuing to take large sips from her glass. I didn't notice the man who took up the empty seat next me since I was so absorbed in the comical conversation with the aunt.

The same school leavers who'd served us drinks then appeared carrying plates they placed down in front of each of us with little care. I looked down at the chicken Kiev, mashed potatoes and peas. The smell of garlic was overpowering and I thought it an odd choice for a wedding lunch.

Just as I picked up my knife and fork, and was deciding how best to tackle the large piece of breaded chicken, I felt a hand on my shoulder. I turned to my right and stared at the man touching me.

'Hello, Dee.' He smiled, showing his nicotine-stained teeth. I knew him well.

'Mark.' I removed his hand and swallowed, not knowing where to look. 'What are you doing here?'

By then Larry had stopped talking to the old boy next to him and was paying attention to our conversation. I felt his hand on my knee.

'Mark, lovely to see you.' Larry cut in extending a hand and doing his best to defuse the tension.

'Lovely indeed.' Mark sat back in his chair and grinned with pleasure. He was enjoying himself.

'So, tell me, how do you know the lovely couple?'

'Groom is my brother.' Mark continued smiling at me knowingly.

'Small world,' Larry was determined to play it cool, 'the bride is my sister-in-law.'

'Is that so?' Mark raised an eyebrow before picking up his fork and stabbing the food. 'Small world indeed.'

'How do you know each other?' The drunken aunt opposite asked, her headpiece slipping down over one eye.

'Met at the pub, didn't we Mark.' Larry was quick to answer.

'Yes,' Mark couldn't help chuckling, 'the pub. That was it.' He was lording it over us and it made me feel sick to my stomach.

Up until Mark's appearance I had been having fun but the moment he sat down next to me that all changed.

I'd met him six months earlier when he came over to the house. He was one of my regular clients. Sitting there next to him at my sister's wedding made me feel sick. What if he said something? What if everyone found out what I did to make money? It didn't bear thinking about.

After the meal was over and the speeches had been made Larry and I made our excuses and left. I'd been on edge ever since seeing Mark and was desperate to get away. We gave the excuse that the children were tired and said our goodbyes. I practically had to drag Sue-Ann away from the dance floor by her hair. The little sod was refusing to leave and causing a scene.

'Don't worry, he won't say a thing.' Larry said getting into the car.

'Oh, I know he won't. He wouldn't want anyone knowing his dirty little secret.'

'So what's upset you, then?' He started the engine and I realised he was way over the limit.

'Just took me by surprise, that's all. I didn't expect to bump into someone like that, especially at my sister's wedding. Not exactly ideal.'

'Don't worry. Just keep doing what you're doing and leave that little worm, Mark, to me.' His hands gripped the wheel and his knuckles were white. I didn't know what he meant so just stayed quiet and watched the world go by out of the window. It had been a strange day.

23

On Tuesday morning I'd just got back from dropping Sue-Ann at nursery when there was a knock on the door. Leaving Robbie strapped in his pushchair I went to answer the door.

'Hello Dee.' Mark stood on the doorstep leaning against the frame smiling smugly.

'What are you doing here? You know my hours are evenings and weekends only.' I started to close the door but before I had a chance he'd shoved his foot in and started to barge his way into the house.

'Don't be like that, Dee. I just wanted to come and say hello.' He was a strong man with large shoulders and big feet. He wore Nike trainers that had seen better days and his work jeans were covered in dust. 'Aren't you going to offer me a cup of tea?' He leant against the hallway wall.

I looked down at Robbie who was chattering happily in his pushchair unaware of the threatening atmosphere that charged the air.

'One cup and then you're gone.' I wheeled Robbie into the kitchen with us, hoping that Mark wouldn't do anything unpleasant if there was a child in the room. 'How do you like it?' I asked through gritted teeth as I filled the kettle.

'Sweet and wet.' His smirk was vile.

We stood not speaking while the kettle took its time to boil. His dirty green eyes didn't leave me for a second. I felt uncomfortable under his gaze and looked down at the tiled floor noticing the muddy footprints he had walked in.

'Larry at work, is he?' Mark already knew the answer so I didn't bother to answer and poured the tea.

'Here.' I considered throwing the boiling liquid in his face before handing him the mug.

'Lovely.' He took a sip and let out a satisfied sigh. 'Now, you and me have got some business.' Mark pulled up a chair and sat down, making himself at home.

'I told you. Evenings and weekends only.' I held my nerve.

'Now, now, that's not very polite. We are basically family now.' He reached out a hand and pulled the pushchair towards him. 'Sweet little fella. What's his name?'

'None of your business.' I growled. 'Get your hands off my son. You've had your tea and now leave.'

'Oh Dee. I'm disappointed. I know you're not much to look at but I thought you had some brains.'

'Get out.'

'No.' He stood up and his large frame overshadowed me. 'Do you want your sister knowing what you do to pay the bills?'

'You don't have the guts.' I spat. 'Everyone would know you pay for it. Your dear old mum would be mortified.'

'My dear old mum can go to hell.' Mark grabbed me tightly around the throat and brought his face within inches of mine. 'And that's where I'll send you if you don't remember your fucking manners.' He continued to squeeze hard before pushing me away and letting go. I fell backwards choking and trying to catch my breath.

'What do you want?'

'I want a freebie.' He grabbed his crotch. 'No, actually, I want lots of freebies.'

'Larry will never agree to it.' I rubbed my throat and tried not to look at Robbie who was sitting silently terrified and watching Mark.

'Larry isn't going to know.' Mark stepped forward and undid his trousers. 'In here or upstairs, it's up to you.'

'Not in front of my boy.' My eyes filled with tears and my voice was cracking.

Mark left an hour later, promising to return at the same time next week. I quickly stripped the bed of the bloody sheets and took them to the bins outside. My groin was sore and so was my throat.

Robbie had fallen asleep in his pushchair and I sat down at the kitchen table and wept.

PART II

24

'That's all well and good Mrs Miller but it's what happened afterwards that interests us.' The detective adjusted his navy blue tie and sat back in his chair.

The interview room felt stuffy. I'd been in there for so long and answered so many questions.

'I don't know what you want me to say?' I pleaded holding my hands out. My solicitor, Carol Winter-Bottom, sat next to me writing down notes.

'We want to know how you were involved in the murder of Mr Mark McCarthy. Just tell us what happened.'

'I don't know. How many times do I have to keep saying it? I. Don't. Know.'

'My client has already told you she had nothing to do with Mr McCarthy's death. Either charge her or release her.'

'Let's go back to that day again,' the detective leant forward and rested his elbows on the desk between us, 'you have confirmed that you saw the victim that morning.'

'Yes.' I was so tired of answering the same question.

'And you have confirmed that you had sexual relations with the victim.'

'Yes I did. But then he left and that was the last time I saw him.' I folded my arms and looked at the man opposite.

Detective Sergeant Dan Small was an average-looking man with brown hair that was going grey at the temples and steely grey eyes. He looked more like a pencil pusher than a policeman. I suppose the two were not mutually exclusive.

'So despite the fact you allege he raped you and then disappeared into thin air, the discovery of his body, buried in your garden, is a mere coincidence and has nothing to do with you?'

'There is no need for sarcasm, detective sergeant.' Carol peered over her glasses at him with her dark blue eyes.

'That's right. I don't know how he got there. I didn't put him there.'

'Well somebody did, Mrs Miller, and it's my job to bring that person to justice.'

I rolled my eyes and turned to Carol.

'I want a break. I want to get some fresh air.'

'You heard my client.' Carol put her pen down and sat up straight in her chair.

DS Small and the assisting officer looked at each other and shrugged. They were tired too. It had been a very long day.

'Interview terminated at twenty-three o seven.'

The detective and other policeman left the room and again I was alone with Carol.

'You're doing fine, Deborah. Just stick to the facts.' She ordered her papers in front of her.

'This is ridiculous. I want to talk to my husband.'

'I'm afraid that's not possible at the moment.'

'How much longer?' I slumped in my chair and rested my forehead on the edge of the table. 'It's been nearly two days now.'

'It's a very serious charge, Mrs Miller.' Carol had a way of delivering every sentence as if she was in court. 'You can be detained for up to ninety-six hours before they have to charge or release you.'

'Either they have the evidence or they don't. They found the body. What more do they need?'

'The pathologist will be gathering forensic evidence. Until all the results come through I'm afraid it's a waiting game.'

'Well, I'm as shocked as the next person. He was a scumbag, but I didn't want him dead and I certainly didn't kill him.'

'Then there won't be any evidence and you will be released.' She looked at me through her glasses and didn't waver from the formal tone she'd taken with the police.

'Larry, when can I speak to Larry? How can I find out what's going on?'

'I'll go and get us a something to drink and ask. Since I'm not his solicitor they are not at liberty to disclose anything to me, but I can try.' Carol stood up and straightened her grey trouser suit. Her dyed blonde hair was tied back in a bun.

'I want to go out for a ciggy.' My frustration was tangible.

'I'll tell the officer on duty.' Carol tucked her leather-bound file under her arm and led me out of the room towards the custody desk.

I was allowed out into a secure courtyard for a smoke and then I was told that the interview would continue later and I was returned to my cell.

I went and sat on the plastic green mattress opposite the door and listened to the sound of the lock being turned in the large metal door. A pair of eyes peered through the small glass window before the shutter was pulled down. I sat alone in the small room wondering what was going to happen to me. The silence was unbearable. For a little while I paced backwards and forwards, replaying the events from April 1989 over in my mind. It was so long ago and my memory was foggy. Did they really expect me to be able to remember that far back? I didn't want to say anything that might implicate Larry but I needed them to know I had nothing to do with it. It didn't look good. The body of a man who raped me was buried in our garden.

I went over the last few days in my head. So much had happened so quickly and now everything was unravelling.

At two-fifteen on the afternoon of January 16th a team of police officers showed up at my door and requested to come inside. Not knowing what was going on I let them in. The kids were at school and Larry was at work.

They proceeded to inform me that my neighbour, who had been laying the foundations for a summer room, had come across what appeared to be human bones at the end of their garden. Since the remains were discovered so close to the edge of our property I was informed that a warrant had been obtained under section 8 of the Police and Criminal Evidence Act 1984, which allowed them access to my garden to carry out an excavation. Realising there was nothing I could do to stop them, I let the team in to begin their search.

I explained that the majority of our rear garden was covered in concrete slabs that needed to be removed before the dig could begin. As the officers set about doing this I called Larry at work. He told me to sit tight and wait for him. He was leaving work early and would make his way over.

The rain was coming down hard that afternoon and the fading light put an abrupt end to the dig. Policemen were left over night to guard the site while Larry and I snuggled up in bed, wondering what would happen next.

On January 18th a police search advisor arrived and took charge. The excavation resumed and by lunchtime a number of human bones had been recovered by two members of the team.

Soon after that we were both brought in for questioning.

Then, I'm told, Scenes of Crime Officers were brought in.

They were there to preserve the evidence found. I was told that the remains were taken to Cambridge Police Station before being transferred to the department of medicine at the university. After being examined there they were then handed over to another doctor whose role it was to establish the identity of the victim. It didn't take them very long to conclude the bones belonged to Mark McCarthy.

I hadn't seen or spoken to Larry since arriving at the police station two days earlier. In that time, I had been subjected to a number of interviews totalling nearly nine hours.

Finally, exhaustion won and I lay down and closed my eyes, pulling the blue blanket up over my head. Re-living the nightmare wasn't helping one little bit.

Then it occurred to me that this was all Dawn's fault. If she'd never married bloody Ian McCarthy none of this would have happened. I clenched my fists until my wedding ring felt tight around my finger. I wanted to scream and felt as if my lungs were going to burst. It wasn't fair and I told myself that the next time I was taken into the interview room I wouldn't cooperate. I'd talked till I was blue in the face and answered all their questions, but that got me nowhere.

25

When I woke up my neck was so stiff. It was the first thing I noticed, even before the cell itself. The feeling in my body was something I didn't recognise. It was age. I was feeling old. Old and tired. And emotional. The older I get the more I know it's time to let go. The bitterness that built up in the teenage me had always been there. For a long time, I'd kept it buried. The happiness I'd found with Larry helped to keep a lid on it. I didn't even know I was unhappy until I met him. He opened my eyes and helped me to see clearly for the first time in my young life.

I thought back to those days and tried to remember the young me. Had I had a crystal ball I'd never imagine it would have all ended here in a police station. Little Deborah Campkin being questioned about a murder. It was unthinkable and I chortled to myself for a brief minute. Then I looked around the cell walls and the gravity of the situation put its hands around my throat and started to choke me. Much like Mark had done all those years ago. I tried hard to remember if that was the beginning or if things had started to unravel before that. The answer was not one I was prepared to face just yet.

At six-thirty breakfast was delivered. It consisted of some lukewarm porridge and a glass of very acidic juice that seemed too alien to be related to an orange. Prison food, I thought to myself. But I wasn't banged up yet. They still had to prove it. And I knew they couldn't.

After devouring all the food, despite the fact it was tasteless, I waited for the next round of questioning that I anticipated was due any moment.

Sitting on the squeaky plastic mattress staring at the heavy door and twiddling my thumbs I tried to imagine what the morning routine looked like for Carol.

Her impeccably behaved children would be eating nicely while her dull yet picture-perfect husband got himself ready for work. No doubt she would spend most of her time checking that she had all the right documents in her briefcase and far less attention would be paid to her family. But I understood that. I could relate to it. She and I probably weren't so different after all. Seeing us as equal for the first time helped me to decide where we could go from there. Until then our relationship had been strained. Of course it had, I'd been arrested for murder; but it was more than that. She was from a different world. A world where families were kind to each other and people wore suits to work. I decided Carol and I would be friends and that made my situation a whole lot easier to bear. If I had a friend in this place, I could survive.

Imagining Carol's family led me back to thinking about my own. Sue-Ann was no longer a problem but Robbie... What had happened to Robbie? Who was looking after him? And little Owen. I hoped they were together and that Robbie was taking care of his younger brother.

I wasn't going to respond to any more questions but I was well within my rights to ask what had happened to my children. Robbie wasn't yet fourteen years old and Owen was only nine. It occurred to me that maybe they were my ticket out of that place. I was a mother, a responsible citizen. How dare they keep me away from my children? Especially given the fact that a corpse had been discovered in the garden they grew up playing in. The poor kids would be traumatised. They needed me then more than ever. With their dad also cooped up in the police station, what those boys needed was some stability. I was it.

The cogs in my brain were turning when a short, slender, Asian officer opened the cell door and ushered me out.

'Come on, Miller.' He was a self-important little bastard.

I got up slowly and stretched.

'Have you ever tried sleeping in here?'

'I've never broken the law.'

'Good for you.' I pulled my jumper down, aware of a cold breeze tickling my stomach and followed him out of the cell. 'I want to know about my kids.'

'You need to speak to the detective.'

'I'm asking you. Where are my kids?' I stopped in the hallway refusing to move.

'I don't have that information.' He stood awkwardly aware of the size difference between us. I was a bit taller and much wider.

'I have a right to know.'

Just then, the officer in charge appeared.

'Come on.' He winked at the little man standing in front of me. 'I've got this.'

'I'm not moving until I know my kids are safe.' I looked at him coldly. The Pakistani officer stood between us waiting for something to happen.

'Your kids are safe, madam.' His sarcasm came as a shock and unaware of how I should respond I simply nodded and followed him to the custody desk.

'I'm not answering anything until my solicitor arrives.' I told him trying to regain some composure.

He ignored me and returned to staring at the CCTV footage on the small screen next to him. That feeling of being invisible returned. I hadn't been that girl for so many years but his dismissal took me back. Feeling like a sulky teenager, I stood tapping my foot on the speckled lino floor. Sick of being treated like a criminal, I looked at the notice board instead of making eye contact with the uniformed men. Their opinions didn't matter to me but I couldn't stand the looks of disapproval. They made me feel like a naughty child and I didn't appreciate it. I was a mother and I knew those looks only too well, having practised it myself a number of times.

Minutes later Carol Winter-Bottom appeared holding her suitcase.

'Good morning, Mrs Miller.'

'Morning.' I wasn't in the mood to exchange pleasantries.

'Let's go through.' She stretched out her arm signalling for me to go first. I plodded along the corridor with my arms folded across my chest until we reached the interview room. I waited for the officer who released me from my cell to open the door before stepping inside. Carol followed me in and then the officer closed the door behind us.

'When am I going to get out of here?'

'The deadline is close. They only have a few hours left in which to charge you or release you.' She sat down at the desk and opened up her briefcase while I remained standing, leaning against the far wall. 'Mrs Miller, as my client I strongly suggest you think back to April 1989 and try to think how it's possible Mr McCarthy came to be buried in your garden. The evidence is overwhelming. You admit that a sexual assault took place and we know that after supposedly leaving your home he was not seen again.'

'I told you it hasn't got anything to do with me. I didn't kill him.'

'Well somebody did and then they buried his body at the end of your garden. I know this is a difficult question but do you know who did kill him?'

'What are you suggesting?'

'Well, Mrs Miller, if it wasn't you then the only other person it can be was your husband. You do realise that by denying the charges you are putting him in the frame?' Her blue eyes looked at me accusingly.

'Larry's not like that.'

'Did you tell him about the rape?' The moment that word left her mouth she started to soften. Unable to meet her eye I stared down at my feet and didn't say anything. 'Look, Mrs Miller, if I'm going to help you I need to be in possession of all the facts. Anything you tell me is confidential.'

'Well, I told him about it afterwards but I can't remember exactly when. It was a long time ago.'

'I see. Why didn't you report it to the police?'

'Back then I was involved with some stuff that wasn't exactly legal and we didn't need the police sniffing round so I kept quiet. It seemed like the only thing to do. Now I wish I'd said something and I might not be in this mess.'

'What do you mean by that?' Carol sprang the question on me.

'Oh, just, you know, being here, being questioned about it and stuff.'

My shutters had come down and she could sense it. She shook her head, gave a little sigh and returned to fiddling with her paperwork.

Ten minutes later the door opened and DS Small appeared with his counterpart. The pair looked very grave and I felt a sinking in my stomach.

'Interview resumed at zero seven twenty between Detective Sergeant Dan Small and Mrs Deborah Miller. The accompanying officer is DS Richard Martin. Also present is Carol Winter-Bottom, the solicitor for the suspect. Have a seat, Mrs Miller.'

Begrudgingly I slumped down on to the plastic chair. I could feel the look of disgust coming from DS Martin. I wriggled in my seat.

'Mrs Deborah Miller, I am arresting you for the murder of Mr Mark McCarthy on April 7th 1989. You do not have to say anything, but anything you do say may be used in evidence against you. Do you understand?'

'Why are you arresting me?'

'New evidence has come to light.'

'What new evidence?'

'There was a thorough search of your house.' Small couldn't look at me. He looked pale. 'We found the axe.'

'What axe?'

'The axe that was used to dismember the body of Mr McCarthy.'

'I don't know what you're talking about.'

'Your fingerprints and DNA are all over the handle.'

'So? You're arresting me for murder because an item found in my house has my DNA on it? It's a joke.'

'This is no joke, Mrs Miller, I can assure you.' Small and Martin shared a look. 'That wasn't the only thing the forensic team discovered.' I held my breath. Carol looked at me and I shrugged. 'We've found an item of your clothing with Mr McCarthy's blood on it.'

'I need to speak to my client.' Carol was flustered and desperate to call an end to the interview.

'Do you have anything you wish to say at this stage?' DS Small added solemnly.

'No comment.'

26

When I discovered I was pregnant a week earlier I had cried. I didn't want my body to be taken over by someone else but felt reluctant to return to the clinic for another termination. I thought all of that was behind me. I'd done with changing nappies and the late night feeds. But Larry said he was pleased and that we should keep it. So we did.

That afternoon I had an appointment with the doctor. Larry wanted to come and took time off from work to join me at the surgery. We sat side by side in the stuffy waiting room watching the clock. The doctor was running late, as usual, and we had to wait for twenty minutes before I was called.

Larry followed me into the room and we both sat down opposite Dr Ling. He was younger than I had expected.

'How can I help you?' he looked from Larry to me.

'I'm pregnant.'

'I see.' He was smart enough not to jump into congratulating us just yet. There was a pause while he waited to see if I had anything to add. When I remained quiet he reached for a cardboard calendar that sat on his desk. 'When was the date of your last period?'

'I'm not really sure.' I admitted. 'They have always been a bit all over the place. But maybe twelve weeks ago.'

'Right,' he looked down at the calendar and started to do a mental sum. 'If that is correct, then your due date is approximately the middle of May. Let's get you booked in for a scan.' He turned to the computer on his desk and started tapping away at the keyboard. 'The hospital will send you a letter with a date for the scan.' His round glasses reflected the brightness off the computer screen.

'Thanks, doc.' Larry stood up.

'Congratulations,' Dr Ling offered as an after-thought without taking his eyes of the screen.

Not knowing how to react I stood up and followed Larry out of the room.

We sat silently in the car on the drive back to the house. My mood was pensive. The visit to the doctor brought the reality of my situation crashing down around me.

After what had happened with Mark all those months before I had contracted an STD. I took a course of antibiotics and Larry made me promise that from then on I'd always use protection. And most of the time I did. Most of the time.

There had been one or two occasions, both about three months ago, when a punter who was a regular paid me extra not to use it. I knew him well enough. He'd been coming to me for months. He was a sad little man whose wife refused to sleep with him since discovering he had an unhealthy obsession with pornography that featured teenage girls. He told me he never slept with anyone but his wife and I had no reason not to believe him. It was funny the things that punters confided in me. I was as much a counsellor as anything else.

Thinking back, I realised it would have been around that time that I last remembered having a period. Sitting in the car next to Larry I tried to push the feeling of dread away. There was a chance the baby I was carrying wasn't his. How could I possibly tell him? I couldn't and I wouldn't. If he ever found out, then I could put it down to an accident. Condoms split sometimes. Mistakes happened.

'I think you should take a break for a while.' Larry's words broke the silence.

'A break from what?'

'From working.' He kept his eyes on the road. 'We've got enough money coming in now and a decent amount saved. It might not be good for the baby if you carry on doing that.'

'I suppose you are right.' It had occurred to me. It wasn't as if I particularly liked my line of work but it paid well and gave me a bit of independence. I hated relying on Larry to pay for everything. My heart sank when I realised I would be going back to being dependent on him.

'My deal with Eric is bringing in lots of cash. Take a break for a while. You can always go back to it later after it's born.'

'I can't imagine many people like the idea of sleeping with a pregnant woman anyway,' I mused.

'You'd be surprised,' Larry chuckled to himself, shaking his head, 'there's a whole world of freaks out there.'

We got home and relieved Alice of her babysitting. Larry gave her some cash and showed her out. The way she used to look at him made me suspect she had a crush.

'Right kids. Mum and Dad have some news.' Larry stood over the children who were gazing at the television and not listening. 'You are going to have a little brother or sister.'

Sue-Ann who was very nearly five turned around and looked at him. I stood by the door watching the conversation unfold.

'Why?'

'Because that's what mums and dads do. They have children. Won't it be nice?' He bent down and ruffled her hair.

She looked at him and thought about it for a moment. 'Babies cry.' She looked over at Robbie who was still transfixed by the cartoons on the television. 'You get cross when we cry. Will you get cross with the baby?'

'Of course we won't.' Larry stood up again and took a step backwards. 'Just watch the TV. Your mum will give you dinner soon. Then it's bed.'

I left the kids in the lounge and Larry followed me into the kitchen.

'She's right you know.' I went over to the fridge and got Larry a beer. 'It's not easy having another baby. Are you sure you want to do this?' I was really hoping he might change his mind.

'Another little Miller, it will be great. I always wanted a big family. Why stop there?' He sipped the beer thoughtfully.

'Are you serious?' I spun around.

'Why not?' Something odd had come over him. He'd never mentioned wanting a large family before. What had changed? I wanted to ask him, but thought better of it.

'Kids are having beans for dinner. Pizza for us tonight?' I picked up a takeaway menu that was shoved into one of the drawers.

'Sure. We are celebrating.'

I stared at the list of pizza toppings and didn't say a word.

'I hope it's a girl.' Larry drained the contents of his beer can and put it to one side. 'Let's find out when we go to the scan.'

I nodded.

'And if it is a girl I think we should call her Paula. I like that name.'

'But what if it's a boy?' I didn't want him to be disappointed.

'Owen.'

'That's nice. Little Owen Miller.' I put my hand on my belly and felt a wave of maternal love for the first time since I'd discovered I was expecting. Perhaps this baby would be a positive thing. After all it made Larry happy and that was good enough for me.

27

That morning I had returned from Cambridge Magistrates' Court. I'd been taken in a police van and hauled up in front of a judge. The police wanted a warrant extended for further detention. The judge granted the warrant and I was returned to the police station where the interview continued.

'No comment.' I was so tired of repeating the same two words over and over again.

DS Small sat back in his chair, loosened his tie and rubbed his chin on which a five o'clock shadow had appeared over the few days since I'd been in custody. It seems he'd not had much time to himself either.

'You aren't helping yourself by staying quiet.' He looked at me deciding to try another tack. 'If you know anything you are better off cooperating. The judge will take that into consideration when sentencing.'

I looked over at Carol, who had dark rings under her eyes where her mascara had smudged over the course of the long day. She nodded wearily.

'No comment.'

'Interview suspended at,' DS Small looked up at the clock on the wall, 'zero nine forty-three.' He stood up and turned to DS Martin. 'I need a coffee.' The policemen left the room and I was alone again with Carol.

'When can I speak to Larry?' I turned to her. She took her black jacket off the back of her chair, stood and slipped it on.

'You can't. It's that simple.' She was tired of talking.

'Then I'm not cooperating. Simple.' I sat in the chair, aware I had been wearing the same clothes for a number of days. I felt dirty.

'That's up to you Mrs Miller. As your solicitor I strongly advise you rethink your position.'

'But I haven't done anything.'

'It is information that they want from you now, not a confession. If you know anything it would be wise to share it.

'You want me to admit I know things when I don't. That doesn't make any sense. How is that going to help anyone?'

Carol stood looking at me with both pity and frustration.

'It's been a long day, but this hasn't even begun yet.'

'And my kids?'

'They have been taken into care, Mrs Miller. And they will remain there until the police get the information they are after.' Her dark blue eyes looked at me coldly. She thought I was guilty. I could see it in her eyes.

'You are meant to be on my side.'

'I am,' she sighed. 'It's my job to advise you. What you do with that advice is up to you.'

'If you don't believe me what hope do I have?' I couldn't help feeling sorry for myself. No one thought I was innocent. 'I'm not a monster.'

Carol put her hand on my shoulder and patted it before leaving the room. A young chubby officer appeared and escorted me back to my cell.

'Can I get some breakfast?' I asked before he closed the heavy door behind me.

'I'll find out.' He couldn't look at me. The revolt he held was palpable.

'Make sure you do!' I called through the locked door between us. 'I have my rights.'

I slumped down on the same uncomfortable plastic mattress and closed my eyes. When would this nightmare be over?

I was woken an hour or so later when the door of my cell opened with a bang. Sitting up and rubbing my tired eyes I saw DS Small standing there.

'Your husband has just confessed to the murder of Mark McCarthy. He says you had nothing to do with it.' DS Small's eyes were scrutinising me.

'Can I go home now?' I stood up expectantly. 'I want to be with my kids.'

'We'll arrange for you to be bailed.' He wasn't happy about it.

There was a long uncomfortable silence while we both stood looking at each other. He didn't like me that was clear, but more than that he didn't trust me. I did my best not to crumple under his gaze.

'Is that it then?'

'For now Mrs Miller.' He turned to leave and then stopped. 'You must be very distraught at this time. You have my sympathies.' He glanced at me, the sarcasm dripping from his words.

'I'm devastated.' I crossed my arms over my chest and looked at the floor of the cell.

'He'll be locked up for a long, long time.' DS Small added enjoying his victory.

'Anything he did, he did for me.' I realised what I'd said too late.

'So you did know?' DS Small was quick to react.

'No, that's not what I'm saying. You're twisting my words.' Suddenly I was flustered and he was in charge.

'The truth doesn't stay buried forever.'

I noticed the discolouring of the fabric of his shirt near his armpits and smirked. He had no idea.

'Something funny?' His eyes were burning with anger.

'No. Not a thing.'

'Good, because if my wife had just confessed to murder I wouldn't be smiling.' With that the grin fell from my face. He was right.

'I don't know how to react, that's all.' I felt myself becoming defensive.

'We will arrange a time for you to come back and give a statement.'

'I'm not stitching up my husband if that's what you're thinking.'

'About the rape, Mrs Miller.'

'Oh. Fine.'

I couldn't understand why he was still standing there. I wanted him to leave and I wanted to get the hell out of that place. I'd already spent too much time in that cell. 'Is that everything?' I could hide my impatience.

'For now, Mrs Miller.' My shoulders dropped. 'Oh, one last thing,' he was playing with me and I felt like a fly caught in a spider's web. 'Do you know the whereabouts of your sister, Dawn McCarthy?'

'No. Why?'

'We spoke to her husband, and the brother of the man your husband murdered. He says he hasn't seen her for years. You don't know where she is?'

'No. We're not very close.'

'It's strange. No one seems to know where she is. It's as if she just disappeared.'

I was escorted home in a police car. At the end of our street a few local reporters had gathered and I was grateful that a police presence guarded the house from the media. I was told that an officer would be there at all times to protect my family and the equipment that would be delivered to the site.

Ignoring their questions and the flashing from their cameras I went inside and closed the door. I'd been told that the children would be returned to my care later that day. For now, I was alone.

Leaving the hallway, I took myself into the kitchen. From the window I could see the tent that had been set up in the garden. A few people wearing white suits were carrying out forensic examinations of the site. A small digger was removing vast amounts of dirt and rubble. I didn't understand what they were looking for. They had already found Mark. DS Small's mention of Dawn flittered through my head.

Pushing the grim thought away I poured myself a large glass of water and tried to steady myself. My hands shook. I couldn't believe I was free. The last few days had been so intense and it had culminated in Larry confessing to murder. I couldn't fathom why he did it. None of it made any sense. He had always protected me and always promised he would. But this was so much more than I had ever imagined. Murder.

I watched as they removed the topsoil using the machine and then began searching the area underneath by hand. Rain continued to hamper the search and threatened to flood the hole. One of the officers told me that a Home Office pathologist was at the site and I wondered if I was meant to be impressed.

Trying not to think about it any longer I went and ran myself a bath. Soon the children would be home and I had to get on with daily life. They needed to be fed and put to bed and that was what I focused on. One thing at a time, I told myself.

Concentrate on what you can control and forget about the rest of it for now.

I took off my purple jumper and jeans and dropped them on to the bathroom floor. The steam rose from the tap and filled the room. I already felt better just being out of those clothes. Next I unclipped my bra and slid my pants down. I sat on the edge of the bath balancing, naked, aware that only a few feet away was an open grave.

For the first time since the whole mess had begun I thought about Ian McCarthy and wondered if nastiness ran through families. His brother had been a piece of work and it turned out he wasn't much better. Looking back over the years at the turbulent marriage of Ian and Dawn, I wondered how different things would have been if they had never married. It all seemed to stem back to them. Everything.

I lifted my heavy frame down into the water and let my troubles soak away. My legs were covered in stubble and I took time and care shaving them with a razor. If I could just clean myself and make myself a little bit more presentable then things would be better, if only on the outside. But it was a start.

After washing my hair, I got out the bath and towel dried myself. The white tiles on the bathroom floor were cold on my feet. Wrapping the beige towel around my body I took myself upstairs to get dressed. The house had never been so quiet and it felt horrible. Suddenly the place was filled with ghosts. I stood looking in at the boys' bedroom. They had bunk beds. The room was a mess. They were due home soon and I wondered what I'd say to them. They would be full of questions. How much should I say?

The idea of having to answer any more questions left me feeling exhausted. But they were Larry's kids too and they deserved to know what was going on, even if I didn't fully understand it myself. The press outside would soon be printing things about us. Lies. It was important that the kids heard it from me.

It dawned on me that from now on I would be a single mother. The realisation hit me hard. Three kids, a husband in prison for murder, no close family around. It wasn't looking good.

Flopping down on to the bed I'd shared with Larry for years I inhaled. His scent lingered on his pillow and I felt close to him there. I wondered how he was coping. I needed to be strong for him.

Shaking myself free from self-pity, I dropped my towel and got dressed. I knew we were sitting on some money and an idea started to brew. If we could get a good solicitor, then maybe Larry would be OK. After all, he only did what any man would do to someone who had hurt his wife. It was almost self-defence. As long as the focus remained on the fact that Mark had raped me, then maybe Larry could get off. It seemed feasible.

I went downstairs and removed my mobile phone from the charger. My hair was still dripping wet. Flicking through my address book I found Carol Winter-Bottom's number and pressed dial.

'You've reached the voicemail of Carol Winter-Bottom. Please leave me a message with your phone number and I'll call you back. Thank you.'

Damn. I hung up. I didn't want to leave a message.

My stomach started rumbling so I made myself a couple of fried eggs on toast. It was so much nicer than the food down at the station. When I'd finished I put my plate into the sink and stood watching the forensics people come and go. They carried bags of evidence back and forwards, via the side entrance, to their van that was parked out on the street and I wondered what it was they were collecting. Bones? I decided not to think about it any longer. The kids would be home soon and it was important I showed them I was together. It wasn't only the kids that were going to probe me. Before too long I knew more press would show up. Vultures always hovered around whenever there was the scent of death in the air. It was only a matter of time before more came out of the woodwork.

In that moment I realised I was so angry and full of hate that I hardly recognise myself. What was happening to me?

28

'I just wish he wasn't so angry all of the time.' Dawn sipped her tea and cradled her daughter with her free arm. The little girl was nearly two years old. She had changed so much and was growing so fast that I barely recognised her.

Since becoming a mother Dawn suddenly had found the desire to spend time with me. Perhaps it was just that she wanted the company of another woman who understood how challenging parenthood could be. Since Daisy was born she would drop in for a natter every couple of weeks.

'He shouts all the time. I can't bear it. Even when Daisy is asleep. It's like he doesn't care.'

I watched my younger sister anxiously twiddling a lock of her long hair between her fingers and I found myself enjoying her unhappiness.

'He's probably just stressed with work or something.' I tried to play it down. Dawn was prone to overreaction.

'It's not that. Things are getting worse and worse between us. I feel like I'm losing him.' Her pretty eyes filled with tears. 'I don't know what to do.'

'Talk to him.'

'He doesn't want to talk and if I ever suggest it he just tells me that I wouldn't understand.' Daisy, who had woken from a nap, was sucking her little fingers. 'It's all since Mark disappeared.'

'Strange business.' I shifted in my seat. 'How long ago was that?'

'Nearly two years.'

'And no one has ever heard from him since?'

'No.' She looked miserable. 'That's half the problem. They were thick as thieves, those brothers. Ian has never been the same since Mark vanished.'

I munched thoughtfully on a digestive biscuit but said nothing.

'Sometimes I'm scared of him. He gets this look in his eye and I think he's going to hurt me.'

'Dawn,' I moved closer to her and put my hand on her shoulder, 'has he ever done anything?'

'No, no. But it's as if he wants to. I don't know I'm probably being silly.' She did her best to convince herself but it wasn't working on me.

'You know, if he ever lays a finger on you then you pack a bag and you come here with Daisy. Larry and I will take care of you both.'

Dawn gave a small grateful smile and tipped her head to one side slightly, looking at me strangely.

'You've changed,' she said, thinking out loud.

'What do you mean?'

'You're so different from how you used to be before you met Larry and had the kids. I hardly recognise you sometimes.' I looked down at my expanding baby bump and rubbed my tummy.

'I've grown up, that's all.'

'No,' Dawn cut in sounding very serious, 'it's more than that. You used to be so shy, so awkward and now you're sitting here giving me relationship advice. I would never have believed this day would come.'

Her back handed compliment felt like a slap to the face.

'I finally worked out who I am. I'm happier now.'

'And so much more confident.' Dawn sat Daisy upright on her lap and handed her a biscuit. 'It's funny how things change. A few years ago I was the popular one. Now I spend all my time being a housewife and trying not to piss off my husband. It's like I'm walking on eggshells. That's how you used to be. It's as if we've swapped lives.'

'In those days you didn't really want to talk to me. You thought I was an embarrassment.' I looked across at her, dead in the eye.

'We were just so different. We didn't have much in common then.' Dawn did her best to sweep the past under the carpet but I hadn't forgotten.

'And now we are even?'

'Yes. I suppose.' Dawn was not comfortable admitting it.

'Well, getting back to you and Ian, if I were you I'd go out and buy some nice underwear. When I want to help Larry relax that's what I do. It works every time. Get a babysitter to have Daisy for the night and look after your man. You'll see, I bet things will improve after a bit of bump and grind.'

'Deborah!' Dawn looked horrified.

'What? You don't think the stork delivered my kids do you?' I couldn't believe she was being such a prude. Out of the two of us she was always the slutty one. 'Men are simple creatures. Learn how to stroke them right and your life will be a piece of cake.'

'I tell you that I'm worried Ian is going to batter me and your answer is what, a blow-job?'

'Why not? Give it a go at least. Unless you want to give up on your marriage before it's even begun.'

There was silence between us for a while and I could see that Dawn was angry. In the background Roxette played on the radio.

'I don't think you understand how much the family were affected. When Mark disappeared it upset everyone really badly. Ian's mother is a wreck. She doesn't know where her son is or why he left without saying a word. Every day she thinks about him, wondering where he is and if he's all right. It's the same for Ian, except it's worse because he has her to worry about, too. It's like time stopped when he went and now all the people left behind are stuck in limbo. It's not right anyone should have to live with not knowing what happened to a loved one. Imagine if Dad just disappeared one day.'

'If only.' I rolled my eyes. 'We wouldn't be that lucky.'

'That's exactly what I was talking about earlier.' Dawn got up and held Daisy against her shoulder and looked at me with disappointment. 'You've changed.'

'Why don't you get down off your high horse.' I stood up and shoved my face closer to Dawn's. 'You think you're the only one with problems?'

'Oh yeah, sure. You're really struggling. You have the perfect husband, two lovely kids and one on the way. You're secure in this house and you don't want for anything. Don't try and tell me you've got it hard.' Dawn picked up her handbag and prepared to march out. 'I came here for some sympathy and this is what I get.' Her cheeks were flushed.

'Sit down, you silly cow.' I backed away putting space between us in an attempt to defuse the situation. 'I'm sorry. OK?'

Dawn stood looking at the door deciding whether to walk through it or not.

'I'm sorry. Come on, have another biscuit.' I held out the packet of digestives as a peace offering and watched as a small smile crept on to her face. I really didn't want her to leave.

'Go on then.' Dawn dropped her bag to the floor and sat back down. 'You know I'm a sucker for a biscuit.'

29

I went into hospital in the early morning of May 14th and by lunchtime had given birth to a baby boy. Owen Miller was born by emergency caesarean section. I was hospitalised for over a week. The complications of the operation left me with a damaged womb. The junior obstetrician who performed the surgery later told me that I would never be able to have a child again.

Although I was not that upset by the news I understood what it meant to Larry. He was devastated. Secretly, I was strangely relieved. I hadn't bonded with my other children very easily and didn't imagine that changing in the future. It was a twisted blessing. But that's not how Larry saw it. He was livid. He blamed the doctor in charge and talked about suing the hospital.

Although I wasn't upset by the news I was infertile I was angry that the operation led to me being hospitalised and severely unwell for over a week. I should have been at home with my newborn and my older kids. Not stuck in a hospital bed suffering from fevers and bleeding from my uterus.

By the time I was released and able to return home I felt

awful. I'd been unable to breastfeed Owen. I was too weak. The nurses had taken over his care and did everything for him. When I took him home I felt as if I was holding a stranger. He didn't feel like my baby.

I still needed bed rest and thankfully Dawn was there to help. She came every day and looked after the children and the house. I think she liked having an excuse to get away from Ian. The irony of it all was that the house was in a far better state than it would have been if I'd been running it. The kids had clean, ironed clothes and the kitchen was spotless. She even managed to cook for us all, as well as keeping an eye on Daisy and nursing me. She was superwoman and I hated her for it. It only added to my feeling of being unworthy and to make matters worse, my kids loved her. Sue-Ann and Robbie loved their Aunt Dawn far more than they had ever loved me.

Lying in bed that evening after Dawn had put the kids to bed and gone home, I waited for Larry to come up to bed. He had been in a foul mood ever since Owen was born. I knew it wasn't directed at me but I felt as if I had disappointed him. I needed to get better and show him that our life could still be good. *East-Enders* was just coming to an end when he came into our bedroom. He'd kindly arranged for a television to be delivered so that I had something to do while I lay in bed. As the bedroom door opened I turned the volume down and propped myself up. I still felt sore. Owen was asleep in a little Moses basket next to me. He was a good baby and so much easier than the previous two. Still I struggled to feel close to him.

'How was work?' Suddenly I was aware that I looked a mess.

'Fine.' Larry started to unbutton his shirt but didn't look at me. I had never felt so distant from him.

'Owen is doing well.' My enthusiasm was strained.

'Good.' I was growing frustrated by his monosyllabic answers.

'Maybe we could take the caravan to Norfolk soon. The weather is nice at the moment.'

'If you want.' He threw his shirt and trousers over the back of a chair and sat down on the bed to remove his grey socks.

'Come on,' I started rub his shoulders, 'things are not that bad.'

'That fucking bitch.' He shrugged himself free. 'How can you be OK with this?' I knew he was referring to the doctor who had operated on me.

'Mistakes happen.'

'She's taken away my chance to be a father.'

'Now that's not true. You have three kids Larry. Some people can't ever have any.'

'But I wanted more.' He sounded like a petulant child.

'Be thankful for what you've got, that's what my mum used to say.' I needed her words of wisdom to get me through.

'But she's dead, Dee. I doubt she feels that bloody thankful.' His words were delivered like a punch to the face.

'Don't speak to me like that.' I swung my legs out of bed and stood up. 'What's the matter with you?' I was tired of trying to make him feel better. Nothing I did was working. 'I'm going to sleep on the sofa. I don't need this shit from you.' Slipping my feet into my old battered slippers I made my way towards the bedroom door.

'What about Owen?' Larry sat on the bed in his underpants looking sheepish.

'You fucking deal with him.' I pulled the door closed loudly behind me and made my way gingerly down the stair. My stiches still throbbed when I walked.

In the darkness I made my way into the lounge. The house was quiet since all three children were sleeping. Carefully lowering myself on to the couch I sat in the blackness thinking about what to do. I couldn't stand any more of Larry's self-pity. It was my body that had suffered the injustice but all he could focus on was his own pain.

Sitting there for a while I contemplated getting up and looking for a book to read. I wanted to escape into something nice and cosy. But the effort of getting up and searching was too much so I stayed put looking at the moonlight filtering through the net curtain on to the wooden floor. Looking around the room but not really taking it in, I suddenly noticed how different it looked. The furniture had been reorganised. On the floor in the far right hand side beneath some shelves were three plastic boxes that hadn't been there before. Squinting in the darkness I could see they contained all the children's toys. I was used to finding building blocks and doll's accessories all over the place. Dawn had worked her magic and in doing so had only added to me feeling useless.

I wish before I'd walked out of our bedroom I'd remembered to get a blanket. It wasn't that warm in the house and I didn't like the idea of sleeping on the couch without a cover but I was not prepared to back down. Larry was being unreasonable. It was as simple as that.

Stretching out on the sofa I realised I'd lost a bit of weight as a result of the op. It seemed that every cloud did have a silver lining. At least something good had come of the last week. I was still quite heavy but any extra baby weight I'd put on had been quickly lost.

As I toyed with the idea of going on a diet I heard the lounge door creak open and looked over to see Larry's face peering round the corner.

'Peace offering?' He was standing in the nude waving his white boxer shorts like a flag before throwing them at me. With my laugh any resentment I'd felt melted away.

'Come in here and sit down, you silly bugger.' I pulled my

feet up and made room for him on the couch, removed his pants from my head and dropped them on the floor.

'I've been a miserable git haven't I?' He put his hand on my cold knee.

'Yes, you have.'

'Sorry.'

'It's OK. This last week has been tough,' I rested my hand on top of his, 'but it's over now.'

'I'm just really angry.' He spoke through gritted teeth.

'I know you are. But you shouldn't take it out on me. It's not fair.'

'I need to take it out on someone.' His large naked frame was lit by gentle moonlight.

'Then do something about it. Be the Larry I married. Don't sit here and wallow.'

He sat looking at the floor silently for a while and thought about what I'd said.

'You're right,' he turned to me, 'something needs to be done.'

The kids had spent their first night back at home. It was so odd being in the house while officers dug in our garden and the press gathered at the end of the road. We were prisoners in our own house.

Sue-Ann asked a few questions about her father but none of them pushed it. They knew I didn't want to talk about it and that the subject should be avoided. What they actually thought was going on I didn't know. I was still in the dark. Information came through slowly from the police and Larry's solicitor was useless at keeping me up to date with any developments.

I told the kids they needn't go to school. It wasn't fair on them to have to face questions and listen to the wicked things other children were saying. Apart from wanting to protect them I also hated the idea of being alone. Since they'd grown up and become able to do things for themselves I found I enjoyed being around them more.

Sue-Ann had grown into a typical teenager. She looked a lot like the feminine version of her father with her dark curly hair and brown eyes. People told me she was pretty. Larry favoured her over the others even though she spent most of her spare time out and about with her friends. She spent so little time at home that he got her a mobile – for emergencies only. They were close in a way I couldn't understand.

Robbie was either found playing computer games or out somewhere kicking a ball. He was always in trouble at school for fighting with other kids. He had his father's temper but my complexion and colouring. It was as if Larry and I had produced little versions of us as the opposite sex.

Owen, who was still very much the baby of the family, was different from the others. He didn't look like either Larry or me. Owen was good as gold and clever with it. It was a mystery where his brains came from. Over the years it got easier and easier to think of him as Larry's son. I never knew otherwise for certain. He was never any trouble. The others looked out for him, we made sure of that. Owen was soft and an easy target for other kids. Sue-Ann and Robbie protected him from the bullies. It made me proud of them in a way I never imagined I would be.

The phone rang again for the tenth time that morning. The press just wouldn't leave us alone. I told the kids not to answer and just keep ignoring it. In the end I unplugged it. Every time it rang it acted as a reminder of the situation we were in.

It had been a while since I thought about dad and although he had been a useless father and a worse granddad I wished he were around. I could have done with some support.

Dad passed away in 1994 after battling with liver cancer. The booze had the last laugh. Despite being told by the hospital that if he gave up the drink he would have longer to live, he carried on not caring. He'd been slowing killing himself ever since mum died. He didn't want to live any more. None of us tried to stop him drinking himself to death. It was too late and our objections would have only fallen on deaf ears.

In the end, even Dawn had given up on him. She used to try. For so long she carried on going over there cooking meals for him and tidying up his place; although she was his favourite not even her disapproval made a difference to him. He was too far gone by then.

When she disappeared that year in June it marked the final nail in his coffin. He just gave up living and let the cancer win. He went into hospital in July. Before his death, I did my best to be a loyal and loving daughter. I visited him every day and spent time by his bedside. He didn't talk much so I took books in and read to him. I'll never know if he listened or appreciated it but I hoped my company meant something to him. He died a few weeks later in August.

His funeral was a tragic affair. He'd lost touch with all his friends over the years and the few that had remained kept their distance in the end. His drinking was too much for people.

Larry and I paid for the service and arranged everything. The funeral was held at Cambridge City Crematorium, outside the town, off Huntingdon Road. It was a grey day.

Despite being situated off a large road, the site was quite peaceful and set in gardens and woodland. We picked the smaller of the two chapels for the brief secular ceremony. The room was painfully empty during the service. It could seat up to fifty-five mourners, but our entire congregation failed to fill half the room.

At the end of the service we all gathered outside. Aunt Mary came over, dabbing her eyes with a tissue, and thanked me for taking care of the funeral. He would have been proud of me, she said. But we both knew that was a lie. I gave her a hug and I asked her to come and visit me and the children soon.

After leaving the chapel I wandered around the grounds on my own for a while, looking at the ornamental shrubs, roses and trees that landscaped the gardens. Every now and then I spotted a bench dedicated to the memory of someone passed. Still walking alone, lost in my thoughts, I passed two large granite books of remembrance that were placed either side of the entrance to the woodland. I couldn't get the image of his coffin out of my mind. It had appeared strangely small. For all of my life I had thought of my dad as a big man. In death, that illusion was shattered.

After leaving the crematorium we drove his ashes back to Harlow and scattered them on Mum's grave in the churchyard. It seemed like the right thing to do. It was sad, though. I hadn't visited Mum's resting place for years. It was all overgrown and shabby. Larry helped me tidy it up before emptying the contents of the urn. Then it really struck me. All my family had gone, and I was the last one left.

Leaving the churchyard, I should have felt sad. I suppose I did, a bit, but I had Larry by my side. He was the only family I needed. Him and the kids.

Now I had to face the prospect of living life without him. It seemed loss, one way or another, had always blighted my life. I couldn't stand the idea of living without Larry – but that was what I was facing.

From the lounge I heard the television blasting and went up to investigate. Sue-Ann was sat on the couch with her legs tucked up and her shoes on the upholstery watching the news. I batted her feet off and scowled at her before I realised what was being reported.

A cocky looking ginger bitch with a nasal voice was speaking into the camera. She stood under an umbrella trying to hide from the rain. In the background I could see our street.

'...Mr Larry Miller of Alpha Terrace was charged with the murder of Mark McCarthy, a local man who had been missing since 1986. A neighbour of Mr Miller's discovered human remains in their garden and contacted the police last week. The investigation is still on-going...'

I picked up the remote control that was lying on the coffee table and hurled it across the room towards the TV.

'Vultures! Bloody vultures.' I stood up, not knowing where to focus my fury.

'Calm down, Mum.' Sue-Ann sat huddled against the arm of the couch.

'Don't ever tell me what to do.' I swung around and without thinking slapped her hard across the face. Her dark brown eyes filled with fear and hurt as her left cheek flooded with colour. She remained silent, too shocked to speak. The palm of my right hand was stinging and I looked down at it and noticed I was shaking. When I looked back at her I saw the tears falling noiselessly down her face.

'Mum?' I turned to see Robbie standing in the doorway looking at me. He had witnessed the whole thing.

'Get out!' I screamed at them both. 'Get out of my fucking sight!' Sue-Ann tripped over her long legs trying to escape the room before I struck out again. 'Get out!' I picked up a cushion and threw it at the door just as it was closing behind them.

Sitting down on the sofa, still shaking all over, I tried to calm myself down. They say that losing your temper never helps a situation, but it sure made me feel better, if only for a moment.

I listened to the sound of the kids' footsteps creeping up the stairs and collapsed into a fit of hysterical tears. By the time the tidal wave of emotion had subsided the children appeared in the doorway holding their bags.

'We are going to stay with Aunt Mary.' Robbie stepped forward to announce their departure.

'You can't!' but my pleading was too late.

'Yes we can. We don't want to be here any more. We don't want to stay here with you.'

I looked to Sue-Ann, who stood behind her younger brother

clutching her rucksack. Her face was bright pink where I'd hit her.

'I'm sorry. I'm under a lot of pressure at the moment. It's not been easy.'

'Save it mum.' Sue-Ann finally spoke. 'We are leaving.'

As both my children headed towards the front door I scrambled out of my seat.

'You can't. How will this look for your father?'

'That's all you ever think about.' She was quivering with adrenaline. 'You never put us first. Never.' Her eyes were brimming with tears again.

'You are both such a disappointment. What did I do to deserve this?' Every word I spoke was soaked in bitterness.

'Fuck you,' Sue-Ann had her hand on the door knob, 'and fuck him, too.'

I felt the rage rise inside me again and Robbie placed himself between us.

'Leave it, Mum,' he warned. 'Let us go. Don't make this worse.'

'Where's Owen?' It suddenly dawned on me that he wasn't with them and I felt a surge of panic.

'We left him upstairs doing homework.' Robbie nodded towards the first floor and I felt my shoulders relax. At least they weren't taking him.

'Well, go on then. What are you waiting for? You know where the door is.' I turned my back on them and started to walk towards the kitchen. The last thing I heard was the door shut loudly as my two eldest children walked out of my life.

That evening when the rain had sent most of the journalists running for cover I ducked out of the house and went to the shop to buy some supplies. I told Owen that his brother and sister had gone to stay with friends for the night and that he had to stay put in the house. He was under strict instructions not to answer the door.

I walked through the cold evening rain getting soaked, despite my so-called waterproof jacket. Shaking myself off outside the door I went in, trying to hide my face from the man behind the till in the Esso garage and the only other customer in there. If felt as if the whole world was against me but they didn't look at me twice, for which I was extremely grateful. My trainers were wet and squelched as I made my way down the narrow aisle in search of something to eat. I went straight to the frozen section and picked up a couple of pizzas. Owen liked pizza and it was easy. I never was much of a cook.

The only other item on my list was cider. I wasn't a big drinker but it had been a very difficult day and I didn't think there was much chance I'd sleep. Cider was to be my short cut to the Land of Nod.

As I approached the till I saw the newspaper stand on my left hand side. Curious to know what the local press, was reporting, I picked up a copy of the *Cambridge Evening News* and put it down on the counter. Pulling a damp ten-pound note out of my pocket I paid for the goods and left the shop.

On my walk home the newspaper grew heavy as it absorbed the rain. I tried not to think about the ink running down the pages. It only reminded me of Sue-Ann's face after I hit her. It had been a rubbish day but I told myself that tomorrow would be better. It certainly couldn't get any worse.

31

I was standing in the kitchen warming some milk for Owen when the news came on the radio. Stirring the formula into the warm water, I listened to the local headlines. There had been a crash on the A14 and the road was partially closed heading east. Nothing new there. It was lethal. People were always having accidents on that road.

As the smell from the milk drifted up with the steam I turned my face away. I hated the sickly sweet odour of it. It reminded me of the nasty rice pudding that used to be served at the school canteen.

Owen was gurgling in his pram by the back door, eagerly anticipating his next meal, as I tested the temperature of the milk by placing a few drops on my wrist. Still too warm. He would have to wait for five minutes.

'...In other news, a healthcare worker was left in a critical condition by an attacker who struck as she left Addenbrooke's Hospital at the end of her shift. Police are linking the incident to the so-called Eye-Sight Killer. And now over to Angela for the weather...'

Checking the temperature of the milk again I finally deemed

it suitable for Owen. I wheeled his pram over and pulled a chair up close to it. He lay on his back, his little feet kicking the air as I guided the rubber teat into his mouth and I watched as his blue eyes rolled back into his head with pleasure. He was a happy little soul.

When the last drop of milk had been drained from the bottle I stood up and rocked the pram backwards and forwards. Afternoon sunlight was flooding in through the window into his eyes so I lifted the hood to shade him from the brightness.

In the kitchen the washing machine was on and spinning at full speed but the noise didn't seem to worry Owen and he started to drift off, happy with his bellyful.

When I was sure he was in a deep enough sleep I rolled the pram out into the garden and parked it in the shadow of the fence. It was building up to be a warm summer and I thought the fresh air would do him some good.

Returning to the kitchen and leaving the back door open so I could hear if he stirred, I turned the volume of the radio up and opened a packet of chocolate biscuits. 'The Shoop Shoop Song' by Cher filled the room and I nodded my head along with the words, feeling good for the first time in a while.

Since our talk a few weeks earlier Larry had perked up. He was back to being the man I loved. My scars were well on their way to being healed and things seemed brighter. Robbie and Sue-Ann were both spending a few hours a day at nursery and so I had time to myself. Owen wasn't very much work. He just slept, pooped and ate. It was easy really. At last I felt I had more control over my life.

Munching on my biscuit I thought about how I was going to fill my days. Now that I'd given up 'work' and the two eldest weren't constantly under my feet, the days looked to be pretty empty.

I missed Trisha. I didn't regret falling out with her but I

wished things had been different. It had been five years since our argument and I hadn't spoken to her since. Sitting at my kitchen table I wondered how different my life would have been if I had returned to working at Woolworths.

Larry had a career, a job he loved and was respected by people. I would never be that person. I'd only ever had one job, working in that scabby store. Then I'd met Larry and my whole world changed. I got married, became a mother, and then... Then I started to make money another way. I wondered when I decided that was an acceptable thing to do. It seems strange but I'd never stopped to think about it until then. It was just something I did. I didn't question it.

From the outside we looked like such a reputable couple. He was an optician and I was... I was the little wife. We had a nice house, a caravan and money to spare. It all looked so tidy. But there was another side to us, to our marriage – A side that would have shocked most people.

Ever since losing my virginity to Larry our sex life was a dominant force in our relationship. We did things that others would have disapproved of. Our appetites were insatiable and we experimented. I discovered a side of myself that I had no idea existed. It was as if I'd been in a deep sleep and meeting Larry awoke something in me. Thinking about it that way it made sense that I ended up making money the way I did. It was the obvious step for me to take and became another thrill – for both of us. Our dirty little secret, he used to say. And it was. It was our private world that no one else ever saw. Yes, the punters were there but they always felt more like extras flitting in and out.

Still, even though I missed the excitement of it I was glad that part of my life was over and done with. It didn't fit with the image we wanted to portray to the outside world.

So instead of using the spare bedroom as a sex den we started to store marijuana plants in there. Before long we had a little farm growing. The money from our sales more than covered what I used to make. Sure it stank a bit but that wasn't a big problem. We only kept it up for a little while. Just until we had enough money to afford to give up growing it.

Larry had a deal with a friend of Eric's. We supplied it directly to him and he took the risk of dealing. We didn't want people coming and going from the house any more. The kids were older and wiser then. It wasn't good to have shifty characters hanging around. The neighbours could have started to notice and that would have been a problem. We wanted to remain under the radar. It's no one else's business, Dee, Larry would say. We aren't doing any harm. And we weren't. Not really.

Leaving Owen sleeping peacefully in the garden I took myself upstairs to get changed. It was a hot day and I'd been sweating. My dress needed changing. Pushing our bedroom door open with my foot I started to peel the dress off over my head. I could smell the faint stink of body odour and reached for a can of spray-on deodorant before looking for something fresh to wear. The cold mist felt good against my under arms and the room filled with the smell of clean linen. Bundling my stale dress up into a ball I dropped it into the overflowing laundry basket. I'd get round to doing the washing at some point. Standing in my underwear enjoying the cool breeze that came in from the slit in the open window I spotted my reflection in the bedroom mirror. My large stomach sagged and I could see a deep red scar left over from the C-section. It was an unattractive sight. My breasts were too big for my bra and bulged over the top of them threatening to show my nipples. I lifted my arms up and stood there looking like Jesus on the cross, just a much larger female version. The weight hung off my arms in sacks. When did I get so fat?

Not wanting to look at myself for a moment longer I dropped my arms to my side and went to rummage through my wardrobe. It was a mess. Most of the clothes had fallen off the hangers and lay in a crumpled pile on the floor. Searching through like a mad woman on the opening day of the January sales, I came across an item of clothing I hadn't seen for some time and held it up. The crinkled slip was the one I wore the first time I had sex for money. Horrid visions of John Boyle's mouth on my face came flooding back and I knew then how glad I was that I no longer did that.

Getting up off my knees I dashed over to the chest of drawers and removed a pair of hair cutting scissors from the dusty top. Frantically I cut and tore at the lace slip until it was a small pile at my feet. I was shaking all over by the time I'd finished destroying the item and I had to sit down on the bed for a moment to catch my breath.

Staring at the pieces of destroyed fabric it dawned on me that Larry and I hadn't had sex for a while. Not since before Owen was born. That bitch doctor had seen to that with her botched operation. But then I remembered my disgust at my reflection and wondered if Larry would ever want to sleep with me again anyway. He had a ravenous sex drive that needed to be fed. If he wasn't getting it at home was he going elsewhere? He'd not laid a hand on me in weeks. I'd been too tired to notice but now that I was feeling better I was flooded with horror and suddenly I knew he must have been sleeping with someone else.

Like a woman possessed I started to through his clothes pockets looking for evidence. In ten minutes flat I had turned the whole room upside down but found nothing. Standing there, still in my underwear, I was hit by a wave of misery. And then I remembered the time. I was going to be late collecting Sue-Ann and Robbie from nursery. Cursing myself for getting so distracted I returned to my wardrobe and pulled a clean turquoise dress from the pile. It needed ironing but I didn't have time.

Taking two steps at a time I descended the stair, grabbed my handbag off a hook in the hallway and left through the front door. It was only when I saw one of the other mother's pushing a pram on her way to collect her child that I remembered Owen.

Not wanting to show the panic I felt, I walked calmly towards the entrance and waited for the children to come out. I reminded myself it was only a five-minute walk home and that he would be fine. The chances were that he was still fast asleep in his pram.

'Not got the baby with you today?' The other mother was wearing sunglasses and had tanned shoulders. I couldn't remember her name.

'Er, no. Erm, my sister has him.' I swallowed hard, feeling the lie stick in my throat.

Before I had to embellish any further the door opened and the children all came running out, holding bright finger paintings.

Not wanting to waste time I took a child in each hand and marched them back down the road.

'Ow, Mummy,' Robbie was digging his heels into the pavement and slowing our progress, 'that hurts.'

'Hurry up and walk now.' The look I gave him told him he'd better do as I asked. He picked up speed and, half-running, managed to keep up. Sue-Ann skipped along happily talking to me all about her time at nursery. I wasn't really listening. I was desperate to get home to Owen and noticed I was sweating again. My brow was damp and my armpits felt soggy.

When we reached our road I noticed Dawn's little red Renault parked outside. I swore under my breath and rushed into the house. She had a key. We had given it to her a few weeks earlier so she could let herself in when she was helping out.

'Hello?' I called out letting go of the kid's hands and

ushering them into the lounge. Flicking on the TV I told them to sit quietly and watch some cartoons.

'Hello?' I called out again, aware of the increasing knot in my stomach. I headed for the kitchen.

'In here.' Dawn sounded stern. Daisy was sitting in the high chair scribbling with some crayons and Dawn was cradling Owen in her arms.

Wiping sweat from my forehead with the back of my arm I said hello and offered her a cup of tea.

'What the hell were you thinking?' she hissed.

'What are you talking about?' I decided that playing innocent was my only option.

'Owen, he was on his own. Where did you go?'

'Oh,' I washed my hands in the sink for something to do so I wouldn't have to look at her, 'he was having a nap and I didn't want to disturb him. I was only gone for a couple of minutes.'

'Only a couple of minutes? Why didn't you take him with you? He was in the pram. He would have stayed asleep. All you had to do was wheel him out. What is wrong with you?'

'I really think you're over-reacting,' the sweat continued to pour down my face and showed no signs of relenting.

'Overreacting? Are you thick? He could have been stung by a bee. The pram could have tipped over. Anything could have happened!'

'Don't talk to me like that Dawn!' I span around growling at her. 'He's my son. Just because you've got a kid you think you're bloody Dr Miriam Stoppard.'

Just then Larry appeared in the kitchen.

'Everything all right, ladies?' his eyebrows were raised and he'd obviously heard the yelling.

'Fine.' I glared at Dawn.

'Hello, gorgeous,' Larry bent down and kissed her on the cheek. I could have sworn I saw her blush.

'How's your day been?' he slid over to me grinning.

'Fine.' I dried my hands on a grubby tea-towel. But things were not fine and I was determined to get to the bottom of what was bothering me. 'You're back early.' I glanced at the clock on the wall.

'The shop was really quiet and Rook told me to knock off early. So here I am, with my two favourite ladies.' I didn't like him feeding Dawn's ego especially given the fact that we had just had words.

'You're not staying for dinner, are you Dawn.' It wasn't a question.

'No,' she wriggled in her chair, 'I've got to get back to Ian.'

'The perfect wife.' I muttered under my breath. Larry flashed a look at me but I don't think Dawn heard.

'Well,' Larry tucked his thumb into his dark grey trouser pockets, 'he's a lucky man.'

Again I thought I saw Dawn blush.

'Put the kettle on, Dee, I'm parched.' He went and pulled up a chair and took Owen out of Dawn's arms. 'How's the little man today?' Larry asked no one in particular. Dawn folded her arms, tucked her chin in and gave me a look.

'He's fine.' I dropped a teabag into a mug and ignored her. 'No trouble at all.'

'Good little lad.' Larry kissed Owen on the crown of his head. 'That's my boy.'

Looking at them both then I knew in my bones that Larry wasn't his father.

32

I was hung-over. Badly. Especially for someone who wasn't a drinker. So when there was incessant knocking on the front door at six-eleven in the morning I wasn't happy. With the taste of flat cider still washing around my mouth I hardly remember opening the door.

'We have a warrant.' He held the piece of paper out but I couldn't focus.

'Warrant for what?'

'To search the cellar.' DS Small had an arrogant grin plastered across his face. I wanted to hit him.

'Come in. Never mind my kid. That's irrelevant isn't it?' My sarcasm wasn't lost on him

'Sorry, ma'am. Just doing my job.' But it was more than that. We both knew it. It was personal.

As he entered the hallway I stopped him and his team.

'I want to read it.' I stood in the hallway wearing the same clothes I'd been in yesterday and tried to feign control. 'Show me or you aren't going any further.' I held my leg up against the wall just like a petulant child. If they touched me, I would cry assault.

'Here.' DS Small eyeballed me. His lack of fear was disturbing.

'I want my lawyer.' I pretended to run my eye over the paperwork. 'Otherwise you aren't coming in.'

'That's the whole point of a warrant, Mrs Miller.' Small stood there looking smug. 'You don't have to agree. You don't really have a choice.' Behind him a group of officers sniggered.

'Fine,' I couldn't think of a clever comeback. 'But I don't have to stand here and watch.' I was thinking the words but couldn't be sure I was saying them. I vowed never to drink again. 'Don't be such a prick.' Did I really say that? 'Let me get my boy and leave before you turn the place upside down.'

If Small had had his way the humiliation would have continued but luckily there was a reasonable person on his team, who convinced him to behave decently.

'You understand there must be someone who accompanies you at all times?' The little man stepped forward. 'You are welcome to get your son and leave but I must accompany you.'

Standing still, blocking the entrance I threatened him with my stare.

'Miss.' His soft voice won me over.

'Fine.' I moved aside. 'Come in and do what you want. But I'm telling you I'm watching. The world is watching.' I realised how pathetic I sounded but it was too late.

The policeman looked at me. His pity was unwelcome. I didn't need his kindness. How dare he.

'Get your boy, miss,' the little officer kept trying to be kind.

I wanted to hate him, I really did. He was barely out of school and didn't appear to have the ability to grow a beard but suddenly that didn't matter. He was a kid just trying to do his job. When I pictured him like that I stopped minding. Skinny and uncomfortable in his own skin, he didn't mean to offend.

'What's all this about, then?' I realised I hadn't washed and felt grimy.

'We've received some new information about the disappearance of your sister, Dawn.'

'Dawn? What's she got to do with anything?'

'I think it's best if you come down to the station and answer some questions.'

'What are you talking about Dawn for?' I had my hand on my hip and tried to ignore the growing feeling of nausea rising from my stomach.

'When did you last see your sister, Mrs Miller?'

'A while ago. Like I said before, she came here when she left Ian. He was not a good husband. Not like my Larry.'

I watched Small raise an eyebrow but decided not to react.

'So she came here, all upset and stuff, telling me how he'd got angry and hit her. I said she could stay for a while. Then one day I came home and she'd gone. She left a letter for me on the table saying she was leaving the area and would be in touch when she got settled. I didn't think twice about it. If I'd married that animal I would have run away too.'

'So when did you next hear from her?' Small pulled out a little leather bound notepad, his biro paused to write.

'She sent a postcard a while back.'

'Do you still have that or the letter?'

'No. Why should I have kept them?'

'Did she say where she was in the postcard?'

'It was from the Costa Del Sol. I guessed she'd gone out there to stay with a friend. Someone she knew from school moved out there a few years back.'

'Can I have the name of her school friend please?'

'Oh, I can't remember. Jane or Janet. Something like that. I'll have a think.'

'That would be helpful.' Small folded his notebook and put it back inside his jacket pocket without having written a word.

'How long did she stay with you for before...' he paused, 'leaving?'

'A little less than a year. We had room so there was no need for her to move out. My kids liked having her and Daisy around.'

'And one day she just disappeared without a proper explanation?'

'Yeah. I figured she got bored of relying on us.'

'I see.' His scepticism wasn't lost on me.

'I still don't get why you're looking in the cellar.' I frowned at him, knowing he wasn't telling me the whole truth.

'Just received some information that suggests we need to have a look around down there.' He remained cagey.

'To do with Dawn?'

'I'm not at liberty to say, Mrs Miller.' He tucked his hands into his navy trouser pockets and rocked on his heels enjoying his moment.

'Whatever.' I returned to the sofa and slouched down on to it feeling the start of a headache coming on.

'Mum?' Owen appeared in the doorway accompanied by an officer.

'I think it's best if he remains with his mum for the moment.' The officer closed the door on us both.

'Mum, what's going on? Why are police here again? And where are Sue-Ann and Robbie?' He looked frightened and I pulled him to my bosom.

'Don't worry. It's all fine. Police just want to come and have a look. They think they forgot something last time. Your brother and sister have gone to stay with friends. It's just you and me, kid.' I ruffled his hair and kissed the top of his head, still aware of my boozy breath. Suddenly I felt exhausted. I just wanted to go to sleep. Reaching for the remote control I flicked the telly on and we cuddled up on the sofa, under a faux fur blanket watching some daytime dross until there was a knock on the sitting room door. Then Small walked in.

'This house is now a crime scene. You need to get some things and leave with your boy.'

'Where am I meant to go?'

'We'll arrange some temporary accommodation for you. Pack some essentials and a car will pick you up. If you need anything more, you can ask an officer to bring it later on.' Small stood looking at Owen with sad eyes. He wasn't enjoying turning my little boy's life upside down.

'Is that it? I'm just supposed to leave my house without a proper explanation?'

'It's a crime scene. You cannot remain here.' When he looked at me his expression had changed. He was cold.

'What have you found? I demand to know.' I stood up throwing the blanket off me. A rush of blood flooded to my head, making me feel dizzy.

'Remains, Mrs Miller. We have discovered another body. The crime scene boys are on their way.'

'Another body? Whose?'

'It is impossible to tell at this stage. One of my officers will escort you upstairs so that you can pack.' His shutters had come down and I wasn't going to get any more information out of him. I doubted there was much more he could tell me at that stage.

'Fine.' I looked down at Owen who was pretending to watch the TV, refusing to take in what was going on around him. 'Come on, up we get.' He did as he was told without saying a word and I followed him out of the lounge and up the stairs. I could feel the weight of the looks from the other police officers who had gathered in the narrow hallway.

I shoved Owen into the boys' room and I told him to pack a little bag then went into my own bedroom to do the same. A fresh-faced officer with ginger hair pulled back in a tight pony-tail watched my every move. I grabbed a few fresh clothes and my toothbrush and phone charger.

'Do you like your job?' I turned to her.

'Yes I do.' She didn't flinch.

'Even when it means evicting a family from their home?'

'Do you really want to stay? Knowing what's in the cellar?'

'I don't know what's in the cellar. That's the point,' I huffed.

'You know enough. If I was you, I'd be happy to get as far away from this place as possible.' She had a point.

'Another body?' I said the words again, allowing them to sink in that time.

'Yes.' She folded her hands behind her back and stood upright. She was on duty. It was that simple.

'Well,' I threw my hold-all over my shoulder and walked past her, 'I know my Larry and he had nothing to do with it.'

On the landing I was met by DS Small who had been listening in.

'My experience is, Mrs Miller, that when a man admits to burying one body on his property, subsequent human remains discovered are rarely "just a coincidence". Mr Miller will be questioned regarding the discovery of this latest victim and I suspect he is going to sing like a canary.'

I couldn't understand why the policeman was taking so much pleasure in goading me.

'Think what you like, detective. I've got my boy to worry about now.'

'Where are your other children?' he inspected his fingernails.

'Staying with friends.'

'Funny that. I thought they were with your aunt Mary.'

'How do you know where my kids are?' I hissed at him. He

smiled but didn't reply. 'The car will be here shortly. I suggest you wait downstairs.'

'Owen, hurry up!' I called moments before he appeared carrying his school rucksack. 'No school for you today.'

'I know that Mum. It's the only bag I've got.' He eyes were wide and his expression timid.

'Right.' I muttered pushing him in the direction of the staircase. 'Say goodbye to the nice policeman. It's time for us to go.'

'OK.' Owen gave a little wave before descending the stairs. 'Where are we going?'

'I don't know, Owen.' I couldn't think straight and his questions weren't helping. 'We'll know when we get there. Think of it as a little adventure.'

'Will we see Dad? Is he waiting for us?' He stood at the bottom of the stairs watching as I lumbered down each step.

'No. He isn't.' I watched as the look on my son's face fell.

'Oh.'

'Go and wait by the front door. I need something from the kitchen.'

Once in the kitchen I opened the two doors on the fridge freezer and started to pile food into plastic bags.

'What are you doing?' asked the ginger policewoman perplexed.

'I'm not letting this food go to waste. God knows when you lot will let us come back. There's a kitchen in this place you are sending us to I presume?'

'I believe you are being sent to a safe house as a temporary measure.'

'You mean until they actually decide what to do with us?'

'Yes.' I admired her frankness.

'Right well, my boy is upset and I know the thing that will cheer him up is a bellyful of home cooking.' I closed the bare fridge freezer doors and gathered the two plastic bags.

'You don't strike me as the motherly type.' She was getting cocky.

'You don't know me at all. You have no idea what I'm capable of. Now get the fuck out of my kitchen.'

'After you.' She held the door open, put her arm out and offered a sarcastic smile.

The panda car drove us through the town to a building in the north side of the city on the outskirts off Huntingdon Road. It was an unappealing apartment block of probably six flats. The metal sign outside read 'Shirley House'.

'This is temporary.' A skinny woman with a gaunt face in plain clothes stood next to Owen and me as we stared at the building. She had introduced herself earlier as a Family Liaison Officer.

'How temporary?'

'I don't know at the moment.' She tucked her dark hair behind her ear. 'Let's get you settled.

I held on to Owen's cold little hand and we followed her into the building. The poorly lit foyer smelt of urine and a rough-looking man whose chin was covered in whiskers shuffled past us.

'You're on the first floor.' The FLO said, leading us up the concrete stairs.

'This place smells a bit funny, Mummy.' Owen whispered clinging on to his bag.

We were led along a dark narrow corridor until we reached a door that had the number three on it. The officer removed a set of keys from her black mackintosh pocket and fiddled with them, fitting them to the unwelcoming lock.

I went in first, casting a reproachful eye over the space. The flat consisted of one reasonably sized kitchen-diner-living-room. Off it were two doors. One led to the small dated bathroom, the other to the bedroom, which was sparsely decorated and had twin beds.

Dropping my bag down on to the floor I sat down on the bed nearest the window. Owen followed my lead and put his bag down on his bed. The officer stood in the doorway looking at us.

'So this is it?' I made no attempt to hide my frustration.

'I'm afraid so.' The officer looked down at her feet.

'Well, you can leave us alone now.'

'Sorry, but that's not the case. I've been instructed to stay around for the moment.'

'So we are kicked out of our home and now we have to have a babysitter?'

Owen buried his face in a comic and pretended not to be in the same room as us.

'Mrs Miller, I understand this is difficult.'

'Difficult?!' I spat, standing up, the bed creaking as I did so. 'Difficult? My life has been turned upside down and I'm being treated like a common criminal. My boy can't go to school and I can't even speak to my husband about all the terrible things you are saying about him.'

'The purpose of bringing you here is for your protection.' She spoke softly and calmly.

'Protection from what?'

'From the press.'

'Fuck the press.' I folded my arms in front of my chest and stood defiantly. I saw out of the corner of my eye that Owen was sneaking a look, presumably because I'd sworn. 'I'm just upset.' I sat back down, apologising to them both.

Owen kept his eyes firmly glued to the comic and the officer, whose name I was struggling to remember, slipped away from the room.

'It's OK, Mummy.' Owen had a decisive frown on his face. 'The bad guys never win in the end.'

'Maybe you're right.' The tears were welling as I lay back on the hard bed and closed my eyes.

I wanted to argue with him, to give him a harsh lesson in life. I wanted to scream, 'You are wrong! The bad guys do win. Often.' But I didn't. He reminded me so much of my younger self. Sitting there with his mind lost in a fictitious world, he was happy and untouchable and it was right that he should remain so.

After allowing myself a period of self-pity I hauled myself to an upright position and decided to see where the policewoman had got to. I didn't trust her on her own.

To my surprise, she was sat on the faux leather sofa waiting for me, her piercing blue eyes full of anticipation.

'Is Owen all right?' She leant forward. She was still wearing her mac.

'He will be.' I could only hope.

'Shall I make us some tea?' she asked getting up and going toward the kitchenette.

'Sure.' I stopped walking and watched her find her way around.

The few cupboards were pretty empty. A few bits and bobs were spread between them. It was like the most basic holiday let you could imagine.

'Do you want me to help you put that away?' She moved towards the carrier bags loaded with frozen food.

'No,' I stepped forward, 'it's all right. I can manage. Would love a cuppa, though.' I dragged the bags towards the ancient fridge, which had turned a tired yellow colour on the outside, and opened the door. No light came on and I felt no blast of cold air. It was empty and silent.

'Oh.' I could tell she wanted to curse. 'They didn't turn it on.' She ducked around the back of the fridge and flicked the switch on. 'There, that's better.'

Artificial light came pouring out on to the floor.

'It's going to take ages to get cold.' I was not prepared to refrain from complaining. 'What about all my frozen goods?'

She came bustling over and opened the freezer door, pulling one of the three drawers out.

'I'm sure they will be fine.' She spoke brightly. 'It's January and this place hasn't had the heating on. They will be fine until it starts to work again.' Bending down she reached for a bag and made a move to help me unpack the contents.

'No.' I barked more fiercely than I intended to and she backed away cautiously. 'You've done enough. Thank you.'

Still she stood there looking at me.

'Look,' I felt an obligation to be honest, 'I know that none of this is down to you. But enough of my life has been turned upside down already. I can manage to put the food away alone. Please, let me have some sort of normality.'

She nodded and backed away, returning to the kettle to make the tea.

And while I was feeling open and honest I added 'I'm really sorry, but I can't remember your name.'

'Helen Thornhill.' She stirred the milk and watched the hot and cold liquids merge.

33

When she showed up at my door her face looked like a punch bag. Her left eye was purple and swollen shut. Her top lip was split and had blood drying on it. Daisy was clinging to her mother like a small monkey. Dawn stood clutching her child in one arm and a suitcase in the other. Her dog, Rollo, a German Shepherd cross, sat obediently by her side.

'I didn't know where else to go.' Tears fell from her one good eye.

'You'd better come in.' I took Daisy from her with difficulty. The child didn't want to come to me and held on to her mother like a limpet.

'Go with Auntie Debbie.' Dawn winced with pain every time she spoke. Her jaw was swollen and red on one side.

Sue-Ann came to investigate and I handed Daisy over and instructed her to take all the children upstairs to play.

Dawn remained outside, trying to hide her face from her niece and nephews. When she was sure they were all out of sight she stepped inside lugging the large suitcase in with her.

'I'll take that.' I pulled the heavy case into the hallway and propped it up against the wall. 'Come into the kitchen.'

Dawn followed me through the house and took a seat at the kitchen table. Despite being so battered and bruised the rest of her appearance was neat and tidy. She had on a pair of light blue jeans, a thin leopard pattern top and a grey cotton scarf. I felt shabby standing next to her in my old slippers, still wearing my dressing gown. It was half-past ten on Saturday morning.

'Here,' I poured a measure of whiskey and slid it across the table to her, 'drink this.'

With a trembling hand she picked up the tumbler and took a small sip. She moved the glass away from her mouth quickly since the alcohol stung her cut lip.

'It will help.' I sat down opposite and encouraged her to finish the drink. She shook her head and pushed the glass away. I picked it up and drank it down in one go. She might not have needed it but at that moment I felt as if I did. 'So, are you going to tell me what happened this time?'

I'd gotten used to Dawn showing up with injuries that were the result of Ian losing his temper. Countless times over the last year I'd told her to leave him. His outbursts were becoming more frequent but every time he hit her she made excuses – It was her fault, he was stressed. In the end I got tired of giving her advice. She wouldn't listen. All I could do was be there to pick up the pieces.

But something about that Saturday felt different. Not only had her face taken the brunt of his rage, when normally he concentrated on her body where nobody would see but that time she arrived bringing luggage. It seemed as if she had finally found the courage to leave the bastard. Those brothers were peas in a pod and I was glad they were out of our lives.

'I burnt the lasagne.' Dawn hung her head in shame. 'Daisy wanted me to play with her in the garden and I just forgot it was in the oven. When he came home he discovered the smell of burning and just lost it. He made me put Daisy to bed and when

I came downstairs he threw the dish of food at me. Look,' she said pulling up her sleeve, 'it burnt my arm.' The skin was red and blotchy and looked sore. 'Then he went mad and started to hit me. I tried to hide under the table to get away from him but he pulled it away and started to kick me in the ribs. I begged him to stop but he wouldn't listen.' Dawn's bottom lip quivered. 'I tried so hard not to make a noise or cry out. I didn't want Daisy to hear me and get scared.'

I reached across the table and took hold of my sister's hand. I, too, was shaking but with anger rather than fear.

'Then he pulled me up by my hair,' Dawn touched the place on her head, 'before putting his hands around my throat.' Carefully she removed the scarf to reveal bruises around her neck. I squeezed her hand, shocked by the extent of the beating she had endured.

'I must have passed out. That's the last thing I remember before waking up this morning on the floor.'

'He's really done a number on you this time. Do you think you need a doctor? That eye looks pretty bad.'

'No I think I'm OK. My ribs are the worst.' She lifted her flimsy jumper to reveal huge bruises all down her right side.

'Jesus,' I muttered to myself shaking my head and wanting to cry.

'As soon as he left this morning I just grabbed a bag, packed my things and came straight over here with Daisy. I'm sorry. I didn't know where else to go.'

'You did the right thing.'

'But he'll know I came here and come looking for me.' The fear returned to her eyes. 'I don't want to bring trouble to your door.'

'Look, I've dealt with worse men that Ian bloody McCarthy in my time,' Dawn looked perplexed. She had no idea about my other life. 'And besides, Larry won't let anything happen. He'll look after us. He's out fishing now but I'll call him on the mobile and tell him to get his bum home.'

I stood and went to get the house phone from the kitchen wall.

'Maybe I should leave. I could go to Spain with Daisy. I have a friend there. He'd never find us.'

'Rubbish. You're staying put. No gutless bully is going to frighten my little sister away.' The fierce protectiveness I'd felt for Dawn when she was younger came flooding back. 'We've got room. You'll stay here until you get back on your feet.'

'But can I ever really move on when I know he is just on the other side of town?'

'Listen Dawn,' I held the telephone receiver in one hand and looked her in the eye, 'I promise you Ian will never hurt you again. Larry knows some people, let's say, who aren't very savoury. It only takes one phone call and well,' I paused not wanting to say too much, 'he needs to be taught a lesson.'

'He won't let me go.' She sounded broken.

'Yes he will,' I held the phone up to my ear and started to dial Larry's number, 'or I'll kill him.'

Larry came home a couple of hours later, empty-handed as usual. He was not a very successful fisherman by all accounts.

I hadn't explained exactly what had happened on the phone so when he saw the physical state Dawn was in he was shocked.

'Bloody animal.' He stood in the kitchen in his old jeans and lumberjack shirt sipping a hot cup of coffee.

'She's going to stay with us for the moment.' I explained to him as I made sandwiches for lunch. The kids were still upstairs playing.

'Sure. We've got room for you and Daisy for as long as you need.' Larry always put family first and I was glad that included my sister and her child.

'I'll go and make the spare room up after lunch.'

'No, please, I can do it. I don't want to be a burden.'

'You're not a burden Dawn,' I turned to her, 'but I want you to listen to me. I think you should go to A&E, get those ribs looked at.'

'I don't want to make a fuss.'

'It's not a fuss. You need to take care of yourself. For Daisy's sake if not for your own.'

'Nah,' Larry put his coffee down and shook his head. 'I think Dawn is right. If you go to the hospital they will start asking questions and they might get the police involved. You don't want them sniffing around.'

'The law might just frighten Ian into keeping away.' I didn't really welcome the involvement of the police but something needed to be done. 'He needs to know he can't get away with this.'

'Let me deal with Ian. I know how to sort out his type.'

'Larry's right,' Dawn pleaded, 'let's not involve the police. That will only make things a whole lot worse. And even if my ribs are broken they won't be able to do anything about it. They need time to mend on their own.'

'They could give you some strong painkillers a least.' I argued.

'No need.' Larry cut in. 'Ice and brandy will do the trick.'

I frowned at him.

'You're not your average optician are you, Larry?' Dawn looked at him fondly. 'I'd love to have a bath. I didn't have time for a wash this morning.' She said turning towards me. Dawn was determined not to go to hospital.

'Fine.' I pushed a cheese sandwich over to her. 'Eat this first.'

It was a bit of a squeeze, all of us around the table but it felt homely. Having the cousins all together was nice. They got on well. Sue-Ann did me proud and helped look after the younger ones.

When Dawn went upstairs for her bath I sent the children into the garden to play and saw an opportunity to speak to Larry alone.

'Of course she's going to stay for the moment. But I know Ian will come knocking on our door before too long. I just hope you are at home when he does. He's a big man, just like that brother of his and I don't fancy my chances fighting him off.'

'He won't lay a hand on either of you. I can promise you that.'

'If you aren't here, there's nothing you can do to stop him.'

'I'm going round there this afternoon.' Larry sat back in his chair and folded his arms.

'What are you going to do?'

'I'm not going to do anything. I'm just going to have a gentle word.' There was a small smile at the corner of his mouth. I knew that look.

'Don't go making trouble.'

'I won't.' He picked up an apple from the fruit bowl on the table and took a large bite.

'We don't want to attract the wrong kind of attention. We've got our kids to think of.'

'I think it will be nice having Dawn around.'

'Why?'

'Why not? She's good with the kids. We can get her to babysit sometimes.'

'I suppose.' I shrugged. It hadn't occurred to me until then that there would be an attractive woman living under our roof permanently. Suddenly I didn't like the idea as much as I had. 'She better not take liberties.'

Larry looked at me thoughtfully.

'What's wrong?'

'Nothing. I just don't want her stuff all over the place. She needs to be respectful. You don't know what she was like when she was a teenager. Dawn has always been selfish.'

'If you say so.' Larry sighed and got up. 'Stay here with the kids. I'm going to pay Ian a little visit.'

'Be careful.' I got up and put my arms around his neck. He smelt like warm sunshine. 'My big bear.'

'It's not me you need to worry about.' Larry had a hard look and I backed away from him feeling uneasy.

'Come back in one piece.' I called out as he left the room.

Sitting down again I felt my stomach knot.

34

'They've uncovered the body of a child.' Helen sat stiffly on the sofa clutching her mobile phone. 'It was discovered buried in the cellar.'

'How awful.' I felt numb.

'Larry isn't saying a word. He's refusing to comment.' Helen's dark bob was neat and shiny and I envied her for it.

'I just can't believe it. Larry wouldn't hurt a child. He loves children.' My voice was shaking.

'I'm sorry.' She couldn't look me in the eye. I could feel the disgust coming from her.

'This can't be happening.' I stood looking out of the window at the grey world outside.

'They think they will have an ID for the female body at some point today. The DNA you gave will help rule things out.'

'You all think it's Dawn don't you?' I turned to her and forced her to look at me.

'It seems likely but until it's confirmed...' her words melted away.

'Then you probably all think the child is Daisy.' I felt sick just saying her name. Helen didn't say anything but I knew what she was thinking. I turned back to the window and watched the rain drizzling down the glass. 'I know what everyone thinks. I've seen the news. People are calling it the house of death. But it's not what they are saying. It's our home. We've got happy memories in that place. It's the only home my kids have ever known. We were happy there. But no one is ever going to believe that now, are they.'

'Shall I make us some tea?' Helen got up and moved towards the kitchenette.

'I don't want any bloody tea. I'm sick of tea. I just want everything to go back to normal. I want to be in my house with my kids. And I want to talk to my husband.'

'I understand how difficult this must be for you.' The kettle whistled in the background filling the silence between us.

Owen was in the bedroom playing on his Gameboy. He was oblivious to the whirlwind of chaos that encircled us. For that I was grateful.

'He wouldn't have hurt Daisy. I just know it.' A large tear rolled down my cheek as I remembered the last time I had seen the little girl. 'She was a treasure. The spitting image of her mother when she was young.'

'I'm sure.' Helen stirred the teabag in her mug and looked solemn. 'Would you like me to go to Blockbuster and rent you a film? Something to take your mind off what's going on.'

'I'd rather read, but I doubt I'd be able to concentrate.'

'Oh, you like books? Me too.' She was trying her best. I couldn't deny that. 'What do you like to read? I'm a sucker for a crime novel.'

'Spoken like a true policewoman.' I mused. 'I don't like all that morbid stuff. I'd rather get lost in fantasy or romance. I like reading about travel.'

'I could go to a bookshop for you if you'd like.'

'Thanks, but I think it's pointless.' I slumped down on to the sofa, put my legs up on the arm and rested my eyes. 'If you really want to help you could go and get Owen a different game. If I have to listen to the bloody Tetris music for much longer I am going to kill someone.' My eyes sprang open and I realised what I'd said but it was too late. 'Sorry.'

'It's OK. It's just a phrase.' She had a kind smile.

'But it's not though, is it? Not under the circumstances.' I sat up and put my head in my hands. 'Why do I feel like I've done something wrong? This isn't fair. It's like I'm under a microscope. I can't bloody breathe in this place but I can't go anywhere. It's worse than being in prison.'

'This won't last forever.' She came over and sat down next to me, clutching her mug in her hands for warmth.

'How do you know? A week ago I had a life. Now there are bodies being dug up in my house. When will it ever stop?'

Helen remained silent looking into her mug.

'You won't find any answers in there,' I told her.

'Mum, I'm hungry.' Owen appeared in the doorway.

'There are crisps in the cupboard.' I pointed.

'I've not had any breakfast.'

'It doesn't matter. You can have crisps. I don't feel like cooking.'

'I could make him something,' Helen sprung up out of her seat and moved towards the fridge. 'You brought lots of food with you, didn't you.'

'No.' I barked. 'I don't want you doing it. I'll make him something. He's my son.' Helen held her hands up and retreated from the fridge as I stood in between her and it, blocking her way. 'What do you want?' I turned to Owen who was still in his Power Rangers pyjamas.

'Waffles and beans?' His little eyes lit up eagerly.

'Good idea.' I ruffled his hair. 'I'll have some too.' I pulled a box of frozen potato waffles from the freezer and looked at

Helen who had returned to the sofa. 'You want some?' I waved the box at her.

'No thanks. I had a bowl of muesli for breakfast.'

'Suit yourself.' I shrugged. Stuck up bitch.

Later that afternoon it was confirmed – the body in the cellar belonged to Dawn.

'I am so sorry, Deborah.' Helen put her hand on my shoulder. I felt numb.

'So what happens now?'

'Larry is being interviewed as we speak.' She spoke quietly so as not to disturb Owen, who was dozing on the sofa.

'I can't believe it.' I shook my head. 'Why? Why would he want to hurt her?'

'Can you think back to the time when she disappeared. Is there anything that stands out? Something about his behaviour? Anything you remember, no matter how small, might help.'

'I really thought she just left.' My throat felt dry.

'It's not your fault. You couldn't have known.' Helen was doing her best but nothing could stop me from feeling guilty.

'Has he said anything?'

'No. Larry is still not talking. Detective Small is interviewing him. It would be better for him if he confessed.'

'You think he did it.'

'Well, yes.' She looked at me strangely.

'But what about a motive? I thought you lot worried about things like that.'

'Small is the best police officer I have ever worked with. I'm sure he will get to the bottom of it.' Is that meant to make me feel better, I wondered. 'He will want to talk to you Deborah.'

'So on the same day it's announced my sister is buried in my cellar I'm meant to skip along to the police station and help you convict my husband?'

'They will have some questions.'

'I've got questions! But nobody seems to give a damn about that.' Owen stirred on the sofa and I remembered not to shout. 'He's going to be devastated,' I said looking at my son. 'All my kids are. They loved Dawn. I don't want anyone else telling them but me. Do you understand? When they hear it it's got to come from me. I don't want a stranger telling them their aunt is dead. This is a family matter.'

'It is also a police matter,' Helen reminded me gently.

'And don't I know it.' I glared at her. 'Now that they know, when do you think we can go home? I'm sick of being cooped up here. I want to get back to some sort of normality.'

'It won't be for some time I'm afraid. There might be more,' the words linger in the air.

'More what?'

'Remains,' she said seriously.

'Are you serious?'

'I can't say for certain, Deborah, but the crime scene officers will be conducting a thorough search of the whole property, given what has been discovered so far.'

'Daisy.' I said her name in a half-whisper. 'When will we know for sure?'

'The pathologist will be checking medical and dental records and of course there is the DNA sample you gave us that helped to identify Dawn.'

'I'm losing everyone all in one go. First Larry was taken away from me, then my kids left and now I find out Dawn has gone, too. What have I done to deserve this?'

'Nobody deserves to have their life taken away.'

I stopped for a moment wondering if she was talking about me or the three dead bodies that have been unearthed. 'No, of course not. I suppose on top of everything else I've now got a funeral to plan.'

'We are a long way off that yet.' Helen looked at me and I could tell that her sympathy was waning.

'Look, no offense but I want to be on my own for a while. Can I leave Owen with you? I'm going to take a bath. This has been a real shock for me. I need time to digest.'

'Of course.' She nodded. 'Take as long as you like. I'll be here.'

'Thank you.' I said, thinking that is exactly the problem.

Once in the bathroom I locked the door. I knew no one would come in but I wanted to be sure of having the room to myself. I perched on the edge of the bath and it squeaked under my weight. Letting out a long sigh I felt my shoulders dropping. Helen's intense scrutiny was beginning to drive me mad. Why did she have to be there all the time? I couldn't breathe. The pressure of the small dark flat was bearing down on me and I couldn't think. I opened the narrow frosted glass window to let cold air circle around the room. I wasn't even sure if I wanted a bath. I just had to get away from her.

I took my mobile phone out of my back trouser pocket and composed a text to Sue-Ann.

'I want to see you and Robbie. Don't talk to the police before you've spoken to me.'

I pressed send and waited for a response. Ten minutes later I was still looking at my phone, willing it to vibrate. I accepted she was not going to answer. She always was the difficult one. Ungrateful.

Still not wanting to return to the living room I closed the window and started to run a bath. I hadn't got any shampoo or body wash with me. We left home in such a hurry that I hadn't had time to think. I regretted the oversight as I watched the bath slowly fill up. Some nice smelly bubble bath would have been just the ticket. On the side of the sink was a new bar of soap, the kind that old ladies use. That would have to do.

Moments after sinking into the warm water there was a tap on the door.

'What?' I didn't even try to hide my frustration.

'Sorry to interrupt, but I've been on the phone to Detective Small. He wants me to bring you into the station to answer a few questions.'

I groaned and let my head sink under the cloudy water.

35

NOVEMBER 15TH 1993

Dawn had been living with us for a while. The spare room had been made into a private place for her, the dog and Daisy. She'd made it very homely. She was clever like that.

I actually quite liked having her around. She helped with the day to day running of the house and was good with my kids. She cooked often and kept the place clean and tidy. In return we didn't ask her for any rent. Occasionally she would do a food shop, though. Ian had been quickly persuaded to give her a monthly allowance. Larry had seen to that.

I will never know what happened between the two men but after Larry paid him a visit we didn't hear a peep out of him. He sent Dawn money and didn't bother her. She and I discussed the possibility of divorce but nothing was ever done about it. She was happy to have him out of her life and feared that involving solicitors would encourage him to turn nasty again. As long as Ian wasn't banging our door down I wasn't going to disagree with her. She knew him better than anyone.

The one thing that did surprise me was how willing Ian was to give up his daughter. He never once tried to see her. Daisy was such a sweet little thing it didn't make sense to me. Before long I started to see her as one of my own. She was a little cherub and I wished I could have felt the same way about Sue-Ann. But Daisy was pretty. It was easier to love her than my own daughter.

Dawn talked about getting a job but I encouraged her not to bother. She didn't have anyone to look after Daisy and I wasn't about to volunteer. She was more use to me when she was around the house. It wasn't lost on me how we had swapped roles. For years I'd looked after her, cleaning and cooking. Now it was her turn. Of course I was still looking after her in a way: she would have been on the street if Larry and I hadn't taken her in. I suppose old habits die hard.

It was a mild autumn that year. I remember finding it difficult to believe that Christmas was only six weeks away. A large watery sun hung low in the sky. The light was beautiful. Sometimes, so that I could get out of the house and away from the noise the kids were making, I'd take Rollo, Dawn's dog, for a walk.

On that day in November as I crunched over the carpet of brown leaves I found myself walking towards the village of Grantchester to the west of the city. Crossing a bridge over the river Cam I found myself on a footpath that followed the river. It was surprisingly warm. I wore only a cotton sweatshirt and jogging bottoms and I flattened anything in my path with my tatty old boots.

It was strangely quiet. The city was so close yet felt so removed. Wandering along the path I watched Rollo bounce about, stopping to pick up a scent or pee every few minutes. He was a happy dog. His tail pointed up in the air and wagged every time he discovered a new smell. It was nice to have an excuse to walk and get away from everything. Living with Dawn only reminded me of how fat I'd gotten. She never carried any extra weight. If anything she was too skinny. I started to worry that

Larry might look at her that way. She was pretty and he had eyes.

To my irritation she would leave her underwear hanging in the bathroom to dry. Her silky knickers and bras were draped over the radiator or hung from the curtain rail. I never understood why she didn't hang them in the garden like I did. But on reflection she always was an attention-seeker. No doubt she did it for his benefit. I should have taken them down or put them in a really hot wash. That would have taught her a lesson.

My relationship with Dawn was complicated and living with her again reminded me of this. Some of the time I wanted to protect her and some of the time I wanted to slap her face. We were so different. If we hadn't been sisters we would never have had anything to do with one another. But I suppose that is the way it is for a lot of families. Sibling relationships are fraught with tension and ours was made worse by the fact that Dawn was Dad's favourite and I wasn't. If mum had been alive things would have been different. She loved me. I was her special girl.

As I walked along the water's edge something caught my eye. The river was narrow at this part and a large dark object was slumped on the bank further upstream. Suddenly I remembered the killer that had been stalking the area. He – everyone always presumed it was a he – was no nearer being caught. I stopped still and squinted into the distance. Could it be a body? Not wanting to get any closer I picked up a stick, teased the dog and threw it in the direction of the mass.

Rollo went skipping over to the stick and returned it to me without noticing the lump by the river. I took a few tentative steps forward. It looked like a corpse. Standing alone, I wondered what to do. I didn't want to get involved but curiosity got the better of me and I made my way carefully towards it. I hadn't realised I was holding my breath until I got closer and realised it was an old coat that had caught on a fallen tree. Of course it wasn't a body.

Rollo was at my feet panting and nudging the stick with his nose. Feeling foolish as well as spooked I ignored the dog's request, turned around and made my way back along the path towards home.

Sue-Ann and Robbie had gone to school when I got back and the house was peaceful. I gave a sigh of relief as I slipped my boots off and left them lying in the hallway. As I passed the lounge I saw Daisy and Owen sitting in their playpen happily together. Rollo pushed past me, almost knocking me over, and bounded up to the kids wagging his tail, still holding the stick he'd been playing with on the walk.

The children squealed with excitement when he pressed his large wet nose through the bars of the wooden pen and tried to lick their faces.

I left them there and went into the kitchen to get a glass of water but was surprised to find it abandoned. Dawn was nowhere to be seen. Going to the bottom of the stairs I called up.

'Dawn? You there?'

There was silence. As I turned to go and check on the kids I heard her call out.

'Yes, just coming. Be down in a minute.' She sounded frantic.

I took my glass of water into the lounge and turned the TV on. Moments later Larry went rushing past on his way towards the front door.

'What are you still doing here? Running late, aren't you?'

'Needed to iron a shirt. See you later.' He said, before I heard the front door close behind him. That's funny, I thought. I could have sworn Dawn had ironed some only yesterday.

Seconds later she appeared in her dressing gown.

'All OK?' She asked me leaning over the playpen and stroking Daisy's head.

'Fine. That dog of yours is relentless. Doesn't he ever get tired?'

'He's still young.' She sat down beside me straightening her satin gown.

'Kids go off to school OK?'

'Sure. All fine. I sent them with sandwiches and crisps. Hope that's OK.'

'Fine. As long as they eat it.' I stared at the TV watching two women on a chat show tear into each other.

'Right, well, I might go and have a bath.' Dawn stood and stretched.

'Didn't you have one last night?'

'Yes. But you are allowed to wash on a regular basis, you know.' She could be so cutting when she wanted to.

'Fine. But remember who pays the bills round here.' It was the best come-back I had.

'As if you would ever let me forget.' She sauntered out of the room leaving me behind in a waft of her sugary perfume. No wonder she wanted a bath. She smelt like a sweet shop.

36

'I really don't know what else you want me to say.' I sat in the horribly uncomfortable plastic chair and stared across at DS Small.

'The truth would be a good place to start.' His mask had slipped and he no longer felt compelled to play the good cop.

'I'm telling you the truth, as I know it.'

'OK, OK Mrs Miller, have it your way. Let's go back to the very beginning.' He flicked through a pile of notes that lay on the table between us.

'If I'm not under arrest why am I here?'

'We are here to talk about the whereabouts of little Daisy McCarthy. I have cautioned you, which means you are not obliged to say anything.'

'I've got nothing to hide.'

'Good. Let's continue then.'

I looked over at Carol Winter-Bottom who sat stiffly beside me. She gave me a definitive nod of the head.

'Fine.'

'What is your relationship to Daisy McCarthy?'

'She's my niece.'

'When was she born?'

'Late 1990, I think.'

'When did you last see her?'

'She was with her mother.'

'When?'

'A while ago.' I shrugged.

'What time of year was it?'

'Spring, I think.'

'Where?'

'At my house probably.'

'Probably? Where in your house?'

'I don't know. The kitchen maybe.'

'And then what?'

'I don't know what you mean.'

'I mean, what happened the last time you saw your sister and her daughter?'

'Don't really remember.'

'What was her reason for leaving the area?'

'I already told you. She didn't actually tell me she was going to leave. I came back to the house one day and she was gone. Left a letter saying she was going to Spain.'

'With Daisy?'

'Yes, I think so.'

'Did the letter mention the whereabouts of Daisy?'

'Probably. I don't remember. It was a long time ago. I can't remember every word of a letter I read years back.'

'What led to Dawn wanting to leave?'

'Nothing as far as I knew. I suppose she wasn't very happy.'

'Did she say that to you?'

'Not in so many words.'

'But she implied she wanted to move to Spain.'

'No.'

'So it was a sudden thing?'

'I guess you could say that.'

'Did you try to contact your sister after receiving the letter she left you?'

'No I didn't.'

'Why not?'

'She didn't leave a forwarding address. She said she'd be in touch once she was settled.'

'At the time she disappeared did Dawn own a mobile phone?'

'I think so.'

'Either she did or she didn't.'

'OK, yes, she did.'

'Did you ever call her on it after the date you say she left?'

'Maybe. Probably a couple of times.'

'And did you talk to her?'

'No. The line wasn't working. I figured it was because she was abroad or something.'

'So, let me get this right: your sister ups and leaves without a word of warning and you can't get hold of her. Didn't you think that was strange?'

'Not really. She was always a bit flaky. Dawn didn't really care about other people's feelings. She always did what she wanted.'

'It sounds as if you were cross with her?'

'No. Why would I be?' I shuffled in my chair wanting to be out of the stuffy interview room.

'Was there a row before she left?' Small's eyes fixed mine.

'No. She and I didn't really argue.'

'Even though you thought she was selfish.' He sat back in his chair looking satisfied.

'I never said that.'

'You sound annoyed, Mrs Miller.'

'Look, she was stubborn. If she'd wanted to talk to me she would have called or something.'

'But she couldn't, could she.'

'No she couldn't. But I didn't know that back then, did I. Like I said, I thought she was in Spain lying on a beach somewhere.'

'Did her husband ever contact you and ask as to her whereabouts?'

'I think so. Once or twice.'

'And what did you tell him?'

'I told him to get lost.'

'Why was that?'

'I told you, he used to beat her up.'

'We've spoken to Mr McCarthy and he denies your claims.'

'Well he would.'

'Currently we only have your word that he ever laid a finger on her.'

'Why would I make it up?'

'Good question.' Small raised his eyebrows. 'Did you discuss her sudden disappearance with your husband?'

'Course I did,' I huffed.

'And what did he say?'

'Ask him.'

'We have. Now I'm asking you.'

'Well, he said she was a grown woman and she had to make her own choices.'

'Were Mr Miller and Dawn close?'

'Not particularly.' Moving in my seat I reached for a glass of water and took a sip. My throat felt so dry. I was sick of talking.

'But they got on?'

'Yeah. He was always kind to her.'

'And Daisy?'

'Sure and her.'

'Did you not worry about Daisy when your sister suddenly up and left?'

'Not really.'

'Why not?'

'She wasn't my kid.'

'And are you worried now?'

'Well, I know stuff now I didn't know back then.'

'So yes?'

'Yes.'

'And you are aware that we have recovered the body of a child from your basement? The same basement your sister was buried in.'

'Yes, I'm aware.' I scowled at him.

'Do you think Daisy is still alive?' Small kept clicking the top of a biro. The noise was driving me mad.

'Could be. I don't know.'

'You don't seem very upset, Mrs Miller,' Small leant forward on his elbows. His shirt arms were rolled up.

'No point in being upset until I know anything for sure.'

'You know that your sister is dead. You know that your husband admitted to killing Mark McCarthy.'

'Yes, well, I'm in shock and I've got my boy to think of.'

'Forgive me for being a sceptic. I've done this job a long time and one of the hazards of it is that people lie.'

'I'm not lying.'

'But you are implicated.' Small's lips went into a thin smile.

'Why?'

'Because bodies have been discovered in the grounds of your home and your husband has confessed to murder.' I immediately looked to Carol Winter-Bottom for help. She sat back in her chair, eyed the policeman and folded her hands in her lap.

'You are aware how serious this situation is, Mrs Miller.' Small continued clicking his biro.'

My right leg was shaking uncontrollably. Carol reached out a hand, under the table and rested it on my knee to signal I should stop the twitch. Then she turned to me and nodded her head once.

'No comment.' I said pretending to examine my nails. 'That's all you are going to get out of me from now on.'

37

Dawn sat at the kitchen table painting her nails a garish shade of pink.

'You're not a teenager any more,' I scoffed.

'Doesn't mean I have to stop making an effort.' She looked me up and down with contempt.

I ignored her look and went over to the fridge and opened the door. I wanted something to eat but I didn't know what. The dog lay dozing on the floor.

'Are there any biscuits left?' I asked closing the door.

'Probably not.' Dawn continued to concentrate on her nail varnish. 'You've probably eaten them all.'

Determined not to rise to her snide remark I went over to the cupboard and removed the biscuit tin. It was empty.

'Go to the shop and buy some more.' I reached for my purse that was lying on the kitchen surface and removed a five-pound note. 'You can get more milk while you're at it.' I held the money out.

'I'm not going anywhere.' Dawn sat up and looked at me defiantly. 'Not with a psycho on the loose.'

'What are you talking about?'

'Another body turned up in the river yesterday. It's grue-some.' She gave an exaggerated shiver.

'Where did you hear that?'

'It was on the TV. Don't you ever watch the news? Sometimes I think you live with your head in the sand.'

'Oh, it'll just be that guy who went missing on New Year's Eve. A drunk who fell in the river, and you know it. Any excuse not to go to the shop.' I rolled my eyes, tired of her attitude.

'Doesn't it worry you, a killer on the loose?'

'Why should it? I'm sure he wouldn't want to kill me. But I can see why you might be worried.' I couldn't contain my smile.

'Bitch,' Dawn muttered under her breath.

'Have you ironed those shirts?'

'Yes. Someone had to.'

'Good. You can sit here and act like a princess. I'll go and get some milk for your kid to drink, shall I?'

Dawn looked up at me her almond-shaped eyes framed by the perfectly applied make-up she always wore.

'You could do with the exercise.'

'And you could do with a slap.' I grabbed my wallet and marched out of the kitchen. I was bursting with anger. She was lucky I hadn't hit out. My size meant that I could cause damage. How I would have loved to wiped that smirk off her face.

It was then that I realised I didn't want her living under my roof any more. That night I would talk to Larry and suggest we tell her to get her life together and move out. She had been relying on us for long enough.

The kids were all in the lounge watching a video they'd been given for Christmas. I stood in the doorway looking at them all. They were so transfixed by the screen they didn't even notice me.

You could spot Dawn's daughter a mile away. She looked so different to her cousins. She was always nicely turned out, her hair brushed and clothes neat. Daisy sat sweetly on the carpet eating an apple while my kids shoved handfuls of crisps into their mouths. Sue-Ann was on the sofa looking sulky. She wanted to go out and play with her friends but I told her she had to stay and help look after the little ones. Her bottom lip stuck out and for a moment I imagined myself slapping her too.

'I'm going to the shop,' I told them. 'Be good.' Not one of them turned to look at me or responded.

Larry came back from work with fish and chips for us all. Said he wanted to save me having to make dinner. I wasn't much of a cook and we all knew it.

Sitting around the kitchen table Dawn, Larry and I munched happily on the greasy chips, dipping them into curry sauce. None of us said anything. I was looking forward to having Larry to myself. I wanted to get him on side and agree with me that Dawn should move out. I didn't want to throw her out with nowhere to go. Nothing so unkind. We'd tell her it was time she got a job and moved on with her life. She didn't really expect to live with us for the rest of her life did she?

From the kitchen I could hear the blare from the TV where the kids were all sitting watching something and eating their dinner. I often fed them in front of the telly. It was easier that way and they never complained.

Dawn had had her fill of food and pushed the paper away dabbing a napkin on her mouth.

'I'm stuffed.' She hadn't eaten half the amount I had.

'More for me.' Larry reached over and grabbed a handful of chips.

'Naughty.' She slapped the back of his hand lightly and smiled.

'I'm a growing lad.' Larry sat back patting his stomach.

'Do you have to flirt like that?' I looked at Dawn angrily.

'Don't be ridiculous. We aren't flirting.' Dawn blushed.

'Don't treat me like a fool. I wasn't born yesterday. Have some fucking respect.'

Larry sat silently, still chewing on a mouthful of battered fish.

'Say something.' Dawn nudged his arm.

'Don't expect him to stick up for you.' I stood up and put my hands on my hips. 'You have pushed me far enough this time. What sort of woman tries it on with her sister's husband?'

'You are imagining things. Larry, tell her please.'

'Dee,' Larry turned to me.

'Don't Dee me. I've had it up to here. We've taken you in and looked after you. But I really think it's time you moved out. Get a job. Stand on your own two feet. Stop scrounging off us.'

'You want me to move out?' Dawn's eyes filled with tears and her bottom lip quivered.

'Yes. I do.' I glared at her, unmoved by her show of emotion.

'Enough.' Larry stood up and slammed his hand down on the table. 'That is enough, Dee. Dawn is family. We look after our own.'

'But Larry–'

'But nothing. This is my house and I say who lives under this roof. Dawn,' he turned to her and put his hand on her shoulder, 'Of course you are staying. Dee is just upset.

I was gobsmacked. I stood there looking at my husband and sister side with each other.

'Why don't you go and sleep in her bed tonight. You're not sleeping in mine.'

Before I even knew what had happened he hit me across the cheek with the back of his hand. It stung and I sat down in shock.

Dawn looked taken back.

'I'm sorry you had to witness that, Dawn.' Larry rubbed his

chin and made an effort to calm himself down. Dawn said nothing. She couldn't look at me. 'Go and have a bath or something.' Larry turned to me. His stare was cold. 'Clean yourself up and then come up to bed.

It was my turn to have tears well up. 'I'm sorry.' My voice sounded hoarse.

'It's fine. Have a bath and then go upstairs and put on that lacy nightdress. You can make it up to me in bed.'

Dawn looked embarrassed and busied herself by clearing away the leftovers.

I nodded and stood silently before leaving the room. My cheek was burning and I could taste blood in my mouth.

'You aren't going anywhere,' I heard Larry say to Dawn as I closed the door to the bathroom.

38

I'm sitting in that dingy flat again, cooped up watching crap on TV. Less than half an hour ago it was confirmed that the body of the child was Daisy.

Helen came in and tried to tell me gently and when I didn't react by breaking down she seemed shocked. I knew it was Daisy. Of course I did. What did she expect? I'm not an openly emotional person. I keep my feelings to myself. What use is it crying and rolling around on the floor? She's dead. The worst has already happened.

'I'll bury her with her mother,' I told Helen as I looked out of the window at a flock of birds that was flying by. 'They should be together.'

'Yes. Of course.' Helen looked sombre but she didn't have the right. It wasn't her family that had been dug up.

'Has Larry said anything?' I was desperate for news.

'He is being interviewed again now. I'll let you know when I hear.'

'I just can't believe it. He's such a gentle man. It doesn't make sense. I just wish that I could talk to him.'

'He will be charged with the murders of both Dawn and Daisy.'

'Has he admitted it?' I didn't know my voice could reach that pitch.

'No. He is still saying nothing. But there is overwhelming evidence.'

'Like what?'

'I can't say. It might jeopardise the investigation.'

'When can I go home?'

'You will be the first to know.'

Owen had been taken into care the day before under an Emergency Protection Order. Social services had whisked him away before I had a chance to object.

'I'm not staying here much longer. Owen needs to be back in his own bed. This place gives me the creeps and the hallways smells like piss.'

'Yes, well,' Helen tried to mask a smile, 'the budget only stretches so far.'

'It stretches far enough to be able to dig up the whole of my basement. I hope your lot put everything back the way they found it when they've finished.'

'If you don't mind me saying,' Helen cocked her head to one side, 'you could do with being a little bit softer.'

I stopped looking at the TV and turned to face her.

'What's that supposed to mean?'

'You are dealing with a hell of a lot at the moment. There is so much to take in. I understand you are trying to keep it together for Owen but it's OK to show your vulnerability some-times. None of us would think badly of you if you did.'

She was trying to be kind. I got that, but it wasn't helpful.

'You think I'm a cold bitch don't you.'

'Not at all. It's just that you come across as very defensive. No one is accusing you of anything.'

'You might not be but I don't think you can say the same for Small.'

'It is his job to be probing in interviews.'

'Downright rude I call it. He nearly came out and accused me of having something to do with the deaths. As if I could ever hurt my sister or my niece. Bloody cheek. As if I haven't got enough to cope with without being made to feel like some sort of criminal. It makes my blood boil.'

Just then Helen's mobile phone rang.

'Sorry, I need to take this.' She said standing up and ducking into the hallway to speak in private.

I could hear mumbled words and turned the volume on the television up. I was sick of the sound of her voice.

A few minutes later her head appeared around the door.

'I've just finished speaking to Small. Larry has admitted to all three murders.'

39

Larry appeared in Cambridge Magistrates' court on three counts of murder and was remanded in custody at Cambridge police station for 28 days. He was to reappear at the court on February 20th.

Larry's solicitor, Howard Bennett, had to give written consent that would allow Larry to be held in the station rather than transferred to another prison. The Home Office gave permission for him to remain there under Section 29 of the Criminal Justice Act under normal remand conditions.

Owen was returned to me but we couldn't go home. Police officers carried on digging in the cellar but hadn't found anything else. I was told that day that a warrant had been granted allowing them to search the rest of the house. Helen told me all the floors would be looked at.

'Who else do you think he's killed?' I was exasperated. 'Will this never end?'

'They have to be sure there are no more remains.'

'He's not some mad serial killer, you know.' Helen remained silent. 'Has he told you why he hurt Dawn and little Daisy? I need to know. I have a right to know.'

'He claims he caught her stealing from his wallet.'

'He wouldn't hurt her over a bloody tenner! There must be more to it than that.'

'Larry told officers that when he found her taking the money he lost his temper and hit her. It seems she hit her head on floor and had a bleed to the brain. It was an accident.'

'But that doesn't explain Daisy.'

'He said that the little girl came in and saw her mother on the floor and he panicked.' Helen placed her hand on my shoulder.

'This is all Dawn's fault.' I sobbed into the sleeve of my cardigan. 'If she hadn't tried to steal then none of this would have happened.'

'I'm sorry to add to your worries but I think you should know that DS Small is currently talking to Sue-Ann.'

'Why? What for?'

'It seems she saw her father burning Dawn's belonging one night. She alerted us to that information and he wants to ask her if she remembers anything else significant.'

'I wouldn't trust a word that comes out of that girl's mouth if I were you.' I wiped my nose with the back of my hand. 'She's been trouble ever since the day she was born. She'd say anything to get her father in trouble.'

'That may be,' Helen look sceptical, 'but Larry has admitted to the killings. Sue-Ann is simply helping the police tie up the loose ends.'

'If she thought her dad killed her aunt why didn't she say something sooner. Can you tell me that?' I looked at Helen defiantly.

'I can't possibly comment.'

'What sort of answer is that?'

'The only one you are going to get.' She picked up her mobile phone and started to compose a text.

40

FEBRUARY 20TH 1998

Larry appeared at Cambridge Magistrates' Court for a second time and was again remanded in custody for a further 28 days while the search of our house continued.

By then I had given up asking when I could return home. It didn't seem like there would be much of a home for me to go back to. By all accounts the place had been turned upside down. The floors had been dug up and excavations made of the entire garden. But they didn't find anything else. I knew they wouldn't.

Our faces were all over the newspaper. Pictures of Larry plastered on the front pages. They called him all sorts. They were vicious. It's as if they forgot he had kids who would read their lies. I was offered so much money to do interviews but I declined every one. No way would I help the press muddy Larry's name.

Despite numerous attempts I didn't speak to Sue-Ann or Robbie. Aunt Mary had taken them in on a permanent basis and she told me they couldn't face me. So I kept my distance and did as she asked. I still had Owen at least and he was a good boy. He never asked questions about his Dad. He just seemed to accept that something bad had happened. I explained to him that his

Dad had gone away for a while. I knew he had seen the papers and the news on the telly but he didn't argue. He was never that close to his dad anyway.

I saw less and less of Helen. Her boss obviously deemed it unnecessary for her to remain glued to my side for any longer. That was a relief. Although, in a strange way, I missed her. She was my only link to the outside world. Apart from bloody DS Small she was the only other adult I communicated with. For the first time since I'd been a gawky teenager I felt alone. Those feelings of insecurity and loneliness came flooding back. I hadn't been that person for such a long time and I didn't know how to deal with it. So I started to drink. I wasn't a drunk. My dad had taught me better than that, but I did enjoy my wine every night. It helped me to sleep better and it numbed the throbbing in my head.

I was a prisoner in that horrid flat. I couldn't go out. My picture was everywhere and the press were desperate to get hold of me. When I did venture out, to get groceries or whatever, I made sure I wore a hat and wrapped a scarf around my mouth. Luckily it was winter so I could hide behind my clothes. Things would have been very different if it was the middle of summer.

A few days ago it had snowed and Owen had asked to go to the park to play. I told him he had to go on his own but he should come straight home after and not speak to strangers. I didn't want to risk being seen by any of the other parents.

Once upon a time I would have been able to call up one of his friends' mum's and ask her to take him out. But people avoided us and didn't want to be associated with me. I didn't mind for myself but I felt bad for Owen. He was suffering and he hadn't done anything wrong. He'd made good friends with an Indian boy in his class who he used to play with a lot, but Owen told me the boy didn't want to be his friend any more. It made me cross. I wanted to march down to that school and give them a piece of my mind. In the old days I would have done just that. But things had changed and me losing my temper would have only made matters worse.

I resigned myself to keeping my head down until the whole horrible business was over, even if I didn't have a clue when that might be.

41

MARCH 19TH 1998

Once more Larry went before the Magistrates' Court. They announced his committal hearing would take place on July 21st. His solicitor explained to me that, because of the nature of his crimes, his case was being referred to the Crown court.

I didn't like Howard Bennett one little bit. He never seemed to want to do anything to help Larry. He saw his task as going through the motions. I'd told him to try and get Larry to retract his confession but Bennett just laughed and said it didn't work like that.

Of course Larry wasn't given bail. The magistrate sent him back to his cell. It was the first time I had seen him since January 18th. He smiled at me across the courtroom. I couldn't look at him, but I felt his eyes on me. Everyone was looking at him but he only had eyes for me.

'I love you Dee.' He called out as he was led away by officers. My heart did a little flip when I heard those words. I knew he still loved me. Some things hadn't changed.

In the lobby Bennett explained that next came the

sentencing and that the prosecution would be asked to present all the facts in front of a judge.

'But he has already pleaded guilty.'

'Yes, but it is his legal right to ask that the facts be presented so that he can dispute anything he feels isn't right surrounding the circumstances. It's standard procedure.' Bennett was looking at his watch and clearly desperate to leave.

'So that's it, is it? He's going to prison for the rest of his life and you're only worried about the time.'

'Mrs Miller,' he straightened his tie, 'your husband has pleaded guilty. There is nothing more I can do.'

'Well thanks for nothing.' I turned on my heels and marched away from him. I was dreading leaving the court. I knew the press were gathered outside like vultures waiting to pounce.

As I neared the door leading to the street I spotted DS Small talking to a woman in a suit. The moment he saw me he made his excuses to her and came over, his hands casually in his pockets.

'Mrs Miller.' He nodded his head.

'Detective.' I wanted the ground to swallow me up.

'You know, there's something bothering me about this case.'

'Oh yeah, and what's that?' I didn't want to listen to his answer and feigned boredom.

'Something about it all doesn't quite add up.' He was playing with me, taunting me and stringing the conversation out.

'Shouldn't you be telling this to your superiors?'

'Oh, don't worry, I already have.'

'Good for you. Well, it was nice catching up, but I've got to get home to my son.' I pulled my coat collar up around my neck and tucked my face down.

'I'm not done with your husband yet,' Small said as I walked away from him.

I stopped still and turned to look at the horrid little man.

'Haven't you done enough already? He's said he's guilty. He's admitted it. What else do you want?'

'I think that Larry can help us with another case. Something altogether separate.'

'What's that then?' He had caught my interest.

'The bodies that kept showing up in the river.' His lips curved into a thin smile. 'I've got a sneaking suspicion your Larry might be able to help us out.'

'That's ridiculous!'

'Is it?' Small turned and walked away leaving me feeling very uneasy.

42

I'd heard the day before that Owen and I could move back into the house at Alpha Terrace. The crime scene people had finished their excavation and were packing up. Finally.

Helen warned me that the place would be in a very different state to the way I had left it. She told me that tonnes of concrete had been used to fill the holes in the basement floor and the garden. Now the council were just waiting to hear that the building was still structurally safe after all the knocking about that had taken place.

'If they've made my home unsafe, what am I supposed to do? Where am I meant to live?'

'The civil engineers will let us know soon enough.' Helen responded flatly.

'I'm never going to be able to sell it am I? Who would want to buy a house that has had bodies in it?'

'I'm sure you don't have to go back there if you don't want to. There must be some other option.'

'No it's not that. It doesn't make any difference now does it? The bodies have been taken away and I just want to get back to how things used to be. A bit of normality will do me the world of good. And Owen. He needs to be a boy again. Go back to school and play with his friends.'

'You're determined to stay around Cambridge?' She wasn't any good at hiding her scepticism.

'I haven't got anywhere else to go.'

'I'm sure I could help you find somewhere that you could both start afresh.'

'No point. My face is everywhere. I'm not ever going to be able to escape what has happened.'

Helen remained silent and looked thoughtful. She knew I was right but didn't want to admit it. She was a glass is half full kind of person. I didn't see what there was to be optimistic about. Maybe if she had spent just one day in my shoes she would have been able to understand why I was resigned to returning to Alpha Terrace.

The strange thing about living through a drama like that are the small details that people forget to think about. I'd lost Larry, my two oldest kids, my sister and my niece which was bad enough but on a practical level I'd lost even more. Larry was the breadwinner. Without his income I wondered how Owen and I would cope. It wasn't very likely that anyone would give me a job.

During their search the police and crime scene investigators had come across the money that we had been hiding in the house. It had been removed and was being used in evidence against Larry, although the prosecution were struggling to link it to Dawn or Mark. In the end I confessed it was money we were saving for our old age but when they asked me where it came from I was not prepared to answer.

The same day I heard that I might be able to return home it was also announced that an inquest date had been set for June 8th. I didn't really understand what it was for but Helen explained that where there is a death as a result of violence or suspicious circumstances then the coroner opens an inquiry. It didn't make sense to me, since Larry had already admitted his guilt but the law has its way of doing things.

Small and his band of idiots had been trying to tie Larry to the killings around Cambridge. Someone leaked it to the press from the force that he was being investigated. It was preposterous. The papers hounded me. Somehow they managed to get hold of my mobile phone number. It rang day and night. They were relentless and would not give up.

Things were made worse when my old friend Trisha gave an interview to one of the big national papers talking about my relationship with Larry. I was so hurt and could not believe her betrayal. She must have done it for the money. That was the only reason I could come up with.

She told the reporter that Larry was controlling and I was his submissive little woman. I was made out to be weak. But that's not me. I'm not like that.

Pictures of our wedding day were added to the article. Trisha had gone so far as to share them with the world. Beneath a picture of Larry and me standing outside the front of the registry office was a sentence in bold back text:

How much did she really know?

I scrunched up the paper and threw it across the room. I'd always known that Trisha loved gossip but I'd never imagined she would have sold me down the river the way she did.

'Fucking woman,' I muttered to myself.

The press called Larry a monster and kept digging into our family. Sue-Ann and Robbie were still not talking to me. I learnt from Helen that Sue-Ann had been responsible for alerting the police to Dawn's disappearance. She said she had seen her father burning Dawn's belonging in the garden one night and had been concerned ever since. She said she had always been frightened of her father and that he had a vicious temper. Of course, none of that was true. She just wanted to be in the spotlight and have the attention on her. He never laid a hand on her, or any of them. Well, no more than is usual in any family. He was a good father.

Even when it came to light that Dawn had been stealing from us, Dawn was still made out to be an angel who fell victim to an evil man. It wasn't like that. It never was. But people had a way of twisting the truth so that they could get their conviction or sell more copies of their papers. It disgusted me, but I was powerless to stop it.

I just hoped and prayed that Larry was sheltered from it. Surely he wouldn't have access to the newspapers in prison, would he? But I worried that other people in the prison knew what was being said. People who were labelled in such a way were likely to have a tough time of it on the inside. I dreaded the thought of Larry being hurt by other inmates or given a rough time by the guards. It made me feel miserable.

Standing in the grotty flat waiting to hear the fate of my home I wondered when everything had gotten so messed up. In so many ways meeting Larry had been like a fairy tale. He'd been my white knight who'd saved me from my horrid life. Then things had started to fall apart. And I knew it all stemmed from Dawn. The day she married that pig everything changed. She always had to ruin everything. Even her death was causing me more grief than it should have. I felt bad about Daisy, of course I did, but it was as a result of Dawn's behaviour. If she had just toed the line they would probably both still be alive.

I went over to the toaster and dropped some crumpets in. I needed some comfort food and crumpets smothered in butter would just do the trick. I looked in the cupboard to see if there was any jam left but remembered Owen had finished it off the day before. Since being moved into that flat I had become a bit of a recluse. I didn't want to go outside and face people. Even menial tasks like going to the shop to get milk had become a big deal.

My life was in tatters and I couldn't help but feel sorry for my boy, my husband and myself. But what I didn't know then was that things were going to get tougher. The worst was yet to come.

43

I t was raining. I remember that clearly. Pouring down.
I had got the go-ahead to move back into the house.
Owen and I were nipping around the flat collecting the belongings we'd brought with us and acquired over the past few weeks.
I was so glad to be leaving that place, even though I knew going home would not be easy. Not having Larry there would be strange and with Sue-Ann and Robbie still with Aunt Mary the place was going to be very quiet.

My mobile phone went as I shoved some of my clothes roughly into a plastic carrier bag. I couldn't see it anywhere and searched frantically before spotting it sandwiched between the sofa cushions. I answered quickly, without even looking at the screen.

'Hello?' I felt out of breath and irritated that I'd been interrupted.

'Mrs Miller?' I recognised that formal tone only too well. Another police officer.

'Yes.'

'My name is Detective Sergeant Cirro. We need to talk to you about an urgent matter. Can you please tell me where you are?'

'I'm in the same bloody flat you lot have been keeping me cooped up in for months.'

'Right. Thank you. An officer will be with you shortly. Please don't go anywhere.'

'What's this about? I'm meant to be moving out.'

'An officer will be there to talk to you very soon. Please just wait.'

'Fine. You've got half an hour and if you're not here by then you can come and find me at Alpha Terrace.' I hung up. I doubted it was anything urgent at all. They always liked to make themselves sound more important than they were.

'Owen?' I called out. He was in the bedroom where he was meant to be packing his stuff.

'Yes, Mum?'

'We've got to wait here for a bit longer. Bloody police want to come and talk to me again. As if they haven't taken up enough of my time.'

Owen appeared in the doorway looking nervous.

'Nothing to worry about, little man. Probably something to do with this flat before we leave. Go play on the Gameboy in our room for a bit, OK. I'll bring you some chocolate biscuits.'

I was looking forward to having a bedroom to myself again. Sharing with my young son had not been much fun, especially since he'd started having such vivid nightmares. Owen would wake up in the middle of the night, covered in sweat, screaming that Aunt Dawn was in the corner of the room and was coming to get him. He told me her ghost wouldn't leave him alone. I hushed him and told him it was just a bad dream but it didn't stop it happening frequently. Despite not believing it myself I tried to reassure him that his aunt was in heaven having a lovely time with Daisy. He didn't believe it any more than I did, but what was I supposed to say? The effort of keeping up appearances and trying to be strong for each other left us both feeling exhausted. That and the lack of sleep took its toll. I hoped that once we were back in our own beds his nightmares would stop.

Twenty minutes later there was a knock on the door. I told Owen to stay in the bedroom while I spoke to the police.

'Come in.' I made no attempt to hide my irritation.

'Thank you.' There were two of them, a young-looking policeman who I guessed was Cirro, stepped inside, the rain-drops on his coat brushing on to my sleeve as he passed. The second officer made awkward eye contact with me and then kept his eyes on the floor for the rest of the visit.

'Sit down, then. Let's get this over with. I've got stuff to do.' I pointed at the sofa and stood with my arms folded. I didn't have a bra on underneath my jumper and felt self-conscious that they would be able to tell.

'Thank you.' Cirro sat down, brushing the rain off the top of his balding head. He was probably not much older than me.

'What's this about then?' I looked at the officers shifting awkwardly in their seats. Neither of them could look at me.

'I'm afraid I have some bad news.' Cirro stood up again, real-ising I wasn't going to sit down. He didn't want to be on a different level to me. 'In the early hours of this morning officers at the prison discovered the body of your husband. I am very sorry.' He bowed his head and folded his hands in front of him.

'What are you talking about?' my words caught in my throat. 'Larry's fine. There's nothing wrong with him. He's fit as an ox. There must be some mistake–'

'No Mrs Miller,' Cirro cut in, 'I'm afraid it appears that he committed suicide.'

'No.' My legs felt like jelly and the world started to spin. 'I don't believe you.'

'I am very sorry.'

Cirro guided me over to the couch and sat me down.

'I am so sorry,' he said again.

'How?' the word came out in a half whisper.

'It appears he hanged himself using his bed sheet.'

I stared blankly at Cirro. He had a kind face, unlike Small, but I could see there was no real pity in his eyes.

'You did this.' My bottom lip quivered. Cirro looked at me perplexed. 'You and your colleagues. You did this to him. He would never have done it if...' My words trailed off.

Cirro sat stiffly on the couch next to me.

'Is there anyone I can call?'

'Like who?' I sobbed. 'Who is going to shed a tear apart from me?' My hands shook and snot ran down my face. 'I want to see him.'

'Once the coroner has had a chance to view the body I am sure that can be arranged.'

'Why didn't anyone stop him? It's a prison, for fuck's sake. The people you lock up should be safe.'

'I am sorry to say that occasionally these things happen.'

'That's your best answer,' I slid away from him putting space between us on the couch. 'When did it happen?'

'Sorry?'

'When did they find him?' I looked at the clock on the wall. 'It's nearly midday. You said early this morning. What time?'

'I don't know exactly.' Cirro looked embarrassed.

'Get out.'

'I'm sorry?'

'Are you deaf? I said get out. You've broken the news and done your job now you can get back to celebrating with your mates.'

'Mrs Miller, I can assure you no one is pleased about this.'

'And I'm the Queen of fucking Sheba. Get out.' I pointed a shaking finger to the door.

'Very well. Someone will be in touch soon.' Cirro stood and I noticed the damp mark he'd left behind on the couch.

'Get. Out.' I was able to say it one final time before the tears erupted again.

When the police had left and closed the door behind them Owen poked his head around the doorframe.

'Can we go home now Mum?' he asked. I wiped my sore eyes with the palms of my hands and looked up at him. 'What's wrong?' his voice was so squeaky he sounded like a girl.

'Come here.' I patted the damp spot on the sofa next to me. 'I need to tell you something.'

Owen had pulled the sleeves of his cotton top down and was holding them bunched over his hands. 'What's wrong Mum?' He didn't move and I could see the fear written across his face.

'I need to talk to you. Please come and sit next to your old mum.' I wanted him close to me. The physical distance between us was making me feel even worse that I could have imagined. 'Please?' I did my best to stop my voice from breaking.

Owen nodded and slowly crossed the room still holding tightly on to his cuffs.

'It's Dad.' I said as he perched down next to me slipping my arm around his shoulder and hugging him close to me. His skinny little body felt so frail as if it might break any moment. 'He died.'

Ten minutes later I was in the car with Owen next to me in the passenger side. We were on our way to Mary's house. I had to break the news to the others. I didn't want them seeing it on the news or hearing it from anyone else. As I drove through the town in the rain my mind was on autopilot. I don't remember actually driving the car at all. I just remember a blur of grey and raindrops pelting the windscreen. Owen sat completely still next to me not saying a word. Every now and then I would remember he was there and glance at him just to make sure he was still breathing. He looked so pale.

When we pulled up outside Mary's house I felt a coldness flooding my veins. I stopped the car and the two of us sat still, neither making a move to open our doors.

'If you want to wait in the car...' I didn't know what to suggest or what would be best. Owen turned his head up and looked at me. There were tracks where tears had been falling silently down his cheeks. I brushed them away using my thumb and tried to smile. 'We will be OK.' It was too soon to know if I really believed that myself but I had to say something.

'I don't want you and Sue-Ann to argue.' His voice was so quiet.

'We won't, I promise.'

'You always argue. I hate it when people shout.'

'You can stay here if you want,' I searched his face for further clues as to what he might be thinking.

'OK. Will you be long?' he looked so scared, like an animal caught in a trap.

'No. I promise. Let me talk to them first and then you can come inside, OK?'

Owen nodded and went back to looking out of the window.

Gripping the steering wheel tightly so that my knuckles turned white I willed myself to get out of the car and walk up to the house. Eventually I found the courage to remove the keys from the ignition and open the door. A blast of cold raindrops came rushing into the driver's seat and I made an effort to move quickly before the inside of the car and Owen were soaked.

'I won't be long,' I told him, slamming the door closed behind me and locking up.

The walk up the small path to the front of Mary's house felt like the longest walk of my life. I was still reeling. None of it had sunk in.

I rang the doorbell. My damp hair stuck to my head and rain

spattered my face as I stood waiting for someone to answer the door. It felt as if time were standing still.

A moment later the door opened a fraction and Robbie's face peered through the crack.

'Hi Rob.' I was shivering but not as a result of the cold. 'Can I come in?'

'Only if you promise not to start an argument.'

'I promise. I just really need to talk to you and your sister. Is she around?'

'She's upstairs.' Robbie opened the door a little more. 'Are you all right?' he looked at me strangely.

'I just really need to come in and talk to you both. Please?'

'OK.' He stepped back into the hallway and let me pass.

'Thanks.' I shook the rain off my head and led the way into the lounge.

Mary had made a lovely home for her family. It had a warm and welcoming feel about it.

'I'll just get Sue-Ann.' Robbie left me standing alone. I didn't know whether to sit or stand. My mind was struggling to make even the most basic decisions.

Moments later Sue-Ann and Robbie appeared huddled together.

'Hi.' I did my best to smile at them.

'We're not coming home.' Sue-Ann frowned.

'No. I know. That's not why I'm here. Please will you both sit down, I need to tell you something.'

Robbie and Sue-Ann looked at each other for a moment before agreeing to my request. They perched side by side on the sofa looking up at me. I lingered near the gas fire trying to find the right words.

'It's your dad,' Sue-Ann immediately rolled her eyes and looked bored and the rage I'd felt on the day I had slapped her came flooding back. Taking a deep breath, I calmed myself before continuing. 'I've got some bad news, kids.'

Robbie looked worried.

'I just found out myself, the police came and told me,' I couldn't find the courage to say the words he's dead.

'Told you what?' Robbie's concern was palpable.

'I'm sorry, I'm so sorry,' the swell of emotion hit me like a punch to the head. 'He died.'

My two eldest children sat perfectly still looking at me. Neither blinked. I stayed quiet for a moment to allow it to sink in. Neither said a word.

'I am so sorry. It seems he killed himself.' I swallowed hard. Still not a word from either of them. 'It's a lot to take in. I know.' I bent down on my heels so that we were on the same eye level and reached out a hand to rest on Robbie's knee. 'It's a huge shock.'

'I'm going to get a glass of water.' Sue-Ann stood up and walked out of the room. Robbie remained sitting on the couch frozen still staring at me with wide eyes. I went and sat next to him and put my arm around his shoulder. His body felt tense.

'Dad.' Robbie spoke in a half-whisper.

'I know,' I cradled his head in my arms.

44

The few weeks leading up to Larry's funeral were hell. I had lost my husband and my kids had lost their dad. The press shamelessly celebrated his suicide. 'One less monster in the world' a headline read. He was called a coward and every other name under the sun. I wanted to scream from the rooftops that that wasn't my Larry, they'd got it all wrong, but I couldn't. It wouldn't have helped. I had to look after the kids and try and keep us out of the news. Journalists swarmed like flies around Alpha Terrace again.

To begin with I was heartbroken and I was angry. I couldn't believe Larry had left me. But the day after his body was discovered the prison recovered a letter he had slipped into a book. It was addressed to me.

Darling Dee,

I am sorry I didn't get a chance to say goodbye but it is better this way. I'm not built for prison. My life should be with you and the kids but now that has gone. I don't want to stick around.

As long as I am still breathing you will never be able to escape the past.

I've loved you ever since I first saw you sitting on that park bench. You are everything to me and I am going to die happy in the knowledge that you can now move on and be free.

I don't want to grow old in this place so I've seen to it that I never will.

Carry me in your heart always and know how much I love those eyes.

Yours,

Larry x

Someone from the prison had seen fit to make a copy. Two days later his private letter to me was on the front of every newspaper.

Sue-Ann refused to talk to me and said she didn't want to go to the funeral. Robbie stopped talking all together and went into himself. They both remained living with Mary.

Owen and I did our best to carry on. It was strange being back at the house knowing that our family would never be together again.

The only person in the whole world who came to see us and shared our sorrow was Eric, Larry's brother. He showed up on the doorstep one day carrying four cans of paint.

'I thought you might want to redecorate.' He stood awkwardly on the street unable to look me in the eye.

'That's a good idea.' I took one of the pots of paint and let him into the house.

We sat silently at the kitchen table both sipping our tea.

'He loved you, you know?' Eric cupped his mug in his hands and looked pensive.

'I know he did. And I loved him. Even after everything.' My words tailed off.

'If you need help organising the funeral...'

'It will be a small do.'

Eric nodded.

'Sue-Ann doesn't want to come.'

'You can't really blame her. The kid must be in such a mess. I thought I knew him, you know? He was my brother and I really thought I knew him.' Tears gathered in the corner of his eyes and for a moment he looked like Larry. A shiver ran down my spine.

'He was a good man. He did some bad things, made some wrong choices but he was a good man. Never lose sight of that.' I reached over and squeezed his hand.

'I'm meant to be the one consoling you.' Eric sniffed.

'We can be strong for each other.' I smiled at him fondly.

'So, are you going to stay here?' He looked around the kitchen.

'No choice. And this is where we were happy. If I leave it's like I've lost my last link to him. I'm not ready to give that up yet.'

'I think I understand.' Eric took a mouthful of hot tea. 'But remember I want you to come to me for anything you need. Funerals are expensive. Let me help you out.'

'You're a kind man, Eric. Just like your brother.'

He smiled, finished his tea and got up.

'Well, better get going. Hope the paint helps.'

'I'll let you know when I have a date for the funeral.' I got up and stretched my arms before giving him a hug. 'Thanks for everything.' It was the first time I had shared an intimate moment with a man in such a long time and it felt strangely good.

'Mum and Dad aren't coming.'

'Oh.' The crematorium was going to be bare.

'They can't face it.' He looked awkward.

'I don't blame them. Bloody press round every corner. Why can't they just leave us alone.'

'Mum's in bits. Has been ever since, well, you know.'

'Yes. I know.'

When Eric left I took a moment to myself and thought about the days ahead. In a way I was pleased I wouldn't have to face Larry's aging parents. I could barely cope with my own grief let alone theirs. No doubt his mother was feeling dreadful. Not only had her son been labelled a murderer but also then she had to come to terms with his suicide. It was all so dirty.

I tried to imagine how she must have felt. It was impossible to envisage Robbie or Owen in prison for killing anyone, let alone having to face burying either of them. I shuddered and went back to sorting out the piles of Larry's belongings on the floor of the sitting room.

On that morning, after I'd put on my black dress and ironed Owen's little white shirt, I sat alone at the kitchen table watching the hands of the clock. In less than one hour I would be at the crematorium watching my husband's body disappear forever. It was so surreal. Owen was in his bedroom reading a book. Earlier I'd taken him some toast and told him to stay up there until it was time to go. I couldn't face him. His little face looked so sad and lost.

Under normal circumstances he and I would have followed the hearse to the cemetery but we were not dealing with normal circumstance. The undertaker, who was very polite and respectful, suggested that they take the coffin directly to the crematorium and that we meet them there. I thanked him for making the suggestion and agreed without hesitation. He assured me that the details of the funeral would remain private and that nobody who worked for his family business would be speaking to the press.

Two days earlier I had visited Larry's body at the undertakers. I'd already chosen a coffin for him and he was laid out in it, looking peaceful. At my request, Mr Armstrong the undertaker left me alone with him for a little while. I stood over his body and stroked his hair. People say that the dead look like they are sleeping. I don't agree. He looked hollow, as if the part of him that made him who he was had left his body.

When I was sure we were alone and Mr Armstrong was not watching I removed a small wooden box with a brass lock and put it in the coffin with him.

'Sleep tight.' I kissed his icy forehead and left the room.

Mr Harold Armstrong was standing respectfully with his head bowed waiting for me.

'Thank you,' I sniffed and pulled my cardigan around my body.

'It often helps, seeing the deceased one last time.' He was a serious man and I found it difficult to imagine him ever smiling.

'I put some personal belongings in with him. Please see that they remain with him until the end.'

'You have my word.' He nodded. I shook his hand and left. It was the last time I would ever lay eyes on my husband.

At eleven o'clock I heard a beep from the street. Our taxi had arrived. I called up the stairs to Owen and put my best winter coat on. The spring sun was shining outside but I wanted to look smart for Larry.

Owen appeared in his dark school trousers and freshly ironed shirt. He'd even put a bit of gel in his hair.

'Very smart,' I told him fixing his tie. 'Your dad would have been proud.'

Owen swallowed back tears and held my hand. Together we stepped out into the warm sunshine and got into the silver Vauxhall that was waiting for us.

I was pleasantly surprised to find a taxi that would collect us from there. The Asian taxi driver eyed me in the rear view mirror. I knew what he was thinking. Everyone in England knew our address.

'Crematorium?' He flicked on the meter, his dark eyes fixing me.

'Yes.'

The car did a rather awkward three-point turn before setting off towards the cemetery. Owen sat silently staring out of the window. I wanted to hug him but feared I might burst into tears if I did.

Just under fifteen minutes later the car pulled into the driveway. The car park was quiet. We were the only car in it. We'd arrived half an hour before the cremation was due to take place but I thought it would be good to wander around the grounds for a while before going into the chapel.

I paid the driver and we got out of the car. The sun was warm on the top of my head and I felt hot in my coat. The diamanté brooch I was wearing glittered proudly in the sunlight and I adjusted it to make sure it was straight.

'Come on, let's go for a wander.' I took Owen's hand in mine and led him towards the grounds. Memories of my father's funeral, which had taken place in the same crematorium, came flooding back. At the time, I thought my father's funeral was a small tragic affair. But this was going to be something altogether different.

We walked amongst the trees, over a carpet of anemones, looking at the plaques of remembrance.

'Why do people have to die?' Owen stopped walking and looked up at me.

'It's just the way it is. Nothing lives forever.'

'Is Dad in heaven?' His expression was so hopeful.

'I'm sure he is.' It wasn't a good time to question the validity of religion.

'So I can see him again when I go to heaven?'

'Yes. But that won't be for a very long time.' I didn't mean it the way it sounded and Owen looked sad. 'I just mean that you have got a long life ahead of you. But Dad will always be there as long as you remember him.'

Owen nodded and we continued walking.

'Was Dad a bad man?' I could tell he was terrified of the answer.

'Well, some people are going to think that. Some people might even tell you that your dad was bad, but they didn't know him, did they. It's not about what they say. It's about the truth. What do you think? Do you think he was bad?' I held my breath waiting for the answer. This was the first time we had discussed the situation properly. He was still too young to really understand.

'I don't think he was bad.' Owen frowned.

'Good. Neither do I. He made some bad decisions, that's all.' Not wanting to talk about it any more I looked at my wristwatch and suggested we head back towards the chapel. 'Uncle Eric will be here soon.'

As we approached the door that led into the chapel a black hearse pulled up outside. The funeral director stepped out and instructed his people to carry the coffin inside.

Owen and I stood sombrely watching as the box was lifted on to the men's shoulders and taken indoors. Mr Armstrong came back and told us that everything was in place and that they were ready to proceed as soon as I said the word. I explained we were waiting for Eric.

Armstrong nodded and disappeared off. He had been so respectful and humane up until that point but on that day I felt as if something had changed. For some reason he couldn't look me in the eye. At the time I put it down to the gravity of the situation.

As I watched Armstrong disappear around the corner with the coffin bearers I heard a car pull up and turned to see that Eric had arrived. He parked, got out and came towards us. His attempt at being smart was somewhat laughable. He had a rather grubby, un-ironed blue shirt on, with a pair of black jeans, trainers and a black tie, which he had no doubt borrowed.

'Morning.' He said scratching the back of his neck.

'Hi.' Owen went over and gave him a nervous hug.

'So, is this it?' Eric looked around.

'This is it.'

'You didn't manage to persuade the others, I'm guessing.'

'No.' The word was clipped. I was trying to ignore the bitter disappointment I felt towards my two eldest children. 'Shall we go in?'

I led the way, followed closely by Eric and Owen.

Once inside the celebrant, Mr Peck, a man with thick glasses and a large belly, greeted us. He put his hand out and we shook.

'I am sorry for your loss.' He sounded genuine and I couldn't contain my surprise. 'Funerals are a difficult business at the best of times. I appreciate this is going to be harder than most. Shall we proceed.'

I nodded and led the way into the empty chapel. The coffin was at the front of the room on the catafalque with only a single bunch of white roses resting on the top. The three of us sat on the front right hand row, all gazing at the wooden box containing Larry's body. It was so surreal.

The room was so quiet you could have heard a pin drop. And then the music started to play. From the speakers on the wall the song 'Behind Blue Eyes' by The Who filled the room. A lump formed in my throat and I swallowed hard, even though I had requested it and knew it was coming. It had been our song. Larry used to play it and said it made him think of me. I thought that was really romantic.

The committal did not take long. It was a very short service. The celebrant managed to say a few nice words and avoid the pink elephant in the room. Then we watched as the curtains closed around the coffin and I looked down at Owen who was sat sandwiched between Eric and me. His little face was pale and he didn't take his eyes off the coffin. Even after the velvet curtains shrouded it he just sat still staring. Then Bach's 'Sheep May Safely Graze' came pouring out of the speakers and we all remained seated trying to make sense of what had happened. As the orchestral piece came to an end the three of us looked at one another and stood in unison. It was over.

We left the chapel and stepped out into the fresh air. Eric removed a pair of sunglasses from his shirt pocket and put them on, shifting awkwardly on the spot. 'So, what do we do now?'

'We go home and try to get on with our lives.'

'OK. Well, I'm glad I came. If either of you ever need anything you know where I am. I'll be in touch, yeah?' he put his arm around my shoulder and kissed the side of my head.

'Sure. Thanks for coming.'

I watched as he went over to his car and drove away. I felt bitterly alone.

'Right, kiddo, let's call a cab.' I started to remove my mobile phone from my handbag when I noticed a figure waving at me from the car park. DS Small was leaning against his car with his shirt sleeves rolled up, his head tilted towards the warm light. I scowled at him. How dare he. Next to him was a police car with two officers standing beside it. I really didn't want to talk to him but I could see I had no choice so I approached the man.

'Owen, go inside and wait for me.' I pointed to the waiting area at the entrance to the chapel. Owen did as he was told.

'What the hell do you think you are doing here? You're not welcome.' I shouted, as I got closer. 'Don't you think you've done enough already?'

'Well hello, Mrs Miller.' Small flashed a row of white teeth at me. 'Lovely day.'

'I could slap you.' I said through gritted teeth.

'Ah, but that would be assault.' Small waggled his finger in the air.

'We're grieving. This is harassment. I'm going to put in a formal complaint.' My chest was all puffed up.

Small looked down at his feet and smiled. 'I think you are going to be spending a lot of time down at the station from now on.'

'What are you talking about?' I wanted to wipe that pompous grin off his face. He looked up at the uniformed officers and gave a little nod.

'Deborah Miller, I am arresting you on suspicion of murder. You do not have to say anything, but it may harm your defence if you do not mention when questioned something which you later rely on in court. Anything you do say may be used in evidence against you.'

I felt the two officers close in around me. My exit was blocked, not that I intended to run.

'This is a joke.' I half-laughed.

'No, madam, this is no joke. New evidence has come to light.'

'What new evidence?'

'The box, Mrs Miller. The box you put into your husband's coffin.'

I felt the colour drain from my face.

'How did you know?' All the fight had left me.

'Let's just say we received a tip.'

I hung my head and let out a long loud sigh.

'You didn't think you'd get away with it?'

'I did, actually.' I looked up and eyeballed Small who took a few steps towards me and slowly lifted his hand to point at my brooch. The little diamanté fox with red stone eyes sparkled in the light and appeared to be taunting me.

'That's an interesting item.' He mused fingering the piece of jewellery.

'Yes,' I said, 'it is. Isn't it.'

45

W hen I was shown into the interview room of the prison, she hadn't arrived yet. I sat down on one of the two plastic chairs and looked around the stark room. High up in the corner of the room was a CCTV camera pointing down at me. The red light on the side of it glowed brightly.

HM Prison Bronzefield is a Category A prison on the outskirts of Ashford in Surrey. It is the only purpose-built high security prison for women in the UK. One of the officers once bragged to me that it was the largest female prison in Europe. As if I give a shit.

I was transferred here when it opened in 2004 from Low Newton prison in County Durham. I don't know why they didn't leave me there. I was getting on OK. I've learnt to keep my head down.

I'm forty-nine years old. In early 1999, when I was thirty-three, I'd received a whole life sentence after being found guilty of the murder of eight people. I will never be released.

I now weigh over sixteen stone and my breathing is not as easy as it once was. My grey hair has been cut really short. A lot of the other girls in the prison keep away from me. Most of them know to give me a wide berth but there's always one who thinks she's tough and wants to show off to the others. I've been in fights a few times. Sometimes I come out of it better and other times I don't. It's the way it is in here.

At least I was given enhanced prisoner status. That means I'm allowed to have my own things around me in my cell. They got me a catalogue so that I could choose some stuff I wanted. I got a bright rug for the floor, some new mint green bedding decorated with little bluebells and a DVD player to watch films on. Believe it or not the prison paid the bill. They said I could order some make-up but I told them I didn't want it. I never really went in for that stuff. And what's the point in here? I'm not a dyke.

I even have a little job working as a cleaner on the wing. They pay me eleven pounds a week. It's better than nothing and it stops me from getting too bored.

Most of the time I wear the green prison uniform but occasionally I put on a grey Adidas tracksuit just for a change. On that day I was wearing my tracksuit. It was a special day.

I heard the door to the room being unlocked and I turned to face the entrance. An officer showed her into the room and then left, locking the door again.

She sat down nervously, placing the Dictaphone on the table between us.

'Hello, Deborah.' She folded her hands together and rested them on the table. I noticed a large sparkling diamond ring on her engagement finger. Lucky bitch, I thought.

'Hello.' I looked at her through my glasses. My eyesight isn't what it once was.

'I'm Verity Holten.' She was pretty and probably not much older than thirty. She wore her auburn hair in a silky bob, which emphasised her delicate jaw and neck. She had large dark blue eyes that were framed with just the right amount of make-up.

'Yes, I know who you are.'

'Thank you for agreeing to talk to me.' I noticed she still hadn't taken her green jacket off.

'Not just down to me. I suppose you had to get permission from the Governor?'

'Yes, that's right.' She was finding it hard to look me in the eye. I was used to people being like that.

'What is it?'

'You look very different from the pictures of you,' she admitted.

'They are old. I was younger then.' I ran my hand through my short hair. 'People change.'

Verity didn't say anything and just sat there looking at me strangely.

'So.' I leant back in my chair and it creaked. 'What exactly do you want?'

'I would like the truth.'

'You mean you want me to spill my guts so that you can splash it all over the front of your fancy paper.'

'I am here for the families of the victims.'

'You're here to sell newspapers.'

'Yes, I work for *The Times* and yes, a lot of what we discuss is likely to end up in my article but that is not my sole purpose for being here.' Suddenly she found the courage to look directly at me.

I examined her face for a moment deciding on my next move. 'What makes you think I am going to tell you anything?'

'The fact that you agreed to meet me suggests you are prepared to talk.'

'Maybe I just thought I'd have some fun.' I looked down at the nails on my left hand.

'Is this fun for you?'

I didn't like her tone. 'I can get up and leave this room any time I like.'

'That is true.' She was keeping her calm and it riled me. 'But before you do walk out of this room I think there is something you should know. My aunt was Joanne Hewitt.'

'Now that's a name I've not heard for a long time.' I leant forward and smiled. Now she had my attention.

'So, will you talk to me?' Verity rested her hand on the Dictaphone.

'Sure. We can talk.'

She picked up the Dictaphone and turned it on.

'Interview with Deborah Miller, May second.'

'So?' I folded my arms and sat back. 'Ask me something.'

'During your murder trial in March 1999 you pleaded not guilty. Can you tell me why?'

'Well, that's a stupid question isn't it?' I chuckled shaking my head. 'I didn't do it.'

'Didn't do what?'

'Didn't do what they were accusing me of.'

'So can you please explain then how you came to have knowledge of the whereabouts of the eyeballs.'

'Like I said before, I found them.'

'Where?'

'In the freezer.'

'And instead of handing the evidence over to the police you decided it should be cremated alongside your husband?'

'He'd already been labelled a murderer and he was dead. I was trying to avoid any more hassle.'

'Hassle?' Verity made no effort to conceal her distain. 'You are talking about the body parts of your husband's victims.'

'Well I didn't know what he'd done until I found them. By then he'd already been arrested. I didn't want to make matters worse for him. And I had my boy to think of.'

'So without hesitation you took the evidence and placed it inside his coffin two days before he was due to be cremated. Did it not occur to you that the families of his victims deserved closure?'

'No. Not really. I had my own family to think about.'

'It didn't occur to you that by withholding evidence you could end up in trouble?'

'I did what I thought was best.' Her look told me that she didn't believe it. 'That's the truth.'

'OK, let's back up. Can you tell me how you felt when you discovered a collection of eyeballs in your freezer?' she asked the question the same way a waitress might ask what you wanted to order in a restaurant.

'Well, I was shocked, of course.'

'Naturally.' Verity's sarcasm was beginning to wind me up.

'If you want me to talk to you, you're going to have to show me a bit more respect,' I growled.

'I apologise.' Suddenly she didn't look so sure of herself and I felt as if I were regaining some control of the situation.

'So,' I said changing the subject, 'Dr Hewitt was your aunt.'

'Yes.' She shifted in her chair looking uncomfortable.

Inside I was smiling. 'Sorry about that.'

'Can you tell me why you tortured her and left her with injuries that ultimately led to her death?' Verity swallowed the words down.

'I didn't do anything.'

'OK, have it your way. Do you know why your husband did it?'

'I suspect he was pissed off with her.'

'Because of the complications when you had your third child?'

'Yes. Because of that.'

'If you don't mind me saying, you don't seem that upset about it.'

'Why should I be?'

'Because a woman was murdered.'

'Rather her than me.' I smirked knowing it would cause a reaction.

'OK. That's it. I'm done.' Verity stood up and grabbed the Dictaphone. 'I thought I could do this but I was wrong. This interview is over.' As she swept past me I grabbed her wrist and stopped her.

'You don't just walk out of here. I'm not done yet.'

'Let go.' I could see the panic in her eyes.

'Fine.' I released her. She took a step back and she rubbed her wrist. 'Do you want to know the truth. All of it?'

'Yes. That's why I'm here.' Verity was clearly shaken up.

'OK then. Sit down. I'll tell you everything.'

She stood for a moment looking at the door, still deciding whether to stay or go.

'Look, we got off on the wrong foot. Sit down.' My voice was softer now. Verity walked back around the table and took a seat. 'Thank you.'

'So tell me about my aunt.'

'No.' I replied coldly. 'Let's go back to the beginning. We'll come to her later.'

'Fine. Where do you want to start?' Verity removed the Dictaphone from her jacket pocket, turned it on and put it back down on the table.

'Before I begin I need you to understand something.' I placed my hands palm down on the table. 'You cannot leave this room until I have finished telling you my story. If you will agree to that, then we can begin.'

'OK. I agree.'

'Good. So, the truth is that Larry was a killer.' I raised one hand to stop her interrupting. 'Let me finish.'

Verity took a bottle of water out of her small black leather handbag and took a long sip. I noticed her hands were shaking.

'I am going to speak and you are going to listen. I will not repeat a single word I say. This will be the last time you ever hear me speak of this again. Understand?'

She nodded meekly.

'Right. I am admitting to the murders of Ms Faulks, Jane Shanks, Rose Delaney, Sandra Morrison, Mark McCarthy, Dawn McCarthy and Daisy McCarthy. I killed them all. Dawn and Daisy were unfortunate. I'll come to that later. As for the rest, every one of them deserved it.' I watched as Verity removed a notepad and pencil from her bag and started to flick through some notes. 'Ms Faulks, as you will know, was my first. That nasty old bitch thought she was so much better than me. But I showed her.' The memory of it made me feel warm all over. 'I owe a lot to her, I suppose. She woke something inside of me. A hunger I didn't know existed and when I'd killed her, and cut out her eyes, I felt more alive that you could possibly imagine.'

The horror on Verity's face only added to my enjoyment.

'The next one, Jane Shanks, needed to be put in her place. I saw her with Larry, talking and flirting. I was so angry. One night I followed her from work. It was dark. I saw an opportunity and I took it. I pushed her over and punched her in the head until she wasn't moving. Then I took out my penknife and carefully removed her eyes. I didn't know she was still alive when I dumped her in the river. I thought she must already be dead.' I paused trying to remember back to that time.

'Rose was next. She was a hooker. I'd seen Larry talking to her when I'd followed him one night. I watched them fuck up against a wall. It made me feel sick. They didn't know I was there.' I lifted my glasses and rubbed my eyes. 'He has such an appetite for sex. It was relentless. Nothing could satisfy it in those days. When I got pregnant with Sue-Ann he didn't want to fuck me any more so he turned his attention to prostitutes. That made me really angry. I knew he was getting it somewhere else so I would follow him. I must have watched him shag lots of different women over the years. In the end I started to find it a bit of a turn on.' I licked my lips.

Verity had turned very pale. 'But why did you take their eyes?' she spoke in a whisper, her voice sounded dry.

'I'll tell you. Larry loved eyes. He said my eyes were the reason he fell in love with me. He was obsessed with them. He became an optician, after all.' I reminded her. 'Ms Faulks was different. I took hers because I didn't like the way she'd looked at me, but with the others,' I paused for a moment trying to order my thoughts, 'I took them because I knew that was what Larry had liked. If he hadn't liked their eyes he would have never slept with any of them. That was his weakness you see.' I looked up at the CCTV camera and spoke directly to it. 'Can we get some tea in here please?'

Verity shifted in her chair and hugged herself. The room didn't feel cold to me.

'Sandra Morrison was different. I did feel a little bit bad about her, I suppose. She didn't do anything really wrong, just wound me up I guess.' I remembered back to the night I had seen Larry talking to her outside a pub. 'He had been trying it on but she wasn't interested. Still that pissed me off. What made her think she was too good for my Larry? Little cow was stuck up and that annoyed me.' I looked up at Verity and saw the disgust written across her face. 'You think you're better than me, too. Don't you?'

Verity said nothing. I shrugged.

'My favourite was Mark. He got what he deserved. He was

scum. He raped me, you know. That was true. I never lied about that.'

'You were a prostitute,' Verity reminded me gently. That made me angry.

'So what? You think hookers can't be raped.' I spat my words across the table and wiped my mouth with the back of my hand.

Just at that moment the door was unlocked and an officer came in carrying two plastic cups of tea. 'There you go, ladies.' He winked at Verity. 'All OK?'

She picked up her tea, took a small sip and nodded.

'Fair enough. You behave, all right?' the gruff officer turned to me.

'Yes sir.' I gave him the finger as he left the room. 'Some of them are real dicks. Some aren't so bad.'

'Do you have any friends in here?' she asked tentatively.

'I do actually. Sonya Lily.'

'The Sonya Lily?' Verity couldn't disguise her shock.

'Yes. As far as I am aware there is only one.'

'I suppose you both have things in common.'

'You're right.'

Sonya was locked up for 12 years for a catalogue of sex offences against teenage girls in her care. She had worked at a children's home, which is where she met her victims. It turned out to be her dream job. She understood what it was like to want to hurt other women and how good it made you feel.

'I've taken her under my wing and been showing her the ropes.'

Verity looked like she might be sick.

'So, Mark McCarthy.' She returned to flicking through her notes.

'Yes. I invited him to come back. Told him he could do what he wanted to me. He was so stupid.' I couldn't help but smile. 'It was a piece of cake. He came over, I took him upstairs and while we were...' I paused for a moment, 'intimate, I put a knife in his back. The look on his face was priceless. I took the knife out and did it again and again until he wasn't moving.'

'They never recovered his eyes,' Verity probed.

'No. I never took them. I didn't want them. He could keep them.' I picked up the tea and took a sip. It was bitter. Normally I liked sugar in it. 'When Larry came back from work I got him to help me bury the body. I told him Mark had come over and tried to rape me again. Said it was self-defence. He felt so bad he hadn't been there to protect me I was able to persuade him to dig a hole in the garden. We chopped him up with an axe and threw the pieces in. It was simple really. Nothing fancy.' I looked down into the watery tea and thought for a moment.

'Everything started to go wrong when Dawn married that idiot Ian. If she hadn't, then things would have been different. Larry might even still be alive.' Even now, thinking about him made me feel sad.

'You loved Larry?'

'He was everything to me.' I looked up at her. 'Don't be so surprised. I'm not dead inside.'

'After Mark, what happened next?' I could see that she was beginning to enjoy listening to my story. The journalist in her had taken over and she was no longer so concerned about her aunt.

'Well, at some point in September 1993 Dawn and Daisy moved in. Ian had beaten her black and blue and she'd had enough. She was my sister and I'd always looked out for her. I was happy for her to stay with us for a while.' I noticed the sadness in my own voice. 'Things were fine for a bit. It wasn't ideal having her there, but we managed.'

'So what happened?'

'I walked in and found her fucking my husband.' I stared

blankly at Verity. 'Dawn could never keep her legs closed and had to take what wasn't hers. That's what happened.'

Verity picked up the pencil and jotted something down on the notepad.

'So that's why you killed her?'

'Yes. She was shameless. Wasn't even embarrassed by her behaviour. I'd welcomed her into my home, not into my husband's pants. She just had to be the centre of attention. That was always her big problem.'

'When he was interviewed Larry told police he killed her when he found her stealing. You're now telling me that was a false confession?'

'Yes I am.'

'So Larry knew you murdered Dawn and was protecting you?'

'No he didn't know for sure. When I walked in on them I started screaming. I was so angry with her. He pulled his trousers on and ran out the room like a kid caught with his hand in the cookie jar. That night he stayed away. When he came back I told him she'd moved out. He never asked what happened and we didn't talk about it again.'

'Did he know about any of them, apart from Mark?'

'I don't really know. I think he must have suspected. Otherwise why confess?'

'Why do you think he did confess?'

'Because he loved me. And he felt guilty about Dawn probably.'

'What exactly happened to Dawn?' Verity's pencil hovered above the pad.

'I strangled her until she passed out. Then I carried her down to the cellar. Daisy saw me dragging Dawn's body down the stairs and started to cry. So I had to shut her up. I grabbed her by the hair and pulled her down to the cellar. She was so scared she wet herself and she wouldn't stop crying. I put a plastic bag over her head and suffocated her. It was all over pretty quickly.'

Talking about Daisy made me feel uncomfortable. I didn't want to dwell on what I did to her.

'Next, that bloody dog started barking. Wouldn't stop. It was giving me a headache so I smashed his skull in. Then Dawn woke up and saw Daisy lying on the floor near her. I was just sitting on the bottom step of the cellar stairs looking at the ground. Dawn started screaming and kept trying to wake Daisy up. I told her there wasn't any point, but she wouldn't listen. I hadn't decided what I was going to do with Dawn but then she told me something that changed everything. She told me Daisy was Larry's daughter.'

I sniffed and wiped a tear away. 'I had no idea they had been sleeping together for that long. As far as I know, Ian found out and that's why he battered Dawn. It all started to make sense.'

'Did Larry know about Daisy?' Verity asked.

'He didn't know she was his kid. No. He never knew that. Dawn never told him. She only ever looked after number one. It suited her to keep the lie going. But when she told me I was livid. I made her tell me everything about her affair with Larry. She said she was in love with him, but she only ever loved herself. We sat in the cellar for hours. Dawn kept cradling Daisy's body. I told her if she didn't tell me the truth I'd kill her too. She really believed I'd let her go. It's funny really,' I shook my head, 'Dad used to say she was the smart one. How wrong he was.' Verity put the pad and pencil back on the table and moved her chair slightly so the gap between us was wider.

'We used to keep the toolbox in the basement. Dawn sat on the floor holding Daisy. She didn't try to get up. I went over to it and removed a screwdriver. Then I prised her eyes out. The axe we'd used to chop up Mark was lying there against the wall in the cellar so afterwards, when I'd taken her eyes, I picked it up and brought it down into her skull. I'll never forget the noise.'

Verity sat, mouth open opposite. 'And there you have it.'

It took her a moment to compose herself.

'What about Joanne? You didn't explain about her.'

'Oh well, that's simple. Larry killed her. I told him to. Told him to make her pay and he did. He really liked it when I suggested he took her eyes as a keepsake. I thought he would.'

Verity buried her face in her hands.

'I'm sorry about that,' I huffed. 'But she ruined me and he was so upset. He needed a vent.'

'You are a monster.' Verity's eyes filled with tears.

'That's not very polite. I've just given you the interview of the decade.'

'Why? Why have you told me all of this?' A large tear rolled down her cheek.

'I'm tired.' I admitted. 'I've been in prison for a long time and a lot of lies have been said about me. I thought it was time people knew the truth. You know I killed one of those bitches when I was pregnant? That's one of the ones I'm most proud of.' I put my hands behind my head. 'Owen stopped coming to see me. I don't have to protect him any more. It's probably better that he hates me. It will be easier for him if he does.'

'You sound as if you actually care about him.'

'I do. He was always my favourite. He was such a good boy.' I placed my chubby hands back on the table. 'So what now?'

'Now I go and write this all up.' She picked up her water bottle and the Dictaphone. 'You know I'll have to pass this over to the police.'

'Do what you like with it.'

'Just one question,' she said standing up, 'Why now? Why confess all this now?'

'Because of you.'

'I don't understand.' Verity looked perplexed.

'When Sonya came to the prison she became my friend. We would talk about lots of different things. I told her I'd been approached by you and she said I should do the interview.'

'Why?'

'Because of your relationship to Dr Hewitt.' I smiled standing up. 'Sonya told me you were Hewitt's niece. She'd read an article you'd written some years ago talking about the trauma families of murder victims faced. It was a golden opportunity.'

'So you knew she was my aunt before today?' Verity looked horrified.

'Sure did.'

'Why didn't you say something then?'

'I thought it might put you off coming and that would put a spanner in the works.'

Before she had a second to react I reached for the pencil on the table. It only took me a second to get around the table and stab her in the eye with it. She cried out in horrendous pain. I pulled the pencil from her left eye, wrestled her to the ground and jabbed it into her right. The popping sound was delicious.

'I'm never getting out of here.' I leant close to her ear and heard the shouting coming from outside the room. 'You were my chance to own another life. To have one more turn at having some fun.'

I could smell the blood that covered her face. Her body twitched beneath me. As I heard the lock in the door turning I pulled the pencil out of her eye socket and threw it across the room and plunged my thumbs into her face. The feeling of wet warmth covered my hands. As I sat back on the ground I looked up at the ceiling, listened to the cries of the officers around me and thought of Larry.

'That one was for you.' I smiled as my face was pushed to the ground and a knee pressed into my back.

'I need some help here!' I could hear the panic in the officer's voice. On the other side of the room Verity laid very still her face covered in blood. The female officer who had rushed to her aid turned to me with a look of terror.

'What have you done?' her voice shook.

'What I always do.' Then I smiled, closed my eyes and let the calm wash over me.

THE END

ACKNOWLEDGEMENTS

Where to start? There are so many great people in my life who have kept me going. My first thank you goes to Jasper Joffe who helped me kick-start my career. As always I am grateful to my wonderful family for putting up with me and supporting my writing. My editor Clare has done a wonderful job and I am thankful for all her hard work. A special mention goes out to Anita Waller who took the time to read the first draft and share her wisdom. Likewise, many thanks to Noelle Holten who put up with me asking questions and advised me on prison protocol. I'd like to show my gratitude to Carol Drinkwater who has given me faith in my ability and shown unprecedented support. To all the fellow authors at Bloodhound Books I am honoured to be amongst you. David Gilchrist and Helen Boyce I am indebted to you for helping me and all the other indie authors out there gain coverage. Finally, I'd like to give a shout out to all the wonderful bloggers and readers out there who help launch and support the careers of indie writers. In particular Emma Welton, Sarah Hardy and Joanne Robertson – You are wonderful.

Printed in Great Britain
by Amazon

31062500R00162